“You *said* you accepted m[illegible] apology,” she [illegible]

hurrying to keep up w[illegible] you forgave me.”

“I did.”

“If you don’t mind my say[illegible]ou don’t look as if you did. In fact,” Julia mused, “you look as though you’d like to peel off the mercantile sign and conk me over the head with it.”

He gazed at the sign in question as they passed by. The speculative gleam in his eye did not comfort her.

“I’m trying to be polite,” Graham said.

“You’d make a more convincing impression,” Julia said, “if you’d stop gritting your teeth.”

The bounty hunter bared them instead, in a toothy smile.

Julia yelped. “Now you look as though you’d like to take a bite out of me!”

“I would.” His swift, heated glance set her blood atingle. “Once I simmer down, I might.”

Praise for new Harlequin Historical author Lisa Plumley

"Lisa Plumley's name on the cover always guarantees a good read."
—Under the Covers Book Reviews

"...an author of exceptional talent whose witty style makes her one of the genre's finest."
—Rendezvous

"Ms. Plumley is a topnotch author whose unique storytelling ability is a blessing to romance readers everywhere."
—Old Book Barn Gazette

THE DRIFTER

Lisa Plumley

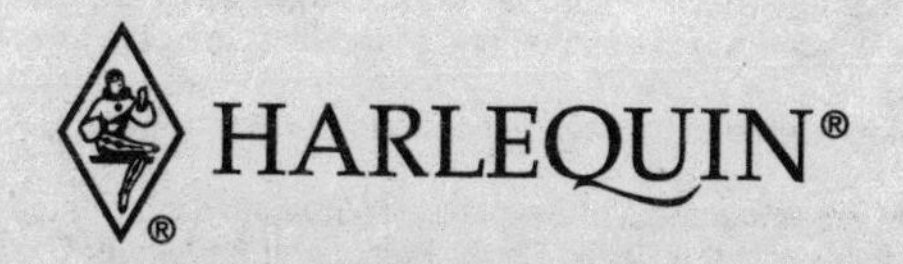

TORONTO • NEW YORK • LONDON
AMSTERDAM • PARIS • SYDNEY • HAMBURG
STOCKHOLM • ATHENS • TOKYO • MILAN • MADRID
PRAGUE • WARSAW • BUDAPEST • AUCKLAND

ISBN 0-373-29205-8

THE DRIFTER

This edition published by arrangement with Harlequin Books S.A.

Visit us at www.eHarlequin.com

Printed in U.S.A.

Available from Harlequin Historicals and LISA PLUMLEY

The Drifter #605

To Jean Price and DeWanna Pace
for their support and encouragement.
And to John Plumley,
because this *doesn't* happen every day.

Chapter One

April 1887
Avalanche, Arizona Territory

Mornings were pure hell, Graham Corley decided on the third day of his latest fugitive-capture celebration. Whether decked out in snowfall, whiskey fumes, or—as was the case today—one thousand proof northern Arizona Territory sunshine, they all left him with the same thought.

Where am I today?

He'd awakened to the thunderous rattle of a mule-drawn freight wagon and the familiar sensation of being lost. Now, he cracked open his eyes in time to glimpse the cockeyed disappearance of the wagon 'round the corner near the Last Chance saloon. Squinting through the plumes of dust settling back onto the main street a few yards away, he shoved himself up on his elbow.

The view straightened itself, revealing several more unpainted lumber-framed buildings, two cowboys passing by on horseback, and the skimpy patch of grass that must have served as his bed last night. He dug his boot heels into a clump of it and pushed all the way upright.

Something rough scratched against his back, scuffing the prime canvas duster coat he'd won in a poker game last night. Frowning, Graham looked over his shoulder to investigate. Cottonwood bark met his disgusted gaze. How had he fallen asleep propped up against a damned tree?

Worse, how had he forgotten doing it?

From beneath his hat brim, he looked higher, idly examining the cottonwood's sturdy trunk and new spring leaves in an effort to gain his bearings. Against the naked sky, the branches swayed lazily in the breeze. More than half of their leaves weren't even unfurled all the way yet…just like him.

He was a slow riser by nature. And a wary one by training. Any bounty hunter who wanted to stay alive had to be. But despite the weight of the Colt strapped near his hip, the knife sheathed in his boot, and the rifle he'd left beneath his unoccupied boardinghouse room's bed, on this particular morning Graham felt relatively carefree.

So far as he knew, no one had tracked him to…where was he again? Avalanche. That was the name of the town. He remembered hearing it when he'd stopped into the saloon two nights ago, dusty and bone-tired after days spent on the twisty mountain trail. *Welcome to Avalanche,* the barkeep had said. *Friendliest town in the West.*

If that was true, he could relax. For the moment, at least. The Hidalgo Kid was safely delivered to the sheriff. The money Graham had earned for nabbing the hoister was safely on the way to his bank account in Baltimore—less enough funds to cover his expenses until he took to the road again. Nothing but endless possibilities stretched before him. And that was just the way his drifter's heart liked it.

With a sigh of satisfaction, Graham tugged his flat-brimmed hat over his unshaven face and patted its low crown firmly in place to shade his eyes. Soothing darkness wiped away his thoughts.

For all of two seconds.

Then the discontentment that had plagued him returned. Like the harsh sunlight overhead, it needled past his defenses and wouldn't be ignored. Swearing beneath his breath, Graham shifted deeper in his new duster coat and turned his thoughts to a surefire diversion.

In his mind's eye, he imagined camisoles and ruby-painted lips. Shimmering paste jewels and lush, curvy bosoms to lay them upon. Satiny garters, and the memory of rolling pale silk stockings down long, curvaceous legs. Sweet feminine seduction, a feather mattress made for two, and…damn.

His mind wandered at the sound of birdcalls nearby, and Graham felt more miserable than ever.

This wasn't working. Not even recollections of the fancy women he'd known on the trail were enough to shove away the niggling doubts he'd carried for the past few months. It seemed there was no getting around it.

His life of adventure had gotten downright boring. Chasing down the same old desperadoes just wasn't what it used to be. Neither were taking pay for a job he'd increasingly lost interest in, and sleeping in musty beds in faraway places…not to mention passing out beneath cottonwood trees.

Opening his eyes again, Graham absently rubbed the well-worn stock of his holstered Colt, and realized the truth that stared him in the face. In truly pitiful fashion, not even pulling iron on the occasional reluctant prisoner was enough to enliven his days anymore.

'Twas enough to give a man the willies.

Especially a bounty-hunting man.

But what was he supposed to do now? Feeling shaken, Graham edged sideways, seeking a more comfortable position against the cottonwood tree. Beside him, a forgotten bottle of Old Orchard tipped and spilled. Its amber contents glugged slowly from the bottle and soaked into the ground. The tang of whiskey filled the air, carried on the same breeze that swept his dark hair from his shoulders and ruffled his coat sleeves.

Hoping to ease his mind temporarily, Graham picked up the bottle and took a slug. The liquor seared a path to his belly. Immediately, he screwed up his face in disgust and shoved the rest of the whiskey aside. Christ! How did anyone in their right mind drink firewater like that first thing in the morning? Obviously, he had no future as Avalanche's town drunk.

On the other hand, he wasn't the kind of man to worry about his future, whiskey-soaked or not. With one last look around the main street, tree-dotted park, and buildings surrounding him, Graham closed his eyes and got ready to catch up on the shut-eye he'd missed while tracking Hidalgo and bringing him into custody.

He didn't know how much time had passed before a feminine voice spoke nearby.

"Have you lost your mind?" its owner demanded. "What are you *doing?*"

The words rushed past in an urgent, Spanish-flavored whisper. Whoever this worrier was, she possessed an abundance of indignation...but on behalf of whom? Remaining motionless, Graham listened.

Someone approached, their footfalls barely discernable against the soft earth and freshly sprouted grass. He sensed a presence beside him—a presence both female and gently bred, judging by the lace-bedecked yellow skirts he glimpsed from beneath his hat, and the subtle fragrance of oranges that swirled from within their depths when she moved.

Too bad, Graham thought idly. A fancy woman might have provided an afternoon's entertainment, at least.

"Be quiet, before you wake him," the possessor of the yellow skirts warned.

Her voice, like the first, was also feminine. But that was where the similarities ended. This new voice, sweetly pitched and vaguely husky, warmed Graham in a way he'd seldom experienced. The sound of it lingered in his ears, combining with the tart, citrus-scented air to leave him languid and content.

"Stay over there," Miss Yellow Skirts went on, speaking in the direction of the street. "If he's not the right one, one of us needs to be ready to summon the sheriff."

Or maybe not so languid and content, after all. Warily, Graham nudged his thumb the barest fraction to the left, ensuring his Colt would be within drawing distance. Woman or not, there was no point letting down his guard now. He'd taken in enough lady sharpers to know the bad guys didn't always wear britches and boots and a long waxed mustache.

"The sheriff?" The lady's companion sounded more worried than ever. "But—"

"Shhh. I think he's moved."

Surprise jolted through him. Had she noticed his thumb edging onto the stock of his Colt? It seemed unlikely. The motion had been slight, at best. And yet…

"Yes, he's definitely moved. Curious."

"Maybe he isn't so drunk as he looks," the Spanish-sounding woman suggested. "Maybe Miss Lillian told us wrong about him."

"Maybe." She sounded doubtful. Curious.

Just the way Graham felt. Were they pickpockets, hoping to help themselves to some poor drunk's boodle? *His boodle?* Or were they a pair of ladies strolling in the park, deciding what to do about the stranger in their midst?

They'd already come too close, though. His only advantage lay in surprise, and Graham meant to use it. 'Til then, he'd have to be still.

The breeze kicked up. The yellow skirts beside him stirred, then billowed higher, momentarily revealing a pair of prissy, high-buttoned shoes and trim ankles. His gaze lingered. Moved upward. Maybe a lady could prove *almost* as entertaining as a fancy woman....

"I still don't think this is wise." The Spanish voice turned louder and quieter by turns, as though the woman kept swiveling her head to keep a lookout.

She could be Miss Yellow Skirt's stall, ready to warn her if anyone approached. She could also be the lady's maid or friend or even her damned chaperone, for all he knew. Graham didn't remember seeing many ladies when he'd ridden into Avalanche—maybe a few more than the typical western town, if that. Nestled in the pine-covered mountains of northern Arizona Territory as it was, perhaps the town attracted more than the usual quantity of families for settlers.

A whole town choked with families. Just his blasted luck.

"Don't be alarmist. Of course it's wise," the lady beside him said. Much to Graham's disappointment, the wind had calmed and so had her fluttering skirts. "Look at him, Isabel. He's perfect!"

"I knew it. You *have* lost your mind. It's all those books of yours. And that fancy college edu—"

"Now, now. Let's not start that again."

Her voice receded as she flounced away on her prissy shoes, saying something more to "Isabel" that Graham couldn't hear clearly. Then she returned, her sunny skirts swaying to and fro above the stubbled grass.

Oddly enough, the image reminded him of his unshaven jaw. And his undoubtedly disreputable-looking clothes. He hadn't seen the point in unpacking his saddlebags for the few days he planned to stay in Avalanche. Now, despite the fact that his white, half-buttoned Henley shirt, tan britches, and duster coat were clean, Graham experienced an unlikely wish they could be unwrinkled and free of the occasional self-made mending job, too.

This, he thought sourly, must be what came of spending too much time in a town populated by families. Three days had been too long. Next thing he knew, he'd be wanting to take up knitting, or something equally domesticated.

Suppressing a shudder, Graham watched the yellow skirts fan out on the grass just beside his knee. Given the fact that his hat brim shaded most of his face, he couldn't make out much more than that fine circle of fabric. The lady's face remained a mystery to him. So did her purpose. Resolutely, he waited for her to make her move…and made immediate plans to pull foot out of family-infested Avalanche as soon as possible. Any place that could make him take an interest in laundry was a dangerous place, indeed.

But no more dangerous than the lady herself. Her

voice swept over him again, with more evident surety than before. ''See what I mean?'' she asked. ''He's absolutely ideal.''

''Oh, *si?* Why is that?''

''Well, just look at him!''

She raised herself upward again, evidently demonstrating the reasoning behind her opinion. Graham watched her curvy little heels tread circles around his resting place beneath the cottonwood tree, then come to a halt a few inches from the boot he sheathed his knife in. Examining her foot—which tapped impatiently as she went on talking—the tremendous difference between their sizes struck him. Whoever she was, she must be delicate.

That, or she had feet like an elf, stuck on an ordinary, woman-sized body. At the notion, his lips quirked beneath the shade of his hat brim.

''This man,'' Miss Yellow Skirts said, ''is exactly what I've been seeking. Can't you see? He's big, obviously strong, well-armed—''

Despite the fact that Miss Know-It-All would probably detect the movement, Graham felt his chest expand a few inches as pride filled him. He was indeed big, strong, and well-armed. He also possessed several other positive—

''—unshaven, shabbily dressed, and he appears to be down on his luck, as well. *He's perfect!*''

—qualities she was obviously too blind to recognize. Feeling grumpy, he decided to cheer himself by imagining the woman's gleeful self tossed into the water barrel beside the Second Chance saloon...starched yellow skirts, and all.

''And he ought to be amenable to my proposal, as well.''

There was a pause as two feminine hands came into view, clad in high-falutin' embroidered lady's gloves with pearl buttons at the wrists. She spread them, palms-down, on the grass beside his knee. Contrasted with his rough and patched-up britches, those gloved hands of hers seemed twice as fancy. Twice as exotic, when compared with the things in his rough-and-tumble bounty hunter's world.

Whoever this lady was, she must be as different from him as the Boston harbors of his boyhood were from the southwestern deserts he'd trekked to get here. Two worlds. Completely opposite. And impossible to put together, short of a miracle.

Despite that fact, momentarily Graham pictured himself unfastening those tiny pearl buttons. Easing the gloves away. Saw her fingers intertwining with his... and figured he must have been out in the sun too long. Mush-hearted imaginings like these were not his way at all.

Miss Yellow Skirts muttered something, then said, "I'd certainly like to get a look at his face first, though."

A flower-bedecked monstrosity of a lady's bonnet loomed suddenly over his thighs. She was bending down to have a closer look at him! Graham closed his eyes, filled with something very near excitement. Which made not a lick of sense. He decided it must be relief that the lady's mysterious mission was about to be revealed—or curiosity about how she must look, crouched on all fours to peer at him—and left it at that.

The fragrance of oranges drifted closer. He wanted to breathe deeply of it, wanted, suddenly and inexplicably, to pull her all the way onto his lap and find out if the lady tasted as good as she smelled. He did neither.

Instead, when he sensed she knelt directly in front of him, Graham opened his eyes.

Staring back at him was an uppity-looking female with dark upswept hair, pretty blue eyes, and a bonnet that looked far too big for her head to keep upright. Just as he'd thought. A gently bred lady. Exactly the type of woman he spent most of his days avoiding.

So why had this one piqued his interest?

She hadn't, Graham told himself in the few seconds that swept past before he could find his voice again. *She never would.*

"Look your fill," he said. He reached out and grasped her gloved wrist, then gently tugged her closer. "And that proposition you talked about before? You'll find I can be *real* amenable...given the right encouragement."

Chapter Two

Oh, my. She was certainly fortunate to have remembered her gloves this morning.

With that nonsensical thought, Julia Bennett gaped into the rugged face—and alarmingly alert features—of the man who'd grabbed her. His self-assured expression jogged up and down as she tottered and fell sideways, landing ignominiously on her backside in the dew-damp park grass. *My, oh, my.*

She'd thought he was asleep. Or unconscious. Utterly oblivious to what transpired around him. With his big body sprawled beneath the tallest cottonwood in the Avalanche municipal park, his battered hat drawn over his face, and an air of relaxation more befitting a tabby cat in the sun than a fully grown man, he had certainly *appeared* unaware.

Looking at him now, though, Julia knew she'd been mistaken. This particular man had probably never been insensible to his surroundings in his life…nor to the ladies within them.

He smiled. His thumb pushed higher on her wrist, flicking past the tidy row of *faux* pearl buttons to caress the base of her palm. At his touch, her fingers flexed helplessly, as though yearning to capture his hand in hers, and a wholly inappropriate—but immensely pleasurable—shiver coursed from her palm to her shoe tips. She couldn't help wondering what the sensation might have been like if she *had* forgotten her gloves. Delightful, most likely.

No. Thoughts like that were entirely unlike her. Undoubtedly, they owed themselves to *his* unsuitable influence. Frowning, Julia fought the urge to wrest her hand from her captor's grasp. It wouldn't do to engage a man like this on his own terms. She'd have to be craftier than that.

She summoned a placid expression. "You certainly seem observant, sir, for a man who has misplaced his bed."

Meaningfully, she looked at the grass beneath them. Then at the thick tree trunk that still pillowed his head. Against the rough bark, his shoulder-length brown hair spilled in disarray. Wavy strands of it were lifted in the breeze, wafting about in the space between his hat brim and long duster coat. It lent him the appearance of a mountain man, especially when combined with his squarish, stubble-covered jaw. But he smelled finer than any mountain man Julia had ever encountered.

And smiled more silkily than any of them had, as well.

"Are you volunteering to help me find it?" he asked. "Or are you offering your services to make this bed more comfortable?"

"Certainly not!" Her scandalized gaze followed his as he outlined a roughly person-shaped area in the tufted grass beside him. "What kind of wo—"

"Either way, I accept," he interrupted. "'Tis the

nicest proposition I've had all day. 'Course, it *is* still early yet...."

The rogue had the gall to waggle his eyebrows in a wickedly suggestive fashion. At her!

"And," he went on while she gawked at him, "I think we ought to at least know each other's names before we go any further. Don't you agree?"

"I—I—" *I'm stammering.* Dear Lord, that had never happened before! "I already know your name, Mr. Corley."

Given the cost to her composure already, Julia couldn't help but embroider the truth a bit. She lifted her chin, and added, "I know a great deal about you, in fact. I know that you're a bounty hunter. That you're considered trustworthy and honest. And that you happen to be between, ahhh, assignments at the moment. That's why I'm here."

The look of surprise that crossed his face told her that, despite whatever else may have gone wrong this morning, she had at least identified him correctly. That was good. On the other hand, Julia thought as his fingers fastened idly on her topmost glove button and began working it through the buttonhole—setting off an array of pleasurable sensations in her hand and wrist—it was also possible she'd underestimated the man.

Not to mention her own reaction to him.

She wrestled her thoughts back on track, doing her best to ignore the pleasant feeling of having her hand cradled in his. Had she underestimated him? And what did that do to her plan? After all, what did she know about bounty hunters? About men, in general, as opposed to in theory? Perhaps the gossip she'd gleaned about Graham Corley had lulled her into a grievously overblown sense of complacency.

He looked up. His eyes were the same shade of blue as the depths of a mountain lake, and equally unnavigable. By strength of will alone, Julia held his gaze. It wouldn't do to appear cowed by a man like this one. Especially not with so much at stake.

He raised his eyebrows. "My reputation precedes me?"

"Nothing so glorious as that. I asked about you in town. As it happens, we don't get many visitors in Avalanche, so you're quite the talk of the community."

"Hmmm." He seemed contemplative, then grinned anew. "You can believe about half of what you've heard."

She couldn't resist the obvious inquiry. "And the other half?"

"Exaggeration. Gossip. *Scandal.*"

A tremor raced through her. She hadn't heard he was scandalous, although the man certainly looked it. Beneath all the grit and long hair and those poorly mended clothes and—she wrinkled her nose—those atrocious liquor fumes, he was probably quite attractive.

In a roguish, low-brow fashion that didn't appeal to *her* at all, of course.

On the other hand, given his renewed grin, it was entirely likely Graham Corley was simply jesting with her. It was impossible to tell, Julia realized with frustration.

Unfortunately, much as it galled her, her inability to decide even that much about him wasn't a surprise. After all, she'd always been better at deciphering arithmetic problems or philosophy questions than at deciphering people. Why should things be any different with a stranger like him?

"Are you scandalous?" she felt driven to ask. "Because if you are, I don't think—"

"Yes, ma'am. I am." A dangerous-looking grin accompanied his words, making them seem indisputably true. "Scandalous as all get-out."

His reply was immediate. *So immediate,* in fact, that it was enough to make her instantly suspicious. She peered at him through the dancing shade of the fluttering cottonwood leaves, at his casual posture and deliberately provocative demeanor, and could arrive at only one conclusion.

"You're trying to scare me away." Julia tilted her head, estimating the rightness of her guess. When his lips tightened, she knew she'd deduced correctly. Satisfied that she hadn't lost her wits completely, she smiled right back at him. "It won't work."

"It's already worked," the bounty hunter countered. "I can feel your hand trembling."

It was true. As though his words had ordered it, her fingers quivered within his grasp. The tips of her gloves rubbed faintly over his big callused hand, proving him aggravatingly correct, and her hand grew warmer.

Not that she intended to address the subject with him.

"No, Mr. Corley, I assure you that I—"

"It's all right." He stroked her palm once more, then released her. "It's not every day a lady like yourself has dealings with a man like me."

Dealings? Despite his placid expression—intended, no doubt to reassure her—Julia felt panic set in. Did he already know about the proposal she had in mind?

At the thought, humiliation washed through her. Gossip ran both ways, of course. Mr. Corley might have heard about her in the same fashion that she'd made it her business to learn about him. Wagging tongues abounded in Avalanche. Even among the marriageable men who were most acquainted with Julia's…unusual situation.

Unfortunately, those same men were stubbornly unwilling to help her with that situation. In general, they seemed to find the notion about as appealing as, well…using a cottonwood tree for a pillow. Which brought her right back to Mr. Corley.

And her proposition.

In preparation for broaching the topic, Julia gave him a vigorous smile. Just then, Isabel rushed to their side.

"I went for the sheriff!" she cried, panting and pointing toward the middle of Main Street, where the road leading to the municipal buildings jutted into the center of town. "He ought to be here right quick."

"Thank you ever so much, Isabel," Julia said, glancing upward from her position atop the grass. She tried to appear as though she were comfortable there, and not as though the brute had hauled her there forcefully. After all, she did have a reputation to uphold. "If you would be so kind as to tell him not to bother coming—"

"Not to come?" Her friend surveyed the bounty hunter with a suspicious look, then turned to Julia with a befuddled expression. "Why ever not? 'Specially now that *he's* awake."

"Because I intend to chat a bit longer with him. About *the subject we discussed*—" as her closest friend, Isabel knew all about Julia's plans, "—and so far, things are coming along quite nicely, too." She gave the man beside her an overly sunny smile. "Isn't that right, Mr. Corley?"

No decent man would purposely embarrass a lady, especially in front of others. It was one of the main tenets she espoused in the dime novel etiquette books she'd become known for writing while away in the East. Bounty hunter or not, Julia was gambling Mr. Corley would maintain that gentlemanly ideal, as well.

He narrowed his eyes at her, briefly, then gazed up at Isabel with a nonchalant expression. "Right enough not to go involving the sheriff, I'd say."

Evidently, Graham Corley possessed a buried chivalrous streak. That, or he wanted to avoid dealing with the law any more than his profession required.

It was a sobering thought. But one Julia couldn't allow to deter her. The man beside her might well be her last chance for getting out of Avalanche in time. She had to do what she could to persuade him into accepting her plan.

"See?" she said, making shooing motions toward Isabel. "Please go tell the sheriff not to bother coming over."

"Are you sure?" Isabel asked.

"Positive." She didn't want the entire town knowing what she was up to. "Besides, I feel certain Mr. Corley and I are about to come to an understanding. It's quite likely our business would be concluded before the sheriff even got here."

"All right." Reluctantly, and with promises to meet Julia later at Bennett's Apothecary and Soda Fountain Emporium, Isabel headed back down Main Street.

Alone with Mr. Corley, Julia felt her resolve waver. She took in his rough-hewn appearance and curiously intent expression, and nearly ran right after Isabel. Then she reminded herself that her future was at stake, and gathered her courage.

Beside her, the bounty hunter crossed his arms over his middle. He watched Isabel retreat around the corner near Miss Verna's mercantile. The moment she disappeared from view, he fixed Julia with a look that made her doubt the wisdom of her whole plan. ''Despite what you told your friend,'' he said, ''we don't have business to conclude.''

''Now, Mr. Corley, let's not be hasty. I believe I—''

''We—don't—have—business. Of any kind.''

It was the same tone of voice he might have used to address a simpleton. For a moment, all she could do was stare at him, agape. No one in Avalanche had ever spoken to her that way.

''Period,'' he added, frowning as though he feared she hadn't understood even his most plainly spoken refusal. ''Understand?''

A smile began somewhere inside her and spread outward. ''Oh, I understand you perfectly.'' *I understand you haven't heard about me already.*

If he had, he'd never have addressed her that way, as though she were utterly lacking in reason. That meant she still had a good chance of accomplishing her goal. Immeasurably cheered, Julia linked her hands atop her skirts.

His gaze dropped to her clasped hands. His frown deepened. ''I don't think you do. Whatever business you have, it will have to be with someone else. I'm not for hire.''

''Of course you are!'' That was the whole point of being a bounty hunter, wasn't it? ''And there is no one else. I'm afraid, Mr. Corley, that my choices are narrowed down to...you.''

After her father's ultimatum nearly a month ago, Julia had begun to despair of ever finding someone in time. Most particularly, someone who fulfilled all the stringent requirements Asa Bennett had laid down to his only daughter. Now, this man was her best and only chance.

"No," her chosen man said flatly. He slouched against the cottonwood tree, yanked down his hat, and from beneath its dark brim, added, "Nice talking to you, ma'am."

Clearly, his tone implied a dismissal. Spoken as it was in that deep, mountain-man's voice of his, it nearly tempted Julia to accept it. Then she thought of living all the rest of her days in Avalanche, surrounded by people...well, people who didn't understand her and didn't give a fig if they ever did, and she just couldn't do it.

"But you don't even know what I want!" she said.

"Don't care."

"You *must* care."

With a subtle shift of his hand, he tipped up his hat partway. He squinted at her from beneath its brim. "Why?"

"Be-because you're a good man, that's why. And, of course, because I'm a lady who needs your help."

His lips quirked. His blue-eyed gaze traveled from her folded hands to her skirts and upward to her bodice, then swept to her new bonnet. At the sight of it, he almost seemed to grimace, which made no sense whatsoever.

"If that's your idea of a proposition," he said, "I can see why you haven't found someone else to help you."

"I resent your implication, sir!"

"I resent being hoisted out of a perfectly good sleep for a lot of idiotic chatter about something you can't even explain properly." Mr. Corley changed the cross of his arms, thrust his chin into his duster coat collar, and pulled down his hat again.

My, he was a grouchy one. Julia hadn't expected that about him. Applying the principles she'd used time and again with her father, she waited. And waited some more. Eventually, as she'd expected, the bounty hunter came around.

His growl of displeasure foretold it. "What in blazes makes you think I'm a good man, anyhow?" he demanded.

She suppressed a smile. Men could be so predictable, especially to a lady who knew how to handle them properly. It seemed Graham Corley wasn't so different, after all.

"Any man who devotes his days to bringing in outlaws *must* be a good man," Julia explained. "Don't you see? I absolutely refuse to believe otherwise. Now, about my proposal—"

"No."

"I'll have you know, I'm about to come into a great deal of money." *If I accomplish this scheme,* she reminded herself. "I can pay you quite well."

"I don't need your money."

Exasperated with talking to his hat brim, Julia snatched the battered headwear and whisked it from his head. "What *do* you need, then?"

He sat up, seemingly oblivious to his missing hat. Without it, he seemed both younger and more like a stranger than before. Nervously, she turned the hat brim around in her hands, waiting for his reply, then realized she was fidgeting and lowered it to her lap instead.

Miss Julia's Behavior Book, volume two: A lady must never allow her person to be beyond her absolute control. Strict self-discipline must prevail at all times.

"What do I need?" His grin vanished. "Well, ma'am, I'll need to think about that for a minute."

For an instant, Mr. Corley closed his eyes. When he opened them again, the message she glimpsed in them was enough to make Julia go still with shock.

I need you.

Spellbound, she stared back at him. Her thoughts whirled. Surely she was mistaken. Surely he didn't mean…

"I need to get out of this damned town," he said aloud. And then he grabbed his hat, pushed to his feet, and strode toward Main Street.

Chapter Three

"I knew this harebrained plan of yours would never work," Isabel said, dunking her cleaning cloth into a wash bucket and wringing it out over the soapy water. She shook her head, then went back to work wiping down the marble countertop at Bennett's Apothecary and Soda Fountain Emporium. "Especially with a man like that."

"Yes, well...he was an unlikely candidate," Julia agreed. "I'll grant you that much."

She glanced toward the rear of the quiet, just-opened shop, making sure her father was still engrossed in the pharmaceuticals he was preparing. It wouldn't do for him to overhear her conversation with Isabel. He didn't know about her plan. With luck, he never would.

He would only approve the results of it.

To her relief, she spied his gray-haired head as he stepped behind a pyramid of brown-bottled Lydia E. Pinkham's Vegetable Compound, then emerged at his worktable. With a frown of concentration, Asa Bennett moved his mortar and pestle to its center, then sprinkled in a quantity of grayish powder. As usual, he seemed engrossed in the task at hand.

"But time is running out," Julia told Isabel, feeling a familiar sense of desperation tighten her middle. "I got another letter from that bigheaded Lucinda Druiry in yesterday's post. She seems to think the position at *Beadle's Magazine* is hers for the taking. And she's not above bragging about it, either."

Frowning, she scrubbed at the soda fountain's silver-plated brass fittings, taking special care with the syrup faucets and draught arm. That done, she rubbed her polishing cloth over the central carbonated water urn, hoping its cold surface would lend her a bit of much-needed clearheadedness.

At her side, Isabel quit wiping, leaving a thin layer of water and soapsuds shimmering atop the counter in the late-morning sunlight. Slapping down her cloth, she put her hands on her calico-clad waist. "That position at *Beadle's Magazine* is rightfully yours! What business does she have to—"

"I *wish* it were rightfully mine," Julia interrupted gently. Surely, she was depending on the income she would earn as the periodical's resident etiquette columnist to finance her new life in the city. "But it's not. And it never will be, if I can't even get out of Avalanche in time to secure an interview with the editor at *Beadle's*."

Beneath her busy fingers, the marble urn gleamed. Sunlight from the apothecary's expensive twin windows danced over its surface. Pausing in her work, Julia smiled over the impressive results. Thinking of Lucinda, her fellow alumna from Vassar College, always put a special vigor in her cleaning.

"And you say that bounty hunter just up and left you," Isabel asked, resuming her wiping, "without so much as a 'how do you do?'"

"Oh, he gave me a 'how do you do.'" If she could call it that. Just the recollection of the way Graham Corley had looked at her in that magical moment before he'd walked away was enough to leave her breathless.

I need you.

Of course, maybe her breathlessness owed itself more to the exertion of preparing the soda fountain for its first customers of the day, Julia reasoned, than it did to Mr. Corley's inexplicably intimate parting look. Yes, that was almost certainly it.

Why, then, did a part of her wish it was something more?

Ridiculous.

"What did he say?" Isabel asked, wide-eyed. "I thought you told me he refused to even discuss your proposal."

"He did." *For now.* Firmly, Julia pushed away those dangerously distracting thoughts of his final, searing glance. "But I have a feeling I haven't seen the last of him. I wouldn't be surprised if he even turned up here."

"Here?"

"Certainly. Why not?"

Giving her friend a teasing wink, she tossed her polishing cloth into the bin beneath the counter, then raised her hands to her hair and checked for tendrils that had escaped her new bonnet. Her hatpins and chignon still felt secure, despite her tumble to the grass earlier.

With a critical eye, Julia leaned closer to the mirrored space behind the soda fountain apparatus. She wanted to make certain no traces of her encounter in the park were visible. She certainly felt changed, somehow. On the inside. But there was no reason she couldn't present the same, unchanging appearance to the people who knew her.

She hoped.

"After all," she continued when she'd finished primping, "this *is* where Mr. Corley will find the mysterious person who settled his boardinghouse bill this morning."

Isabel gasped. "You didn't!"

"I did. If there's anything I know about gentlemen, it's that not one of them can bear being beholden to a lady. Mr. Corley will come back, all right." Julia smiled at her reflection. "And he'll be looking for me when he does."

"Oh, *Madre Dios.*" Swiftly, Isabel crossed herself. "Your papa will kill you when he finds out."

"My father isn't going to find out."

"He...might."

"What? How?" Turning at the curious, singsong note of warning in Isabel's voice, she caught sight of her friend's face. She looked worried. But then, that was Isabel. A mother hen, even before she'd been out of short skirts. Whatever had her riled up now, it was probably nothing to panic about.

Or maybe it was.

Julia followed her friend's gaze to the front of the shop, just as a dark-hatted figure moved briskly past the plate-glass windows. Nearly past the entrance, a hairsbreadth from the ornate show globe that designated the place as a pharmaceutical shop, he paused. He squinted through the glass. Then, with an abrupt shove of his hand, he opened the door.

The bounty hunter entered.

In his wake, the bell chimed merrily. The man stopped for an instant, obviously getting his bearings in the merchandise-packed shop. He frowned. Standing amidst the pharmaceuticals advertisements, shelves of goods, glossy fixtures and stacked displays of medicinal remedies, Graham Corley looked twice as rugged. Twice as fearsome.

And all at once *she* felt twice as foolhardy, for entangling herself with a man like him. But what choice did she have? None, really, Julia reminded herself.

Nevertheless, as his gaze finally reached her—pinned her, examined her, *touched her*—she felt rooted in place. When he started toward her across the oak plank floorboards, Julia had to stifle a very real impulse to flee. Staring straight at her, Graham Corley strode toward the soda fountain. His footsteps were loud and ominous in the sudden stillness.

For one giddy instant, Julia imagined herself lifting one of the high wrought-iron soda fountain stools, aiming it bottom-first at the bounty hunter, and forcing him backward like a lion tamer determined to keep his most savage pupil at bay. But that was ridiculous, she told herself. If her plan was to succeed, it would require her and Mr. Corley to remain much closer than a chair's distance apart.

Much, *much* closer.

At the thought, she suppressed a cowardly urge to duck behind the counter and hide. Instead, Julia made herself stand upright while she awaited his approach.

Miss Julia's Behavior Book, volume one: Ladies should avoid staring openly at people to whom they have not been properly introduced, as this is ill-bred and unbecoming, and shows a serious want of dignity.

She realized she was indeed gawking at him with a lack of dignity that probably went far beyond unbecoming, and lowered her gaze. If this transaction were to proceed as she hoped, she couldn't afford to take any actions that might offend Mr. Corley.

Not that a bachelor like him would be likely to notice. Still, as the town's sole etiquette expert, she did have a responsibility to uphold.

"Mr. Corley!" She summoned a shaky smile and gestured toward one of the stools lining the soda fountain's long marble countertop. "How pleasant to see you again. I believe you've already met my friend, Isabel Deevers."

He nodded to a gaping Isabel, who muttered a greeting in response, then retreated to serve a customer who had followed the bounty hunter inside the shop. Julia watched her friend all but run to the opposite end of the soda fountain counter, and had the feeling that, in this instance at least, Isabel might very well be the wiser of them both.

Bravely, she looked up at the man she'd maneuvered into seeking her out. He glowered back.

What in heaven's name had possessed her to choose *him?*

Desperation.

And it hadn't abated a bit.

She fluttered her fingers toward a stool, hoping he would take a seat. Maybe then he wouldn't tower over her in quite so daunting a fashion. "I—I trust you had no trouble locating my father's fine establishment?"

"None at all." He ignored the stool she'd indicated. Standing beside it, he bared his teeth in what she supposed passed for an answering smile. "I asked in town about you. Where could I find Avalanche's most fancy-talking, won't-take-no-for-an-answer, busy-bodiest female? I asked. You must be talking about Miss Julia Bennett, everyone said. Just go straight on over to Bennett's Emporium."

Wanting to cringe, Julia lifted her chin instead. She

could well imagine what folks in town would have told him about her. *Uppity. Peculiar. An overeducated excuse for a spinster.* She had heard them all, and more. As the town misfit, she should have become accustomed to it.

She hadn't.

The comments still hurt. Now, and every time she heard them. They were one of the reasons she needed to escape back to New York, where she could be safely anonymous again.

Of all the things she'd learned at Vassar, the most important had been the revelation that she could live her life *without* feeling like an outsider. Without feeling as though she didn't belong, and never would. In the city, no one cared if she could figure enormous sums in her head, or memorize great spans of text and formulas and theories. In the city, she was just another person.

It was a feeling Julia would give almost anything to experience again. At the moment, stranded as she was in rustic Avalanche, that goal seemed almost impossible. But she had experienced freedom once, and she'd vowed to do so again.

Even if it meant forging an alliance with the intimidating, unpolished and unlikely man frowning at her from across the soda fountain counter.

She untied her apron, using the task as an excuse to stop looking at him. "You can believe about twenty-five percent of what you've heard about me, Mr. Corley," she said crisply, tugging it from her waist. She turned away from him and, with trembling hands, hung her apron on the hook beside the stacks of stemmed soda glasses. "And as for the rest—"

"As for the rest, I'd rather come to my own conclusions."

His voice came from directly behind her. How had he slipped past the counter without her noticing? Julia felt his breath blow gently against her nape, stirring the delicate hairs there. Then she sensed the warmth of his presence...and its disturbingly rousing effect on her emotions.

For the space of a breath, she yearned to lean back against him. To absorb some of the strength he used so effortlessly. To let herself be sheltered by someone bigger and stronger, even if only for a moment. Fortunately, a lifetime's self-preservation set itself into motion just in time.

"Good. You're an original thinker." She smoothed her apron strings. Tucked them into her apron's pocket. Made doubly sure the garment was secure on its hook...and, all the while, tried desperately to appear as though she stood within touching distance of a man every day of her life, and was thus unaffected. "Then perhaps you'll listen to my prop—"

"I'm not finished talking."

"Neither am I!" Overcome with the frustration of trying to speak with a man who obviously had no sense of common politeness, Julia drew a deep, fortifying breath. "And I never will be, if you don't stop inter—"

Turning, she found herself nearly squashed between his broad chest at her front and the pile of glasses at her back. The rest of her planned speech emerged in a squeak. "—rupting me!"

A tinkling sound, coming from the vicinity of her skirt's bustle, warned of an imminent crash. Calmly, the bounty hunter reached past her hip, steadied the stack of stemmed soda glasses with one large hand, and then took a step back. Fresh air swept between them.

"I've been thinking that you might benefit from one

of my etiquette guides, Mr. Corley,'' Julia told him, raising her eyebrows. ''Perhaps the volume I wrote as an aid to bachelors who want to enrich their lives with the benefits of marriage and family.''

His eyes gleamed dangerously. ''Not a chance.''

She shrugged. ''I see. It's possible that the volume containing hints and helpful guidelines on the art of conversation would be more to your—''

''Miss Bennett—''

''—liking.''

''It's possible, as you say,'' he gripped her elbow, drawing her closer, ''that you are the one who needs your etiquette books.''

''What? Sir, I do not!''

''That's debatable.''

''It's preposterous!'' Julia said, offended at the very suggestion.

''It's true. True as what I came here to tell you today, before heading out of town.''

Out of town? This wasn't proceeding at all as she'd planned. Bothered by that fact, but unwilling to reveal as much to him, Julia jerked her arm out of the bounty hunter's grasp. She darted a nervous glance at her father's bowed head. Thankfully, he still seemed absorbed in his work—for the moment.

She gazed back at Mr. Corley. He stared down at her with barely suppressed impatience. Maybe it was best to humor him before presenting him with her proposition, Julia decided. In that spirit, she gave him the most innocent look she could muster. ''Very well. You came to tell me something?''

''You had no business paying my damned boarding-house bill,'' he said. The hard set of his features left little doubt he meant it. "Graham Corley pays his own way. I'll be beholden to no one."

"Well. You already are."

His gaze darkened. Flippancy didn't agree with him, it seemed. In a quieter voice, Julia said hurriedly, "But not for long. You see, all I ask in return is that you consider my proposition. It won't take more than a few minutes. I feel sure you'll want to discuss it."

"Sure enough to bribe me into coming here to do so?"

"Irony is unbecoming in all its guises, Mr. Corley."

He rubbed his hand over his dark-stubbled jaw, looking aggravated. "So is trying to force a man into listening to you."

"I simply want to hire you," she said.

"I already told you. I'm not looking for work."

"Perhaps not yet." Julia waved away his refusal, then reached beneath the soda fountain counter to retrieve her reticule and gloves. Pulling them on, she stated the obvious. "But every man has his price. It would save us both a great deal of time if you would tell me yours. I assure you, I can afford to pay it."

If possible, that statement drew an even more forbidding expression from him. Could it be that she'd chosen the wrong tactic for dealing with a man like him?

If so, it was too late to correct the matter now. She'd simply have to forge ahead.

His unshaven jaw took on an obstinate angle. He folded his arms across his middle—a gesture, Julia couldn't help but notice, which effected an interesting contrast between his sun-browned skin and plain white shirt. In fascination, she watched the play of muscle and sinew against the faintly nubbly cotton, then realized what she was doing and jerked her gaze upward.

He'd caught her at it. The knowing grin on his face told her so. To her surprise, that moment's weakness on her part seemed to soften him. Just a tad. But perhaps it would be enough.

It was.

"All right, Miss Hoity-Toity," he said. "Tell me what you want."

It took Miss Julia Bennett thirty-odd minutes, one change of gloves, a church social's worth of inane chatter to the people in her father's shop, and about fifty yards' worth of walking to reveal her proposition to him. And even then Graham couldn't tell what the hell it was.

It was written down.

He stared at the paper she'd handed him, vaguely aware of her moving around inside the small clapboard structure behind Bennett's Emporium that she'd led him to. With a brisk motion of her arms, Julia snapped open a pair of shutters to his right, then another pair at the rear of the building. Sunlight flooded in. A steady beam of it filtered between the crates and bottles and dust motes, illuminating the fancy script letters that faced him.

Graham squinted harder. The curlicue-adorned script merged into a spidery mess and made his situation all the worse. Christ. It figured that an uppity woman like her would want to hire him with a written agreement. After their encounters so far, the last thing he wanted was to admit he couldn't read it.

Julia stepped between a stack of pine crates and a table piled with a jumble of what he assumed were dusty pharmaceutical supplies. Her skirts whispered in the stillness, yellow and lacy and far too fancy for plain surroundings like these. Still, she seemed oddly at home in the cluttered shed—and more at ease than he'd seen her so far.

It made him wonder about her, something Graham had done far too much of already. He should have left Avalanche when he had the chance. No matter how much she intrigued him, or how much being indebted to her pained him. Now he was stuck with a lady he couldn't get out of his head and an offer for another bounty hunting job he didn't want.

It ought to be a simple thing to turn her down. Strangely enough, Graham wasn't in a hurry to do it. From the moment she'd tumbled to the grass and blinked up at him with those wary eyes of hers, he'd been stupidly—and temporarily, he felt sure—smitten. It was just his blasted luck.

Aside from Frankie, he hadn't known many real ladies. Graham figured that was the reason this one fascinated him so much. Anything more didn't bear wondering about.

"This was the original shop my father opened when he and my mother settled in the Territory," Julia offered, indicating the little building and its furnishings. "We don't use it much since the Emporium was constructed—a schoolroom for a while, before my mother died—but it's out of the sun and well away from the street. We'll have the privacy we need here."

"It'll do." Clearing his throat, he looked again at the paper in his hand. He could make out his name, the name of the territory, and a few of the smaller words. Nothing more.

"I thought a written agreement would suit best for this situation," Julia said, coming closer. She stopped beside him, angling her head to read the paper, and the scent of oranges wafted upward. ''I wouldn't want there to be any misunderstandings between us...especially with so delicate a situation as this. I'm sure you understand.''

Not at all. '''Course.'' Feeling damnably awkward and uncertain, Graham thrust the paper onto a barrel beside him and then retreated to familiar territory. ''But I usually work on a more informal basis. Why don't you tell me exactly what you need?''

Her pretty face turned pink. ''I—I was hoping to avoid that, actually. It's...well, it's rather embarrassing.''

Finally. A hint as to what she wanted. 'Twas probably a runaway fiancé that Julia Bennett was wrangling for him to find, Graham figured. No wonder she was skittish.

Hoping to put her at ease, he pushed his hands in his pockets. He looked through the shuttered windows with a deliberately casual air, as though studying the painted sign visible through the glass on the side of the Bennett's Apothecary and Soda Fountain Emporium building.

''I assure you,'' he said, idly watching a stagecoach pass by between the buildings, ''you're not the first lady to request this sort of thing.''

''I'm not?''

''Happens more than you'd think.'' *But he'd be damned if he'd haul the poor knuck back to face a wedding noose.* Not for her. Not for anyone. ''But like I said, Miss Bennett, I'm fixing to head out of Avalanche today. I'm not—''

''Please! Just consider it. I wouldn't be asking you now if I didn't truly need your help.''

Again she shoved the paper toward him. Reluctantly,

Graham took it. He frowned down at the indecipherable words written on it, and discovered there was no sorrier feeling than knowing a lady was relying on you...and the only way to help her was to make yourself look like a blasted fool.

He looked up at her. Worriedly, Julia nibbled at her lower lip while she read the paper once more—looking for whatever he might have objected to in it, most likely. Teeth caught on the fullness of her lip, she looked up and caught him staring. To Graham's dismay, even the little wrinkle between her eyebrows appealed to him. Beyond all reason, experience and common sense, he wanted to help her.

Lord, she was pretty.

Lord, he was in trouble.

He'd never gone spoony over a woman like this in his life. Spooked at the sensation, Graham took a step back. He needed time to think. He needed distance to plan. In the park this morning, trying to scare her away hadn't worked. But what would?

And did he really want it to?

Yes, a part of him yelled. *Hell, yes.* He was a drifter. A man who belonged on the trail, not lodged in a town overrun with families and irrepressible bookish females.

Graham peered at the paper. What he needed was a gentle way to turn her down. He opened his mouth, and could scarcely believe what emerged. "If you want my help, you'll have to tell me what you need straight out. I can't read this."

Looking aghast at his revelation, Julia snatched back the paper. She folded it in half, then folded it again and again, muttering a string of apologies. "Oh! Oh, I'm so sorry, Mr. Corley. I never guessed—I mean, you seem so...well. Well."

Silence descended. Graham couldn't stand it.

"I can still find your damned fiancé for you," he said, driven to make the offer by the utter dismay that had clouded her delicate features. "I'm good at what I do. Ask anyone."

"I know you are. That's part of the reason I chose you."

This was more like it. "Never lost track of a man I was after. Or a woman, for that matter."

"Oh, I'm sure you haven't," she agreed, nodding.

Clasping her hands behind her back in a prim gesture, Julia marched to the window and looked outside. Outlined in sunlight and blue skies, her figure looked womanly enough to warm a man for all his days...and all his nights, too. Graham couldn't help admiring the sweet side-to-side swoosh of her skirts as she paced nearer to him again.

She paused before him with a decisive tilt to her chin. "But I don't want to hire you to find someone," she said.

"You don't?"

"No."

Graham watched as she opened her reticule and tucked the folded paper inside it. For a woman who'd just given up on the man she had hoped to snare into wedlock, Julia Bennett seemed remarkably serene. "What about your fiancé?" he felt compelled to ask.

"I've already found him." At his doubtlessly confused expression, she actually laughed. "From the moment I saw him, I knew he'd suit perfectly. Or, that at least he could be made to suit perfectly. It's you, Mr. Corley."

"Me?" He rubbed his jaw in aggravation. "What

about me? I already told you, I'm headed out of town this after—''

''Why, I want to hire you, of course,'' Julia interrupted, looking far too much like a cat with cream to suit Graham's peace of mind. ''To be my fiancé. And I'd like to get started right away, too. That's why privacy was required.''

Privacy. At her softly spoken explanation, a dozen ribald thoughts chased themselves through his mind, doing more to spark his blood than anything had in months. Maybe years. Maybe a lifetime.

It was worse than he'd imagined. Graham shook his head to clear it. Unfortunately, the motion did nothing to dislodge the sense that he'd gotten in over his head this time—and there were thunderous rapids and a waterfall further on down the line.

Beside him, Julia smiled brightly. Now that she'd finally gotten her proposition said and out of the way, she seemed visibly cheered.

''Shall we shake hands on the deal?'' she inquired. ''Or will my word be good enough for you?''

Chapter Four

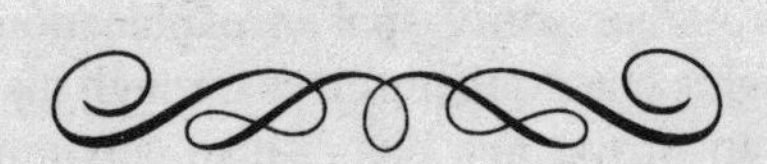

Graham shook his head. Either his brains had been scrambled by all the whiskey and five-card stud he'd indulged in over the past three days, or Miss Julia Bennett had actually suggested she needed to hire a fiancé.

More specifically, needed to hire *him* as her fiancé.

Standing before him still, she awaited his reply, her gloved hand outstretched as though he might actually agree to shake on her preposterous proposal. She'd cocked her head at an expectant angle, putting her hat at serious risk of toppling sideways, and to all appearances, Miss Julia Bennett meant what she'd said.

Why, I want to hire you, of course. To be my fiancé.

To cover his befuddlement at this unexpected turn of events, Graham gave her a grin. "I'd say a woman like you, Miss Bennett, could have her pick of fiancés." *So long as they didn't mind being jawed to death with conversation.* "Why hire yourself one?"

Impatience flashed across her features—that, and something that looked an awful lot like...embarrassment?

"It's expedient, Mr. Corley," she said, as though a rapid answer could erase the vulnerability that had showed, so briefly, in her face. "A modern woman deliberates, makes a reasoned assessment and then acts accordingly. I see no reason why matters of the heart should be conducted any differently, or any less rationally."

Graham folded his arms and looked her up and down. "A rational person generally chooses a fiancé she's acquainted with."

"This is a special situation." She lowered her hand, evidently sensing he wasn't ready to seal their deal. "Requiring special measures."

"I see." *No, he didn't.* "But why hire a stranger for a fiancé? There must be dozens of unmarried men in Avalanche."

"None who'll have me," he thought he heard her mutter as she moved past him toward the window. *"Blast it!"*

Graham blinked. He couldn't have heard aright, that much was plain. He decided so when he looked at her again, and saw that Julia had fisted her hand in her skirts. With her back straight and her chin lifted, she looked every inch the ruffle-clad warrior princess going into battle. A woman like that would not admit a weakness of any sort. He had to admire her spirit, even as he wondered at her motives.

"Besides, I don't want a *genuine* fiancé," she explained.

"Now there's a relief," Graham said, even more confused than before.

"What I want is a *seeming* fiancé—"

"A pretend fiancé. A counterfeit."

She ignored the plain face he'd put on her plan. "Someone who can make my father believe he's wild with love for me." At this she blushed, but continued on, nonetheless. "Someone biddable, temporary and eager to leave town once this is all over with. You fit the bill on all three accounts, Mr. Corley."

"Biddable?" He couldn't help but grin at the unlikeliness of it.

"Hirable, at least," Julia amended. When she turned from the window to face him straight on, he saw an answering smile on her pretty, lively face. "And who could be more temporary than a bounty hunter who, by his own admission, can't wait to leave Avalanche? As I said in the park, you're ideal."

"True as that may be—" Graham delighted in her open-mouthed expression as he agreed with her assessment of him as an ideal man "—your telling me what kind of bogus fiancé you want doesn't explain why you need a sham engagement in the first place."

It also didn't explain why he cared at all, why he hadn't already pulled foot for a less complicated town, inhabited by less mystifying women. Frankie would have said 'twas Fate that kept him here...but then she'd always had a touch of the fanciful in her, despite the circumstances of their growing up. Graham had known better. Almost from the start.

Julia sighed. Her gaze measured him, examined him, and in her face he saw the same kind of quick-mindedness that helped him nab slippery desperadoes time and again. Perhaps they had more in common than he'd thought, he and Miss Julia.

"Very well," she said briskly. "I can see you're a man of exceptional perceptiveness. I suppose I owe a man of your powers of deduction a tad more explanation."

He tried not to smile anew at her praise. 'Twas uncommonly hard to resist, Graham discovered to his dismay. He *wanted* to smile at her...wanted to see her smile at him, in return.

Had so little time in domesticated, family-packed Avalanche softened him as much as that? Or was it something in Julia herself that made him think such mush-hearted thoughts?

"The truth is," Julia continued, not looking at him as she fiddled with her reticule, "I have an urgent need to travel East in approximately one month's time. I'm recently returned from attending college in the States—"

"Ahh, that explains it."

"Explains what?"

"Your highfalutin' ways. I understand higher learning sometimes affects females that way. Makes 'em uppity. Understandable, really," Graham said, "given the way education crams a woman's head with information she can't put to use."

"I'm a Vassar alumnus, yes." Her voice had suddenly filled with starch. "And given the urgency of my situation, I'll have to let your woefully misguided views on the subject of women's education go unchallenged for now."

"Misguided?" He liked sparring with her, Graham decided. Liked witnessing the swift workings of her mind and hearing the remarkable things she said. "Says who?"

She didn't rise to the bait. "I'd rather not discuss it." Primly, Julia went on explaining. "My father worries about me. He refuses to allow me to revisit the East unless I'm accompanied by a husband—one who loves me completely. One who, furthermore, fully supports my professional aspirations in New York City. That's why I need...someone like you."

Graham let the subject of "loving her completely" rest for now, intriguing as it was. "Professional aspirations?"

She stiffened still further, as though his simple question insinuated something very different. "I have an opportunity to be hired as an etiquette columnist at *Beadle's Magazine.* It's something I've worked toward for years now."

Etiquette columnist. He shuddered. "And?"

"And I won't be able to accept unless my father believes I've found a husband in time to make the trip. Thus, my need for a fiancé to set things in motion."

Her expression earnest, Julia came closer. Evidently, her desperation to hie herself off, to New York City, of all places, overrode both her etiquette training *and* her wariness of him.

"It won't be a real marriage, if it comes to that. We can obtain an annulment the minute we leave Avalanche. And I can pay you well for your trouble. My mother's legacy was substantial. I'm sure that—"

"I don't need money."

She snapped her mouth closed, but not before her gaze whipped over his much-mended clothes and disreputable-looking boots, lingering just long enough to put his dander up.

"And I don't have any interest," Graham continued, frowning over her continued skepticism about the state of his finances, "in being any woman's fiancé—or, God forbid, her lapdog husband—at her beck and call for even so little as a month."

At that, Julia snorted. Graham raised an eyebrow.

"As though," she said, looking not the least bit abashed at having emitted such an unladylike sound, "anyone could expect that of *you.* Why, you must be the least malleable man I've ever met."

Paradoxically, her observation made him feel slightly more agreeable. *Mold me,* he thought, distracted again by thoughts of her hands against his skin, her touch gentle as the kiss of rain on the parched desert ground. *Let me show you how amenable I can be.*

"And as for that lapdog nonsense you mentioned—" she must have glimpsed the heat in his gaze, because her eyes widened and she stepped backward again "—well, pish posh. I'm sure I won't be requiring your services in such a manner."

"You won't?"

"Certainly not."

But she sounded uncertain, even intrigued, by the intimacies her scheme suggested. And despite himself, Graham was, too.

"I can be persuaded, even made a bit more malleable," he told her, quietly. Unable to resist, he raised her hand from her skirts and clasped its gloved softness in his. Looking into her eyes, he rubbed his thumb over the expensive kid that kept their bare skin from touching. "And I understand a bargain as well as the next man. What I can't see is what I stand to gain from this scheme."

Julia's mouth opened, then closed again as she visibly struggled for words. Her gaze swerved from his face to their joined hands, then skittered away to the cast-off furnishings surrounding them. "Money. You stand to gain money, as I've said."

"Not interested." And those prissy gloves of hers had separated them long enough, Graham decided. He worked the first button through its loop, already anticipating the warmth of her skin against his. Unbelievably, she didn't stop him.

"Favorable mention," Julia said rapidly, "once I'm ensconced at *Beadle's?* It's quite a popular periodical. The publicity might well improve your hiring rate."

Graham shook his head and freed another two pearl buttons. "I have all the work I want. When I want it."

She trembled in his grasp, but gamely continued to bargain. "The satisfaction of having aided a lady in need? Even a rogue such as yourself must—"

"Ahhh." His smile widened. Another button came free, exposing a tender glimpse of bare skin. "My reputation *does* precede me, then. Graham Corley...bounty hunter by trade, rogue by reputation, drifter by choice."

Squirming, whether with frustration at her bargaining gone awry or something sultrier, Julia gave a frustrated sound. "There must be something you want!"

Graham paused. With utmost care, he slipped away her glove and set to work on its mate. When it, too, was tugged from her hand, Julia released a pent-up breath. Shakily, she grabbed for her gloves, and came up empty when Graham tucked them playfully behind his back.

"There is something I want," he said. Looking down, he thought he saw defiance whisk over her features...defiance, and a hint of curiosity, too. "Something I've wanted for a very long time. And this seems just the opportunity to get it."

Thoughtfully, he rubbed his fingers over the gloves he'd captured. Somehow, they seemed to symbolize the differences between them...Julia, so refined and pure. He, so rugged and careworn. After a moment, Graham fisted the gloves in his hand, and felt the pliant leather yield to his strength—the same way Miss Julia Bennett would yield, if he had his way, to all that he wanted.

She simply didn't realize it yet.

Truth was, Julia was too busy believing she had the upper hand to allow anything else to interfere. Graham meant to turn their dealings onto a more even footing. Now, or later. He was a patient man.

"What is it?" she asked, her voice betraying not so much as a quaver. "What do you want?"

"If you give it to me, I'll agree to your fiancé scheme—even a sham marriage," Graham told her. "For up to a month."

The fact that they would be deceiving the townspeople and, most importantly, her father, bothered him. But not enough to change his course and not enough to still the idea that had taken hold inside him. Graham couldn't let himself be swayed by other people's foolishness. He'd been on the road too long now, depending only on himself, to believe otherwise. And if Asa Bennett didn't already realize what a schemer he had for a daughter, he deserved his fate.

"A month should be enough time," Julia said. "That's the term stipulated in the, um, er—" She broke off, gesturing awkwardly toward her reticule, where she'd stowed the multi-folded hiring agreement Graham hadn't been able to read. "That's what I was hoping for. But what do you want in return?"

She bit her lip, awaiting his reply. Graham leaned closer, the better to give his answer in the privacy it deserved.

"'Tis simple," he said. "I want you to teach me to read."

Bewitched by the enraptured look on the bounty hunter's face and feeling at a decided loss without the safe barrier of her gloves, Julia didn't fully understand what he'd proposed at first. Once she did, her first sensation was one of disappointment…disappointment that Mr. Corley hadn't touched her since removing her six-button French kid gloves, and dismay that she craved such personal contact at all. It was wildly improper, and decidedly unlike her.

"Oh!" she cried, desperate to seem as though she hadn't just been lost in a world of completely inappropriate desires. "Teach you to read, you say?"

"Yes."

His dangerous blue gaze dared her to ridicule his request. With her heart still thumping from her recent glove-removing adventure, Julia found she didn't have the strength to do so, much less the will. Against all reason, she liked Graham Corley. Liked his straightforward manner, his easy way with a smile, his surprising perceptiveness.

She might have liked the tumultuous feeling being close to him gave her, as well…had it not reminded her so powerfully that becoming smitten with a man had ended many a woman's ambitions toward greater things. Being in the city at college had been the most at home Julia had ever felt. There, she'd *belonged.* In Avalanche, she did not. And there was no power on Earth strong enough to convince her to rusticate here. Not while an avenue away remained open to her.

"I'd be delighted to," she told Mr. Corley, and it was true. She'd enjoy a chance to help him. "I fancy myself a passing fair teacher and you seem a quick learner."

His devil-may-care smile flashed again. This time it made her weak in the knees.

"I usually get by well enough," he said, "with the few words I've picked up here and there, from Wanted posters and saloon signs and letters from Fr—"

Graham stopped, making her wonder what he'd been about to say. *Letters from Frances? Frederica?* Did he have someone special in his life already? The notion bothered Julia more than she wished.

No, never mind if he'd already given his drifter's heart to another, she told herself sternly. It wasn't his heart she wanted, was it? It was the appearance of devotion, a *seeming fiancé,* that she was after. That would have to be enough.

No matter how much she might yearn for more, herself, someday. From someone...

"When that fails," Graham went on, as though he'd never faltered at all, "most towns have someone willing to read letters and contracts or scribe correspondence for a fee. Often the saloon owners or barkeeps. I get on well enough."

"But it's not enough," Julia said, sensing that much.

He shook his head, his unruly dark hair brushing the tops of his shoulders. "Not nearly enough," he said, his voice suddenly raw.

As though he couldn't bear to discuss such things without some action to deflect the feelings they aroused, Graham turned away. Purposefully, he began moving the dusty crates, clearing a space amongst them.

"I want to read a newspaper," he said as he worked. "To get lost in a book. To know the worlds that have been denied to me." His hands fisted on the box of discarded patent medicine bottles he held, and Graham stared fixedly at their varied shapes. *"I will be good as any man, or die trying."*

Her heart squeezed at the determination in his expression. Wanting to go to him, but knowing she should not, Julia tried a jest, instead. ''It shan't be *that* difficult,'' she offered. ''I've yet to have a student turn toes up on me.''

Graham's face cleared, but for the gratitude—if she wasn't mistaken—she glimpsed in his rough-hewn features. ''You've tutored others before me, then?'' he asked gruffly, setting the box down with the others.

''Not precisely,'' she admitted. A moment lapsed before Julia spoke again, a moment during which she found herself quite fascinated by the play of muscles in Mr. Corley's back and shoulders as he continued stacking crates in an orderly way. Giving herself a mental shake, she continued:

''But I have inadvertently found myself in such a position before, yes. When I returned from Vassar, with my three published etiquette guides tucked in my trunks and what I suppose was a newly acquired gleam of Eastern sophistication—''

''I'm sure you positively sparkled.'' The scoundrel paused in his work and winked at her.

''Suddenly, the ladies in town seemed willing, eager, even, to follow my lead. In matters of etiquette, social interaction, taste and even fashion.''

''Fashion?'' He cast a doubtful eye over her dress and hat, then grinned. The rascal.

Raising her chin, Julia finished. ''Despite what you may think, I seem to have started all manner of fads since my return. So you see, I've become quite the instructress, without having even tried. I'm sure that, with some determined efforts from you, we'll have you reading the likes of Shakespeare and Wordsworth in no time at all.''

She smiled over the notion of a rough-and-tumble

man like Graham Corley sitting down with a volume of romantic poetry. He'd more likely fancy one of *Beadle's* dime adventure novels, or an issue of *Punch.* But of course, she couldn't begin with such lowbrow material, Julia reminded herself. As an etiquette instructress, she owed it to everyone around her to be a model of perfect behavior.

Miss Julia's Behavior Book, volume one: To be a well-trained woman is to be courteous, cheerful, polite, pious, moral and benevolent, and to avoid gossip, slander, tale-telling, fault-finding, grumbling and public display of quarrels. Decorum is all.

Even while deprived of one's gloves? Julia wondered mischievously, and her smile took on a new width. The feelings Mr. Corley aroused in her were scandalous, indeed.

The man himself paused at that instant, and caught her bemused expression. Dropping the final crate, Graham narrowed his eyes and put his hands on his lean, twill-covered hips.

"What's so funny?" he demanded.

Julia started, embarrassed at having been caught. "Nothing! I was merely, er, contemplating our first lesson."

His expression darkened. "I warn you," he said. "I'm not above exposing your secret if you expose mine. I'd lay odds you won't want the town to know you hired me to...what was it? Be wild with love for you."

Recognizing her own intemperate words, she looked away. No, indeed she would not want the town knowing she'd hired a man. Especially for such outwardly bawdy purposes. Misunderstandings were bound to result.

Amidst her silence, Graham Corley stalked closer, all hard man and unknowable, roughly clad threat.

"Even a man who *loves you completely*—" his fierce, half-growled delivery turned the words she'd uttered earlier from an innocent requirement to a sensual promise "—can be pushed too far. Understand that, Miss Bennett?"

She gulped as he stopped before her. "Yes! Yes, I understand you perfectly. I won't reveal your tutoring without your approval, I promise." She drew in a breath. "Although my father will have to know, of course. It will provide us a reason to appear together."

Graham nodded, a barely perceptible tilt of his head.

"We—we have a deal, then?" she croaked out.

How she'd found the courage to validate their bargain, Julia would never know. But she did—and found herself steered, inelegantly, toward the seating area Mr. Corley had fashioned from several stacked crates. He swiped one clean with the sleeve of his duster coat, then seated her on it.

"A deal?" he repeated, raising his eyebrow. "Yes, we have a deal...and now we're going to confirm it."

"Confirm it?" Julia tightened her fingers on the crate beneath her. It felt strange and rough to her ungloved palms—as strange and rough as the bounty hunter suddenly seemed, looming over her with an unreadable expression on his face. "With a handshake, you mean?"

Gamely, she extended one hand. The scoundrel scoffed.

"With a promise?" she guessed, her heart beginning to pound with the anticipation of having her way at last. "I could write a—"

He shook his head, and his smile turned wolfish. "I didn't move these crates so you could sit and scribe. I moved them so you wouldn't swoon from the pleasure of what came next.''

''Whatever do you mean?'' Julia asked, wrinkling her brow. Men really did seem to complicate things unnecessarily. ''It's simple, really. In order to be binding, our agreement truly ought to be sealed—''

''With a kiss,'' Graham finished, and he'd scarce got the words from his mouth before he came forward, bent on one knee, and moved to claim his prize.

Chapter Five

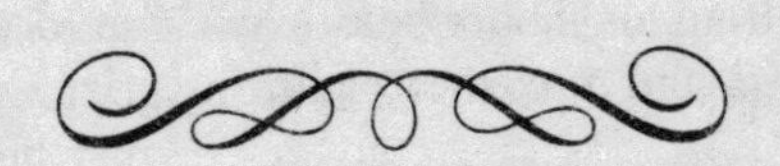

"Damnation, Corley! What the hell happened to your face?"

At the question, Graham squinted through the gloom of the livery stable he'd just entered. Reflexively, he put one hand to his left eye, and felt the lump that had grown up below the socket. "Got on the bad side of an ornery female," he muttered.

The men murmured in commiseration, making way for him in their group around the unlit potbellied stove. As in many other towns scattered throughout the Territory, the livery stable in Avalanche was both business and sanctuary for the local males. Within its two-story, boxlike space and unpainted lumber walls, everyone was equal—and equally deserving of sympathy.

"A filly you ain't had long can be like that," said the night man, putting away the last of the harnesses he'd been cleaning. "Pure temper. Once she gets used to you, she'll settle down."

"That's right," chorused the other men. "Hell, yes."

Graham had his doubts about that.

Nevertheless, he made a noncommittal sound and withdrew a cheroot from his duster pocket. Lighting it, he settled on the edge of the assemblage to listen, soaking up the tone and tempo of town news the way he'd first learned to do as a green bounty-chaser.

He steadfastly did *not* point out that the ''filly'' who'd walloped him had two legs, not four. Nor that she wore an outrageous flower-bedecked hat instead of a bridle. He left the men surrounding him to their assumptions. They did not need to know it was feisty Miss Julia Bennett who'd planted a sockdolager to remember on Graham Corley's face...no matter that he had the blackening eye to prove it.

Who'd have thought he'd lose his knack for sweet talk, and so rapidly, too? One minute, Julia had been all doe eyes, fluttering eyelashes and quivering hopefulness beside him. The next, she'd waylaid his intentions to seal their bargain with a kiss—by planting her hand on his chest, grabbing the nearest object at hand, and beaning him with it.

Unfortunately, that object had turned out to be a half-pound bar of pressed castile soap, discarded in a box of herbal nostrums. Graham supposed he ought to count himself lucky that Julia hadn't snatched up the heavy earthenware bottle of cod liver oil or package of anti-pain plaster stowed along with the soap...but he didn't. Not when the soap had encouraged a shocked Julia to blurt, ''Perhaps *that* will clean up those vulgar notions of yours!''

At the time, he'd been too surprised to do more than gape as she'd exited the cast-off building behind Bennett's Emporium with her head held high and her skirts in a flurry. But now, with his shiner ripening like a sour plum several hours later, Graham was starting to feel a bit testy.

He'd stolen countless kisses in his thirty-odd years of

prime bachelorhood. He intended to go on stealing many more. If prissy Miss Julia didn't want to count herself on the receiving end of one of them, that was just too bad for her, wasn't it? It wasn't as though he'd ever swooned in on a woman who didn't want to be kissed, after all.

No, sir.

And it wasn't as though she hadn't been wearing all the right signs, either, Graham reminded himself. For a single instant, as he'd leaned forward to kiss her…Julia had closed her eyes and actually swayed toward him. Near enough that he'd felt the whisper of her breath across his lips. He figured he might be able to live on the memory of that moment alone for quite a while.

'Course, a heartbeat later she'd poleaxed him with a cake of P. Q. Brown's Original Castile. But for an instant, she'd almost yielded. And that was all he needed to know. For now.

With talk still humming around him, underlaid by the sounds of animals shifting in their stalls and the clank of the blacksmith's shop nearby, Graham puffed his cheroot and breathed deeply. The comforting, earthy smells of horses, feed, manure, leather and hay were a balm to his wanderer's soul.

No matter how far afield he went, in every town the livery stable remained the same. Its constancy could be relied upon, from the walls covered with tin signs advertising all the same equine patent remedies, to the blackboard keeping track of which horses and carriages had been rented. Here in Avalanche, as in most every other town, a hand-lettered sign had been hung over the door:

WHIP LIGHT, DRIVE SLOW. PAY CASH BEFORE YOU GO.

Looking at it now, Graham grinned and carefully stubbed out his cheroot, pocketing the remainder for safekeeping against fire. He'd do well to go slowly with Miss Julia, too...else he might never discover what drove him to accept her wild proposition in the first place. If there was one thing Graham Corley couldn't tolerate, it was not knowing the whys behind things.

'Twas probably the same poor impulse that had driven him to ask to be taught to read. He still couldn't believe he'd done it. Yet at the prospect of shouldering into that long-forbidden world, a part of him felt as excited as a boy. Surely the promise he'd made in exchange wouldn't be that difficult to keep...would it? How thorny could it be to woo a lady, pretend to be her fiancé, and fool a town into thinking the two of them head over feet?

Well...when one of those two was uppity etiquette book authoress Julia Bennett, it might be pretty difficult, Graham reflected. Frowning over his remembrance of the Castile soap incident—and its implications on his current predicament—he cleared his throat and addressed the men around him.

"On the subject of ladies," he said, speaking on the heels of a joke about a farmer's daughter and a medicine show drummer, "where are the marriageable females in this town? I've got my mind set on finding the future Mrs. Corley while I'm here."

Ten pairs of masculine eyes gaped at him in astonishment.

"I'm terribly sorry, Miss Libbie," Julia said to her fourth soda fountain customer that afternoon. "You know I'm not permitted to make a gooseberry soda for

Herbert, no matter how much he wants one. I'm afraid you'll have to take him outside."

Libbie, nine years old and Julia's neighbor since her birth into the packed O'Halloran clan two doors down from the Bennett household, stared disconsolately from the opposite side of the counter. In her arms she clutched a white Bantam rooster with a red comb and an eager expression.

"But I earned the money especially for this treat, helping Miss Verna dust the shelves in her mercantile," Libbie protested. "Herbert is very fond of gooseberry sodas."

"And you're very fond of Herbert."

The girl nodded. Her red-gold curls bounced against her shoulders, partially obscuring the bird tucked so closely against her calico and lace gown. "He's my best friend."

She ducked her chin and whispered something to the rooster, then smoothed her cheek gently against his head. Herbert shook himself, then gave Julia a beady-eyed look.

Julia could recognize a fowl threat when she saw one.

But in this instance, she'd do better not to relent. No matter how the sight of Libbie hugging her "best friend" tugged at memories of Julia's own lonely past. Like Libbie, Julia had wanted someone of her very own to love, someone who would love and accept her in return. She simply hadn't had the necessary audacity to claim that affection in whatever form it came...even poultry.

She'd like to think she'd grown out of such soft-hearted yearnings. Truth was, she hadn't. It took nothing more than a glimpse of a courting couple sharing a ginger soda, their bodies close together at one of the

Emporium's intimate round wrought-iron tables, to remind her of that. Even something so commonplace as a pair of lady friends out shopping together, or a mother and daughter whispering over the choice of one of her father's patented cold remedies, had the power to touch that raw place in her soul. It never eased. Julia had begun to fear it never would.

Plainly put, she was different. From an early age, she'd been able to cipher sums that stumped grown men. She'd easily memorized great quantities of literature and history. She'd understood the way things worked in an intuitive fashion that set her apart from all the other children in Avalanche's one-room schoolhouse, and even from her schoolteachers. Having those abilities didn't make Julia need acceptance and caring any less...it only made finding them even more difficult.

At least it had, until she'd discovered Vassar College, and the safe anonymity of the city two days' ride away. There, no one had looked askance when she'd spent a day reading books. No one had ridiculed her interest in poetry, or her talent for quoting great philosophers. She'd been free. A bit lonely...but free. And honestly, she'd become accustomed to the loneliness. A person did, after a while. Which brought her right back to Miss Libbie and Herbert.

Julia smiled at the girl. Really, she'd be doing Libbie a favor if she encouraged her to stop buying treats for her pet and put Herbert back in his chicken coop. Doubtless, the other children made fun of Libbie for having such an unusual companion. And Julia knew only too well the pain of being laughed at. Teased. Excluded.

A small "harrumph" from her father, at his post at

his druggist's counter, brought Julia back to the present. She glanced at him, and saw the quick shake of his graying head that told her she was meant to make Libbie and Herbert leave the Emporium.

"Listen closely, Miss Libbie," Julia said, leaning farther over the soda fountain counter to speak with the child. "I have a plan."

At the whispered confidence she shared, Libbie looked up, wide-eyed. "Do you really mean it?" she asked. "About Herbert?"

Julia nodded. Then she snatched up a fountain glass, expertly worked the ornate levers on the fountain's dispensing nozzles, and emerged from behind the counter shortly thereafter with two fizzy gooseberry sodas balanced on a tray.

A few minutes' consultation with her father produced the efficient—if somewhat skeptical—moving of a table and two chairs to the boardwalk out front. With Libbie and Herbert preceding her—and Isabel taking charge of the fountain for the next little while—Julia carried the drinks outside.

"There!" she pronounced, setting down the tray. "A most elegant dining experience. *Al fresco,* as I've heard it's done in Paris, France."

Libbie jumped up and down and giggled, causing Herbert to ruffle a few feathers. Asa Bennett gave another "harrumph" and retreated to his druggist's counter again. And Julia sat down, crooked her pinkie, and initiated the soda-drinking. Libbie joined her quickly, spooning foamy gooseberry-syrup-infused carbonated water from her glass and patiently feeding the treat to the rooster perched on her lap.

Passersby gave sidelong glances to the doubtlessly strange sight of a girl, a rooster and an apron-clad etiquette instructress sharing gooseberry sodas in the middle of the afternoon. But Julia didn't care. If everything went as planned, because of this Libbie would soon have more friends—of the *non*-feathered variety—than she ever had before. And that would make it all worthwhile.

After walking from the livery stable down the length of Main Street, locating the perpendicularly situated Fir Tree Lane, and muttering his way past seven separate houses, Graham stood at the gate to the eighth and squinted speculatively. The setting sun threw the house into partial shadow, and put a chill in the air that made him grateful for his newly won duster coat. Despite the poor lighting, Graham decided, this had to be the residence he sought.

For one thing, the place wore gingerbread trim like Julia Bennett wore lace—to excess and without apology. For another, its two stories, fancy peaked rooflines, and primly painted three-quarters porch reminded Graham strongly of the fancy-frilly architecture of the dress she'd been wearing earlier. And for a third, its prominent three-bay glass window fairly screamed wealth—the same way Miss Julia's manner did, when she looked down her nose at his trail-ragged duds. Yep, this was the place all right.

Graham opened the gate and started up the brick walk. The fragrance of flowers reached him as he passed orderly beds; the solid clunk of well-tended painted lumber met his boot heels as he ascended the steps. Growing increasingly uneasy, he ducked beneath the decorative spindled archway that led to the entry, then stopped on the mat and regarded the imposing front door.

It had been years since he'd entered a respectable home on a social call like this one, Graham recalled suddenly. Years since he'd had occasion to sit in a parlor instead of a saloon, making polite conversation instead of finagling a bounty-hunting deal.

The last time he'd faced a proper front door like this one, he'd been eight years old and hopeful as a puppy with a bone too big...and he'd wound up leaving soon after, with his tail between his legs, too. In the end, it had always turned out that way for him. He'd learned to quit hoping, had gotten good at moving on. Now he didn't quite remember what it was like to stay put.

Not that he wanted to, Graham reminded himself staunchly. He'd chosen a drifter's life and it had always suited him. The sooner he finished this charade with Julia Bennett, the sooner he could return to that life.

Ignoring his tightening throat, he sucked in a deep breath and knocked. Moments later, the door opened. An apron-wearing, sour-faced maid stood in the entry.

"Yes?" she asked, her attention all for her floury hands and water-spotted apron once she'd sized him up. "May I help you?"

"Graham Corley to see Miss Bennett," he said. His voice boomed in the small space, overly loud and rough as gravel to his ears. Defiantly, he squared his shoulders and silently dared the woman to refuse him, the way he half expected.

"You must mean Dr. Bennett," she told him dismissively, waving her arm. "Use the side entrance. That's where all his customers go to, once the Emporium's closed for the day."

She began closing the door. Graham jammed his boot into the passage. "I mean Miss Julia Bennett, not her father. I've come to call."

A confused look met his statement. "You've come to call on Miss Julia?"

"Yes."

The woman's perplexed expression only grew. Did no one ever call on Miss Julia? Or did no *gentlemen* ever call on her? Against all reason, Graham hoped it was the latter.

"She's expecting me," he added.

"Have you a card?" the woman asked. Her pinched face begrudged him every syllable of the question. "I'll see if she's at home."

He stared at her work-roughened, floury hand, outstretched to receive his calling card, and realized, in that moment, exactly how ill-equipped he was to enter his supposed "fiancée's" world. A bounty hunter carried no card, had no credentials save his record for captures and a hard-earned reputation. The reputation Graham had made—for patience, tireless pursuit, shrewd captures and honest dealings—would hardly carry weight in a world where ladies pretended not to be "at home" to disreputable elements.

Disreputable elements...like him.

"No card?" the maid asked. She arched a brow. "Miss Julia is not at home to you, then. Good day."

Frowning, he made ready to leave. The maid's obvious disapproval pushed at him in ways he hadn't experienced since his days in Boston. He thought only to escape it. For an overlong moment, Graham felt crushed beneath it, desperate to strike the trail and put Avalanche, with its close-knit families and respectable ladies, firmly at his back. The way he always did. The way he always would.

But then something inside him caught hold, and he stopped with his body only just turned away. The chill of the deepening twilight swirled past him with his return to face the maid.

"I've no card but this," Graham said, snatching a dollar coin from his pocket and holding it out to her. "I'd say it's fine enough for now."

Her eyes widened. "What'd you say your name was?"

"Graham Corley." He said it proudly, the consequences be damned. Miss Julia Bennett and her family would accept him as he was, or not have him at all. "To see Miss Bennett."

"Fine, then." Instantly, her demeanor changed to one of cooperation. "I'll tell her you've come."

The coin disappeared. So did the maid. And a moment later, the woman who'd filled his mind with visions of lace, his senses with the fragrance of oranges and woman, and his dreams with foolish hopes better left unspoken, arrived in her place.

Julia.

The very sight of her revitalized him, brought him away from the childhood memories that plagued him back to the life of the man he'd become. Graham felt calmer, clearer—utterly purposeful. The past was behind him. This—*she*—was his future, and he meant to make good on the bargain they'd made.

She stood on the threshold, dressed in a new gown of deep blue and ruffles, and gawped at him as though she couldn't quite believe her eyes. Clearly, Graham decided, Julia could not believe her fiancé prayers were being answered quite so swiftly…and so masterfully. Mustering a bow from some mostly forgotten sense of gallantry, he angled himself before her and then rose with a grin on his lips.

"Let the games begin," he said.

Letting out a squeak, Julia grabbed his coat sleeve and hauled him inside the foyer, slamming the door behind them.

"Sweet heaven, you're really here," she muttered, her gaze roving from the top of his head to his boot heels. In the distance, the sounds of conversation and clanking cutlery were heard, betraying the presence of other people in the house, but Julia's attention was all for the man standing nearly noses-touching in front of her. "What in the *world* have I done?"

Chapter Six

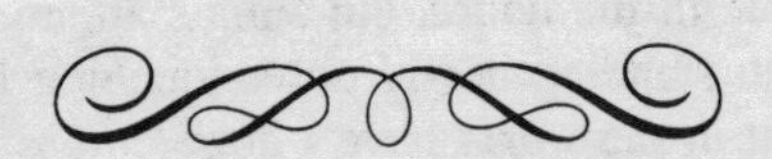

"What have you done?" Graham repeated. Stepping still closer to her in the foyer, he gave her a widening, bedazzling smile. "Why you've bartered yourself a man to come courting, Miss Julia. And I'm here to fulfill my end of the bargain."

"Now? Like this?" Panic poured through her at this unanticipated development, and suddenly Julia wanted nothing more than to take back her desperate scheme. "You can't!"

"I can. *I am.*"

"Paying calls after five o'clock simply isn't done," she returned inanely, taking refuge in the security of her etiquette books. "We're already at dinner."

Graham wrinkled his brow. He glanced at the octagonal foyer's elegant furnishings, taking in the mauve velvet drapes, glossy parquet floor, standing fern, and upholstered settee as though noticing them for the first time.

"I've been afoot for so long now, I've lost track of such things," he admitted. "I'm sorry to disturb you. I can see that your dinner is important to you. Its interruption has you fair worked up."

His gaze shifted to her hand, still fisted on his coat sleeve. Beneath his flat-brimmed hat, his eyes sparkled with teasing humor. At once, Julia became aware of the hoydenish way she'd dragged the bounty hunter inside the house with her, and wanted to close her eyes with embarrassment at the memory of it.

Miss Julia's Behavior Book, volume three: Unseemly and impudent contact should never be tolerated. No proper woman permits a man to be so familiar as to toy with her hands, encircle her waist with his arm, or otherwise encroach intimately upon her person.

How much worse, then, was it for a *woman* to handle a gentleman in such a fashion? If she continued to behave so recklessly, she would lose what little respect and admiration she'd earned in the community since her return. Seeing her plan through, Julia realized, would require far greater self-control than she'd thought. It would be risky, in the extreme.

Something about Graham Corley, though, brought out a kind of irresistible wildness in her. An urge to throw caution afield and do…*something.* She didn't know what.

"Or maybe it's me," Graham said, breaking into her thoughts with his rumbling voice and good-natured manner, "that has you in such a state. *My* presence that's got you all aflutter. I wonder…."

Experimentally, he moved closer, angling their bodies more nearly parallel. Julia found herself unable to move away, helpless to do more than hold her breath and wait to discover what came next. A taut expectancy took hold of her, thrumming through her with an excitement that was wholly unwise…and completely overpowering.

The bounty hunter's coat whispered with his continued movement, brushing against her skirts. His dark hat dipped low to shade his whiskery face. With his free hand, Graham touched his fingertips to her chin, and tilted her face upward toward his. The heat of his body made her skin fairly tingle.

"Standing this way, so close with your hand on my arm, 'tis almost an embrace," he observed. "Nearly a lover's hello."

Only he could have turned her embarrassing social *faux pas* into an opportunity for seduction, Julia thought crazily. Yet for a heartbeat, it seemed almost as though Graham truly craved that fond greeting he'd mentioned. The harsh angles of his face softened as the bounty hunter spoke of it, and his eyes darkened with anticipation.

His fingertips stroked her, once. Julia leaned nearer, her heart beating wildly, momentarily fascinated by the change in him.

"If I didn't know better, I would swear you hold me like this because you can't bear to let go," he said, some hitch in his smile betraying an earnest hope behind his lightly spoken words. "You're a woman of passion, Miss Bennett."

Leisurely, he lowered his hand. Julia refused to admit that she felt the loss of his touch.

"'Twill make our charade go easier," he added, eyes sparkling. "I'm pleased to learn it."

"I'm sure to deny it!" She found the will to loosen her grasp at last, and tucked her fist safe at her side amidst her skirts.

"Ahh, but will you deny it truly? Or would that be a lie?"

Without awaiting her answer, Graham shucked his coat and hat and hung both on the mahogany coatrack beside the front door. Then he stretched his arms high, groaning with unconscious pleasure at the movement, and stepped with heavy footfalls a few paces farther into the house. His attention was drawn to the table, where he touched the calling cards in their silver plate receiver.

For some inexplicable reason, he dropped a coin into their midst, looked at it with something close to satisfaction, and then continued his survey of the house.

His shrewd assessment was unnerving. It was as though Graham saw and measured everything in the blink of an eye. Doubtless the ability served him well in his notorious profession, but heaven help her if he ever decided to turn his talents toward her! She'd have nary a secret left, nor the will to keep one from him.

The thought jolted Julia into action. She needed to take the upper hand, here, else risk losing it forever. As it was, her sense of control was sorely slipping away.

"Perhaps if you'd care to wait in the parlor," she began, walking toward him with hopes of guiding them both into the adjacent room, "we could—"

"Get better acquainted? I'd like that."

He turned the whole of his focus on her. The effect was enough to stop her where she stood. My, but the man had a wickedly charming manner, when he chose to!

As though he'd guessed what she'd been thinking—and approved—Graham's smile broadened. "A man should know his betrothed. *As thoroughly as possible.*"

"We could have a proper visit, after dinner," she finished staunchly, willing herself to seem unaffected, and untempted, by his outrageous suggestions. "With a chaperone, of course."

His answering expression of disappointment was nearly her undoing. It seemed as though Graham truly wanted to be alone with her—to get to know her—and the notion was a heady one, indeed. The man was a rogue, it was true…but he was a likeable one, too.

Trying to hide the strange, topsy-turvy feelings being near him gave her, Julia indicated the parlor with one hand. Amiably, Graham edged past her in a graceful movement she wouldn't have expected in a man so powerful.

Their bodies nearly touched as he left her, and she found herself entranced by the glimpse of bare, tanned throat and masculine chest his partially unbuttoned shirt afforded her, right at eye level. It was with unfamiliar awareness that Julia watched him turn away and stride to the center of the parlor.

"A chaperone?" Turning to her, he raised his eyebrows. "Are you afraid to be alone with me, then?"

Yes, suddenly. So long as he wore that predatory aura and expression of masculine surety, she would be. Never mind the fact that she'd soundly discouraged him once before—with a cake of soap, no less—and that he had the bruised face to show for it. In matters of men and women, compared with the bounty hunter's greater experience, Julia was at a disadvantage.

And she knew it.

"Being alone together wouldn't be proper," she said aloud, following him inside the room.

"It would be enjoyable."

"Not once someone found out. Even betrothed, we'll need to take care, else risk both our reputations."

He made a small sound, one that richly expressed his disregard of a proper reputation. Unnerved at this reminder of the risk she was taking in bargaining with him, Julia hid her dismay with a burst of activity. It wouldn't do for the bounty hunter to guess she had anything less than utter command of herself and her future.

She took a few minutes to adjust the love seat and chair pillows and to light additional lamps for his comfort. That accomplished, she looked upward to discover him regarding her seriously.

"We're alone right now," he said, as though no break had taken place in their earlier conversation. "It can't have escaped your notice."

It hadn't. Julia had the trembling fingers and unusual urge to look her fill of his rugged features to prove it. The last thing she meant to do, however, was reveal that fact. At least not until she thoroughly understood her fascination with Graham herself.

"I'm aware of our situation," she said instead, busying herself with arranging sheet music atop the parlor piano. "It's most out of the ordinary for me, Mr. Corley, and I assure you—"

"You have nothing to fear from me, Miss Bennett. Nothing at all. No matter how beautiful you look, with the lamplight shining on your face that way."

Julia stilled, the husky sound of his compliment still echoing inside her. A thrill enveloped her, and she dared to send a forthright glance his way.

He stood, unapologetically blunt and unfortunately bruised. Graham nodded once, almost tenderly. "'Tis true. The dress becomes you as well. I noticed while you lit the lamps."

At a loss for the flirtatious response that was clearly called for, Julia brushed her palms down the dark bombazine skirt of her gown. Her heart felt too open to him, all at once, her soul too hungry for acceptance, to pretend otherwise with a careless remark or coquettish gesture. It was as though, somehow, this unlikely man saw inside her to what she needed, and could not wait to provide it.

Which was foolish, of course. Why she should feel such a pull toward him, Julia didn't know. And until she did, she, who was accustomed to understanding all the things in her world, was afraid to reveal as much to him.

So she looked away, and busied herself with the ornaments on a side table. "You needn't flatter me so, Mr. Corley," she told him evenly. "It isn't part of our agreement."

"Perhaps," Graham said, and there was undisguised bemusement in his tone. "But courting you *is* a part of it, and so is paying calls, like this one."

Of course. He'd merely been fulfilling the terms of their bargain. In the future, Julia reminded herself, she'd have to take care not to be naive enough to take everything that passed between them at face value.

"You asked me to call on you," he went on. "Here I am."

"Indeed." She needed to return to dinner, she thought wildly. Her father and Aunt Geneva would be wondering what had happened to her. But Julia found herself curiously reluctant to leave her bounty hunter. And so she lingered. "Do you need anything before I go? I could send Alice 'round with refreshments for you."

At mention of her household's longtime servant, Graham grimaced strangely. But all he said was, "No. Thank you."

"Very well, then. I suppose I—"

"What's this?" came a booming interruption from the passageway between the parlor and the adjacent dining room. The twin walnut doors dividing the areas slid

aside with a thunk, and Asa Bennett emerged from between them. "Refreshments for the man, when we're right in the midst of dinner? Come now, Julia! Let's show the proper courtesy to Mister...?"

He extended his hand to the bounty hunter, a jovial grin playing over his usually serious face. Graham clasped it, and they shook solidly.

"Corley," he replied. "Graham Corley. I've come to call on your daughter, Mr. Bennett."

"Asa!" her father insisted. He rubbed a hand through his graying hair, then let his palm rest on the waistcoat of his tailored brown suit, just above the paunch his skinny frame supported. "We don't stand on formality in this household. Not amongst our friends."

He laughed aloud, and Julia gaped at him. Her father typically stood on utmost formality with his *family,* and certainly with acquaintances. What had gotten into him?

Whatever it was, it was growing increasingly worse, she learned next.

"You hear that, Geneva?" her father called, leaning sideways toward the dining room beyond. "Young Mr. Corley here has come to call on our Julia!"

"Oh, my goodness!" Geneva Whitcomb, Julia's aunt on her mother's side, bustled into the room, almost as though she'd been waiting for exactly such an opportunity. "My dear boy," she called to Graham, "do come in. *Such* a pleasure to meet someone of Julia's acquaintance."

Geneva's gaze flickered meaningfully to her brother-in-law, then back to Graham. Julia watched the byplay in befuddlement, at a loss to discern what caused her family to behave so atypically.

"I was just explaining to Mr. Corley that I'd need a chaperone if we were to spend more time together, Aunt

Geneva,'' Julia said hurriedly. ''I wouldn't presume to—''

''Nonsense!'' Geneva, tall and elegant in a green gown with her dark hair twisted in a ribbon-embellished chignon, waved her hand dismissively. She'd come to live with them since shortly after Julia's mother had died, and was very much a respected authority in the family. ''These are enlightened times. And you're an eminently trustworthy person.''

At that, her aunt and father both looked inexplicably pained. Nevertheless, Geneva hurried on: ''A trustworthy person *of a certain age,* to boot. With your family right in the next room, we hardly need to stand on such ceremony. Wouldn't you agree, Asa?''

''Indeed.''

Julia boggled, but her father continued on blithely—and, she could add, utterly uncharacteristically.

''Especially where Mr. Corley, here, is concerned,'' he said. ''As a matter of fact, Mayor Westley and the sheriff were both in the Emporium today, telling me all about this young man's efforts on behalf of Territorial justice.'' Beaming, Asa clapped Graham on the back. ''Excellent work nabbing that Hidalgo character, young man.''

Conversation turned rapidly to the criminal capture that had brought the bounty hunter to the Arizona Territory, and to Avalanche. Julia stood by in stunned amazement as the lively talk continued between her family and her imminent fiancé. If she'd expected them to be taken aback at Graham's unusual occupation, she'd been mistaken.

''But why are we going on and on, here in the parlor,'' Asa said several confusing minutes later, ''when Mr. Corley is doubtlessly hungry?''

"Oh, yes, please do join us for dinner," Geneva urged.

Although she did not actually seize Graham's arm in encouragement, she did plant herself directly in his path...with her elbow conveniently crooked. With a wink for Julia, Graham did his duty and escorted her aunt.

"Thank you," he said, grinning. "I'd be happy to."

His boots rang loudly against the polished floorboards, and his rough clothing contrasted madly with the painstakingly stylish furnishings around him. Graham's easy ways took the place of proper manners, and his ready laughter belied all decorum. But despite all that, her father and aunt clustered around the bounty hunter. They watched with satisfied eyes as he sat at the table, and quickly summoned Alice to serve him.

And that was how, against all reason and expectation, Julia found her choice of a temporary fiancé welcomed into the bosom of the Bennett family. It was almost simple enough to cause suspicion...if she'd been a mistrustful sort of person. Which, of course, she wasn't.

Or hadn't been. Until now.

The dining room of the Bennett family, Graham discovered during more than an hour's worth of eating and conversation, was every bit as idiosyncratic as its inhabitants. The table itself was carved wood in an English style. The urns of colorful peacock feathers in each corner were vaguely exotic. The brick fireplace with its warm crackling flames was rustic, the mullioned windows were modern, and the table settings themselves...never in his life had he come across so much varied china, cutlery and linen.

He hadn't the scarcest idea of what fork to use when,

nor where to put his hands. Suddenly, they seemed overlarge, even for a man as big as himself. His knuckles grazed the glass goblets, nearly overturning them. His squarish fingers fumbled over the salt cellar and rewarmed beef roast that coin-hungry Alice brought from the kitchen for him. And his conscience nagged at him all the while, for the deceit he was about to practice upon the people who had welcomed him into their home.

But Julia sat across from him, lovely in the golden glow of the small lighted chandelier overhead. And Julia smiled at his jokes, and worried over the adventures he'd described of his bounty hunting days. He felt fair giddy in her presence, and to see the interest and absorption in her face made any discomfort worthwhile. By the end of the meal, Graham felt sure he'd have happily hung a fork from his shirt and called it a four-in-hand necktie, just to hear her laugh.

He hadn't expected to find a welcome here. Had steeled himself against the lack of it, in fact. The familiar tightness in his neck and shoulders told him that much. 'Twas as though he'd brought along five pairs of the iron shackles he carried for reluctant prisoners, and had worn those 'round his shoulders instead of a plain shirt to match his britches.

The time he'd spent with the family, though, had eased him somewhat. Rolling the kinks from his muscles with a few discreet movements, he reconsidered his situation.

Asa Bennett and his sister-in-law Geneva were uncommonly open-minded people, Graham decided. He didn't want to enjoy their wholehearted welcome…but he did. The coziness and laughter around their table did much to restore a man who'd awakened that morning with nary a notion where he'd drifted to now. Or where he'd be going to next.

"Ahhh, here's Alice with the plum tart now," Geneva said, breaking into his mawkish thoughts. She smiled brightly as the maid carried in a porcelain plate filled with pastry. "Do give Mr. Corley the first piece, please, Alice."

"I'm near too full to eat another bite," Graham said, watching as the maid expertly cut and served a crumbly piece of fruit tart. But as she slid a plate before him and the aromas of sweet plums and fresh-baked pastry drifted upward, he couldn't resist. "It does look delicious, though."

"Every man has room for something sweet." Geneva gave an overly innocent smile as she helped pass more plates of dessert. "Do sample *all* the treats our household has to offer, Mr. Corley. I insist."

Julia's mouth dropped open. "Aunt Geneva!"

"What? I'm merely urging our guest to enjoy himself."

"That's exactly what I'm concerned with!"

"Pshaw. Your Mr. Corley knows precisely what I mean." Geneva turned to him, her merry hazel eyes twinkling brightly enough to rival her fancy earbobs. "Don't you, sir?"

He did. The double entendre contained in her words was ribald enough to take its place amongst the farmer's daughter jokes at the livery stable. Unable to contain a grin, Graham said, "'Twould be a shame not to end such an excellent meal with a proper finale, I'll agree. I'm all for something sweet."

Geneva straightened, looking delighted. Alice left the dining room carrying the rest of the tart, looking smug. Asa Bennett devoured his pastry, looking ravenous. Julia watched Graham cut a bite of dessert…looking nervous.

He gave her his best roguish wink for reassurance, and then began to eat. Availing himself of the household's other delectables would just have to wait for a better time.

The first tender forkful was fruity and sweet and unlike anything Graham had ever sampled. The buttery pastry nearly melted on his tongue, and the tangy plums brought his senses alive. "Mmmm. Delicious," he said, closing his eyes to better savor the taste.

When he'd finished the first bite, Graham opened his eyes to see Julia across the table from him, an enraptured expression on her face. She watched his mouth avidly, her fingers gone still on her own cutlery. Her gaze was alive with a hunger he doubted she recognized, and several moments passed before she realized he'd noticed her.

A becoming blush rose in her cheeks. "I—I'm so glad you enjoy your dessert," she said, clearing her throat against a sudden hoarseness. She shifted in her chair. "Is, er, plum tart a special favorite of yours?"

Asa and Geneva looked on, with avid interest. Graham sensed their gazes, but somehow couldn't tear his attention from Julia. Something drew them together, he felt sure, but was at a loss to describe what it was.

"I've never tried it before," he told her. "Nor most other sweets. They're not easy to come by, for a man on the trail. As a child, I sometimes had penny candy—" *nicked from a shop during an outing with Frankie and the others* "—but that was all."

"No Christmas treats?" Geneva asked in surprise. "No birthday cake?"

Graham turned to her. The words he'd never meant

to say were out before he could stop them, loosened by conviviality and encouraged by the ease he felt. "I don't know my birthday, ma'am. Never have."

The three of them looked shocked. Graham felt equally shocked that he'd ever revealed such a thing. It was unlike him. Shoving aside the rest of his tart, he made ready to leave. He didn't want to have this conversation, and had stayed overlong, in any case.

He'd grown complacent, in this place. Already. Bargain or no, Graham couldn't allow it to happen again.

"No birthday?" Asa said, breaking the silence with an awkward chuckle. "Damned shame, sir. Perhaps you could adopt one, on your own? I see no reason why not. Holidays are set in just such a manner, and—"

"Hush, Asa," Geneva said. With a sympathetic sigh, she reached for Graham's forearm. "I'm so sorry, Mr. Corley. I'm sure we didn't mean to be intrusive. Please forgive us."

"The fault is mine." Stiffly, Graham rose.

As though she'd only just now recovered from the surprise of his announcement, Julia looked up. Regret softened her features, that and...pity? 'Twas more than he could bear.

"Please, don't leave," she said quietly. "I didn't mean—"

"I know." Straightening to his full height, Graham met their expectant looks with a straightforward one of his own. Hard-earned pride stiffened his shoulders as he explained.

"I was a foundling child, discovered on the streets of Boston and taken in by the Sisters of Mercy. 'Tis why I have no birthday. And why I've had no plum tart 'til now." He tried for a grin, but it felt strange on his lips. "Doubtless 'tis why I can say goodbye to you so well right now, given the practice I learned in their care.''

Some strange emotion welled inside him, and Graham brutally pushed it back. ''Thank you for your welcome, and for the meal. I'll see myself out.''

He saw nothing but the blur of the household passing him as he left, heard nothing but the thunder of his boots against a floor too fine for the likes of him. And it wasn't until Graham felt the gentle touch of a hand on his shoulder and turned in the midst of putting on his hat and duster coat that he realized Julia had followed him.

He ducked his head and made a gruff sound, embarrassed to have her see him in so unguarded a state. ''You see now why this was a mistake,'' Graham said roughly. He shook off her hand to finish pulling on his hat. ''I told you so in the park this morning.''

For a long moment, she only looked at him. Looked at him in a way that made him feel *seen,* and woefully uncomfortable.

''Please,'' Julia said. ''Please, come back. If not now, then tomorrow. Will you promise?''

He gazed back at her, fighting a fierce urge to cradle her face in his hand. Graham wanted to discover if she gave a kiss as passionately as she wielded a cake of Castile soap, and as sweetly as she'd savored his pleasure in the taste of a tart. But a kiss to Julia would mean more to her than he could give. Graham forced himself to stand steady.

''I don't know if I'll be back,'' he answered, as truthfully as he could. She deserved that, at least.

Then he slipped out the door, into a night that felt more welcoming for its familiarity than anything indoors ever could...for a drifting man like him. And he waited for relief to strike, knowing he'd taken his leave of Julia and her family before things became even more tangled.

Oddly enough, relief did not strike. For the first time, Graham had allowed himself to want. And what he wanted, what he needed, was the woman he left farther behind with every step.

Chapter Seven

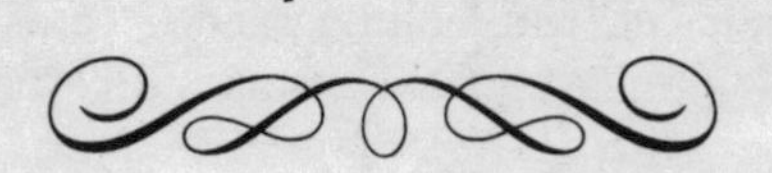

Two days passed. Julia had no word from Mr. Corley, and at first feared she never would.

Without meaning to, her family had hurt him, during their dinner together. As open as the bounty hunter had been about his foundling childhood, it had been as plain as his rigid shoulders and stoic expression that it pained him to speak of it. He would not want to come back for more.

Doubtless, Mr. Corley would leave Avalanche far behind—and with it, his intentions to hold fast to their bargain, too. Julia had reasoned as much during that long first night. She'd curled into her quilt, cold and unaccountably lonesome, and known in her heart it was true.

But then her intellect had come to her rescue, and had delivered a plan so clever she felt sure that Fate had a hand in it. Thus far—much to her relief—it had been functioning perfectly. The latest evidence of that fact stood before Julia right now, in her father's Apothecary and Soda Fountain Emporium.

Patrick O'Halloran, Libbie's eleven-year-old brother and Asa Bennett's drugstore delivery boy, panted as he looked up at her. Beneath his strawberry-blond hair, his cheeks were rosy with the effects of running in April's early-morning chill.

"All finished, Miss Julia," he said. He cast a furtive glance toward her father, busy behind his druggist's counter. "Do you have something for me?"

"*If* you have something for me." Julia fetched a stack of colorful, chromolithographed cards from the pocket of her soda fountain apron and casually sorted through them. "What news of Mr. Corley today?"

Another furtive look. "Mrs. Harrington told me, when I took her delivery of Hostetter's Stomach Bitters to her, that the bounty hunter spent the night at her boardinghouse. Same as last night," Patrick confided. His gaze followed the cards in her hands with a collector's interest. "And this morning, he was at Cutter's Restaurant, havin' eggs and taters, when I took in a bottle of Lydia Pinkham's Compound for Mrs. Cutter."

"He was? Did he seem all right to you?" She bit her lip, awaiting his answer.

Patrick wrinkled his forehead. "All right?"

"Yes. You know, cheerful. Happy?" Since Graham's revelation—and sudden departure—from her house two days ago, Julia had become increasingly worried about him. She knew her family's intrusion had wounded him…and the proud, pain-filled look on his face as he'd left haunted her still.

"Oh, yes, ma'am. He looked fine to me. I guess."

"Truly?"

"Sure." The boy shrugged. "Saloonkeeper Cole over at the Last Chance says types like Mr. Corley are ornery at the best of times. The bounty hunter didn't shoot nobody over his eggs not bein' cooked right, if that's what you mean."

Julia grinned. That would have to do for now, she decided, her mind somewhat at ease.

In thanks, she fanned out the cards, watching as the richly illustrated images sifted through her fingers. Left at the Emporium by drummers and representatives of various companies, the cards were in fact advertisements, meant to be distributed to potential customers. They had become popular collectible items among children like Patrick, though...and Julia was a very reliable source.

"I overheard Mr. Corley sayin' he'd be heading out to the livery stable after breakfast," Patrick added, still eyeballing the cards. "He's probably there right now."

Grinning, Julia ruffled his hair. "*Excellent* spying, Patrick! I don't know what I'd do without you."

But I do know what I'll do with a certain wayward bounty hunter, Julia thought. And once she'd handed over several coveted cards to a beaming Patrick, she set out to do exactly that.

At the livery stable, Graham rolled his cheroot between his fingertips, watching a slender wisp of smoke curl from the thin cigar's lighted end. All around him, local men discussed the business of the day, talking over feed prices and politics and all the latest news on who'd taken ill in Avalanche.

'Twas the most mundane conversation he'd been treated to since arriving in town.

And all when he most needed something illicit, illegal and untoward, calling for a bounty hunter's skills to bring about the proper justice. Did this milk-instead-of-whiskey place breed no ruffians, no criminal types? He could scarcely believe his poor luck.

He'd already had time to see to his horse, groom the

animal from forelock to fetlock as he did daily, and dole out an extra ration of oats for the restless bay gelding. All the while, the men of Avalanche had talked about quinine, hay bales, ague, President Cleveland's veto of Civil War veterans' pensions, and whether or not carbonated soda waters truly carried the medicinal and healthful benefits they claimed.

This last reminded Graham of the Bennett family's soda fountain and emporium...and of Julia. Remembrances of the way she'd felt, soft and delicate beside him as they'd stood together in her fancy foyer, nudged into his mind and refused to be shoved aside. She'd smiled at him. Talked with him. Responded to him—at least until he'd blurted the truth of his past—as a woman does to a man.

Curiously. Needfully. Passionately.

But he wasn't the kind of man Julia needed. Not even for a sham courtship. He must have been daft to agree to such a nonsensical scheme in the first place. And Graham meant to remedy that mistake by leaving. Soon. Before the pull between them grew even deeper.

Before he revealed even more of himself to her, and lost the will to go, altogether.

'Twas past time for action, he decided as the talk turned to hair tonics and the new barber at the shop inside Mulligan's hotel. With a frown, Graham finished his cheroot and stubbed it out, then pocketed the remainder. If he couldn't find work in this town, there was always another farther down the line. He'd just have to go out and find it.

And if he felt unaccountably sad at doing so...well, 'twas probably nothing more than unease at remaining here so uncommonly long already, that he felt. Graham could credit nothing else. Not even once he'd turned to fetch his horse, and spotted through the stable windows a woman in yellow walking purposefully down Main Street.

His heart jolted. Squinting, Graham looked again.

It had to be Miss Julia Bennett. No other woman, save her, wore hats as gaudy as the overlarge fruit- and flower-bedecked one he spied. No other woman made her skirts sway quite so bewitchingly as she moved. No other woman would have dared call out to a roomful of men, every one of them surly and hunched at a female's approach.

"Yoo-hoo!" she called, waving the closed parasol in her hand. "Good morning, gentlemen. How are our menfolk, this fine day?"

Graham couldn't move. He stood there as though his boots were nailed to the dirt, and watched as Julia stopped in the doorway and looked from one to another of the men gathered around the livery stable's potbellied stove. She hadn't noticed him yet. He melted into the shadows behind him, and waited for an opportunity to slip away.

After all…leaving was what he did best.

"We're fine, Miss Bennett," muttered one of the men. Reluctantly, he tipped his hat. "And yourself?"

"Very well, thank you." Julia nodded.

"You ain't come to bring us more spittoons, have you?" asked another. "'Cause we don't need 'em in here. I swear, if a man can't spit in the dirt, where can he?"

Murmured agreement was heard. Julia made a face, involuntarily glancing down at the hard-packed earth beneath her skirt hems. "No, I haven't come for that. I—"

"We don't need no dancing lessons, neither," interrupted one of the men, a volunteer from the local firehouse. "My Rebecca told me how you got the ladies all fired up about havin' a Spring ball here in town. She 'bout wore me out, talking about it."

Several of the men grimaced. Graham bit back a smile. He had his chance to leave and should be taking it, 'twas true. But somehow, seeing Julia again made a new batch of trail dust seem a lot less appealing.

"No, the plans for the Spring ball didn't quite work out, I'm afraid," Julia said. "In truth, I've come—"

"To make us all wear neckties?" asked another man, yanking at his shirt collar. "That town dress code idea of yours darn near caught on, Miss Julia, 'cause the ladies were so taken with it. But speaking for me and the boys—"

"—we're not having it!" said the night man.

"We don't care what those books of yours say," interrupted someone else. "We ain't layin' down on horse dung just so our wives can keep their shoes clean!"

A chorus of approval rose to the rafters. Looking abashed, Julia stared down at her parasol for a long moment. Although the men loomed closer, clearly a little aggravated by her activities in town, she did not back down.

"That was a metaphorical example, Mr. Chasen," she told the last man, raising her head to look him bravely in the eye. "I merely meant to illustrate the proper lengths to which a gentleman will go to shelter his companion from the unpleasantries of urban life. Nothing more."

Chasen shifted and spit, clearly unhappy at being corrected in front of his friends. The anti-necktie brigade shuffled their feet and murmured about "bunch of damn dandies, that's what we'll be!"

The man nearest Graham's spot in the shadows nudged his neighbor. "No wonder my Myrna didn't want her in the ladies' sewing circle," he said, tipping his head toward Julia. "She'd like to drive a person crazy, with her highfalutin' ways. Got more book-learning than is right for a woman, that's the trouble."

"She made my Annabel all wrathy, too," agreed the second man, "correcting her figuring of the prices on fabrics down at the mercantile. Too good for the likes of us, that's how Miss Julia sees herself."

In the doorway, Julia jerked her head sideways. She gazed with pretend interest into the depths of the stable, chin held high as the men's conversations picked up speed and swirled around her. Despite her proud posture, though, Graham detected a wobble in her lower lip and a gleam of moisture in her eyes, and knew she'd heard their thoughtless comments.

He recognized the stiff set to her shoulders, felt it as his own. He heard the telltale rasp in her voice before she cleared it away, and understood the pure stubborn will that let her speak at all.

"I have not come here to harass you, gentlemen," she said. Her knuckles showed white on her parasol handle. "I've merely come to make an inquiry, if you please."

Tom, the livery stable owner, stepped up. With a compassionate look, he inclined his head toward her. "You'd better say your piece and leave, Miss Bennett. These knucks are still all worked up over your marriage scheme from a month ago, and that editorial piece you wrote for the newspaper didn't help matters none. They didn't like hearing you lambaste 'today's gentlemen' for being too cowardly to wed properly."

Graham edged closer, intrigued by the mention of her

marriage scheme. Had Julia approached many men before turning to him? The notion was nearly unthinkable...except for the fact that he'd learned, when dealing with her, that most anything was possible.

"I meant that remark in the most general of terms," she returned tightly, the doodads on her hat quivering. From beneath its brim, she examined the faces surrounding her. "How dare they take offense?"

"Well, ma'am," Tom replied soothingly, "you did call unmarried men past the age of thirty spineless, indolent, lack-witted cretins, too afraid to assume responsibility for the well-being of—"

"Yes. Well. I may have been feeling a bit passionate toward my subject on the day I wrote that editorial," Julia admitted. She bit her lip, continuing to search the group of men. "There are, of course, exceptions to every rule. Like you, for instance, Tom. You're a wonderful man."

She patted the stable owner's arm, seeming to cheer a little. Then her gaze lit upon Graham's gloomy corner. Instinct kept him still...that, and a feeling he was in over his head with her, and it was likely to get worse if he stayed here much longer. Surely she couldn't see him. It was too dark, too—

Her gaze swept on.

The rumblings around him grew louder, punctuated with random curses. Graham saw Julia's face go pale, saw her hands tremble slightly as she grasped her parasol.

"I'm looking for the bounty hunter, Mr. Corley," she said, raising her voice to be heard. "Has anyone seen him?"

Instantly, all the men around him shifted so their bodies shielded him from view. Or would have, had any of them been tall enough. Before Graham could so much as clear his throat to reply, a half-dozen denials were heard.

"He don't want spittoons or neckties or dancing lessons, neither," said one of the men. "So you might as well head out."

It was true. Graham wanted none of those things. But he did want the woman who'd tried to organize their presence in Avalanche, however unsuccessfully. And no matter how much he tried to make himself leave, he hadn't been able to hit the trail yet. There had to be a reason for it.

He hesitated for an instant, feeling himself in sudden danger from something he could not name. 'Twas true that Miss Julia was bossy and opinionated, with a penchant for paying his boardinghouse bill and invading the town's sole male sanctuary to find him...but he couldn't be in danger from her. And although the place was strange—Graham was sure he'd seen three little girls carrying pet chickens on the way to the livery stable this morning, and the druggist's delivery boy somehow kept popping up everyplace Graham did—Avalanche was not a hazardous place.

Except maybe to his heart.

For in the next moment, Graham shifted his hat and shouldered forward through the crowd, and went to meet his fate.

"I'm here, Miss Julia," he said. "What do you need?"

Graham had looked so masterful, so *welcome,* coming toward her from the shadows, Julia mused a bit later. She'd been so relieved to see him that she drank in the sight of his tall, rangy frame, his fine-looking face, and even his rascally growth of whiskers. Watching him approach her had filled her with a sense of gratitude so profound that she'd nearly released the tears she'd been so diligently holding back.

He hadn't left. She'd made it in time. And he seemed strong and cheerful, too, compared with the silent man who'd left her standing alone in her foyer two nights ago.

Yes, she'd been wondrously happy to see him and to hear his voice...until Julia had remembered the livery stable had but one entrance. Which meant that Graham Corley had listened to the men in town attack her, merely for her efforts to bring some much-needed culture to Avalanche. He'd listened, and hadn't tried to help.

He'd listened, and worse. Now he knew the full extent of how she was shunned in town. She would never live it down.

But that had been nearly ten minutes ago, and now Graham strode through one of Avalanche's side streets, headed alongside her toward the Emporium. His face was dark beneath his hat, his expression stormy, and if she hadn't known better, Julia would have sworn he still hadn't forgiven her.

"You *said* you accepted my apology," she pointed out, hurrying to keep up with his powerful steps. "You said you forgave me."

"I did."

"If you don't mind my saying so...you don't look like you did. In fact," Julia mused further, "you look as though you'd like to peel off the mercantile sign and conk me over the head with it."

He gazed at the sign in question as they passed by. The speculative gleam in his eye did not comfort her.

"I'm trying to be polite," Graham said.

"You'd make a more convincing impression," Julia said, "if you'd stop gritting your teeth."

The bounty hunter bared them instead, in a toothy smile.

Julia yelped. "Now you look as though you'd like to take a bite out of me!"

"I would." His swift, heated glance set her blood atingle. "Once I simmer down, I might."

Julia shivered. "I had to say *something* to those men. They would have wondered why I came down to find you."

"Let them wonder."

His bad attitude was unrelenting. With a sigh, Julia touched his arm. Graham stopped instantly, leaving her scattering dust beneath her skirts as she scrambled to match him.

"I care about my reputation," she said. "Deeply."

Understanding flashed on his face. Steeling his features against it, the bounty hunter looked at the buildings surrounding them, the clear blue sky above them, the mounted riders and wagons passing by them in the distance—anywhere but at her. Finally, he spoke.

"I know you do," he said. "But you didn't have to say you wanted to discuss the delivery of a remedy for mmmmph."

"What?" Courageously—or foolhardily, depending upon one's point of view—Julia leaned closer. The breeze tugged at her hat, forcing her to clap one hand atop its crown. "I can't understand you."

"Mmmmph!" Louder, this time.

"Honestly, Mr. Corley. You'll have to enunciate, if I'm ever to—"

"Male troubles!" he yelled. "You told them I

needed Doctor Whittaker's patented remedy for male troubles!"

"But—"

"I think I can hear them hooting and hollering, still," he grumbled, setting himself in motion again. With a muffled curse, he sent her another scathing look. "I do *not* have male troubles."

"I'll admit you don't seem to." Julia lifted her skirts and scurried after him. "Why, you must be one of the most virile, masculine-seeming men I've ever seen."

Hardly mollified, he kept walking.

"But even you must agree," she went on, "that I needed a valid reason to come searching for you. Saying I'd come to deliver your Whittaker's remedy was perfectly reasonable."

"I liked it better when you were prattling on about my manliness."

"Very well. You've a fine growth of whiskers, there."

He grunted.

"And...and a powerful set to your shoulders. An exceptionally lengthy stride." Julia hurried to keep up, searching for something else to please him. "And, er, your gun belt coordinates quite nicely with that shirt."

She beamed. Graham turned, saw her smile, and shook his head. "Coordinating gun belt," he muttered. "You don't know what Doctor Whittaker's formula is designed to cure, do you?"

"Of course I do!"

"Mmmm?"

His rumbled inquiry only served to set her off. "Aside from curing general neuralgia, it's designed to remedy any man's weakness of body or limb, give strength and vitality, and generally invigorate the male constitution.'' Pleased with her answer—recited in part from the bottles on her father's shelves—Julia raised her parasol and gave him a self-satisfied smile. ''So there. You'll find, Mr. Corley, that I'm knowledgeable about a great many things.''

''Not this one, you're not.''

''I resent that!''

''I know you do.'' The bounty hunter swiveled abruptly, smoothly, placing his body directly in her path. He searched her face. Just as she was about to ask what was wrong, Graham raised his hand to sweep a lock of hair from her brow, and his blunt fingertips lingered, just for a moment. She might have sworn, daft a notion as it was, that his attention centered on her lips.

Why that should make her feel so breathlessly excited—especially given the Castile soap incident—Julia did not know.

''But don't worry,'' he told her. ''One of these days, I'll demonstrate to you exactly why I don't need Dr. Whittaker's remedy. You'll see it's got *nothing* to do with my gun belt.''

His gaze fairly smoldered as he said it. Julia was left with the indisputable impression that Mr. Corley's promise meant far more than his words suggested. Curious, she leaned nearer. But he only ran his hand lightly down the side of her face and then turned away with a rueful look.

''I'll have plenty of time for it, too,'' he said as they began walking again, ''since I seem to have an unbreakable commitment here in Avalanche.''

Elation rushed through her. ''Do you mean you're staying after all?''

His grumbled reply was surely meant as agreement.

''Because I wouldn't want to have to seek you out

each day, inventing a new malady to cure you of as an excuse each time. That would be most inconvenient."

Graham raised his eyebrows. "A jest, Miss Bennett? That's so unlike you."

Julia twirled her parasol and gave him a grin. "You'll find I can be quite unpredictable, Mr. Corley. Quite unpredictable."

"I know." They reached their destination, the shed behind the Emporium. The bounty hunter held open the door, and ushered Julia inside. He followed her into the secluded space. "You'll find I carry my share of surprises, too," he said, and then moved closer. "Here comes one, now."

Chapter Eight

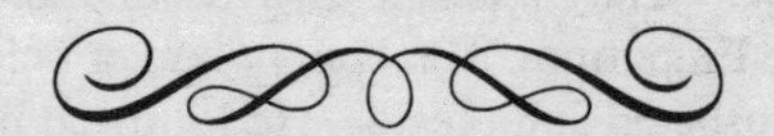

Inside the abandoned building, sunlight beamed in through the gaps in the shutters. The scents of lemon oil and soap lingered in the air as though the place had been recently cleaned, and the orderly placement of blankets atop the stacked crates—forming a seating area and table—confirmed that it had. In the center of the room, Julia propped her parasol beside a crate topped with a stack of books.

"I cleaned everything myself, and arranged it, too," she said in a businesslike tone. "I thought we'd begin with the McGuffey First Eclectic Reader, just to see where your skills lie, and then...did you say, surprise?"

She stopped, only just then seeming to realize what he'd said upon their entrance into the building. "What kind of surprise?"

She seemed alarmed. Likely, 'twas due to his earlier attempt to seal their bargain with a kiss—not a mistake Graham would be likely to repeat. He meant to move gradually but surely with Julia, now that he'd decided to stay.

"'Tis not so dangerous as your wide eyes suggest," he told her, stifling a grin. "Come closer, and find out."

Julia narrowed her eyes. "Is this a trick?"

"Ah!" He pretended to thrust a dagger into his heart. "You wound me. Do I seem a man given to deception?"

"You seem a man given to improprieties and stolen kisses," she answered crisply, but came nearer, all the same. Her curiosity shone in her eyes, and in the inquisitive tilt of her pert, fine-boned face. "But I suppose I must trust you, given our arrangement."

"You must," he agreed. "Now hold out your hand and close your eyes."

After a moment's pause, Julia ducked her head and then raised her arm, gloved palm upward. He found himself staring at a brilliant red velvet flower at the crown of her finery-bedecked hat, and couldn't help but chuckle.

"I'll not be fooled by your hat brim," Graham said, unable to hide his grin. "Raise your head, and this time, close your eyes."

As he'd suspected, she'd been gazing steadily at her hand from beneath her hat. She made a face, and did as he'd asked.

From his duster coat pocket, Graham withdrew the slender box he'd been carrying for the past two days. His heart hammered oddly as he carefully set it on her upturned palm, then closed her fingers around it. "Open your eyes."

She did. "A gift? Oh, Mr. Corley!" Julia said, hugging the box against her bosom. "You shouldn't have."

"This is no time for false humility," he said, pleased at her expression of astonishment. "Open it."

"No, I mean you *really* shouldn't have! As I said clearly in *Miss Julia's Behavior Book, volume one,* the only proper gifts for a young man to give the lady he fancies are trifles such as flowers or candy.''

With dismay, she jerked the box out at arm's length again and examined it, as though continuing to cradle it close might endanger her sense of propriety even further.

''A lady must not allow herself to be compromised with a less-perishable gift,'' she went on. ''After all, what if our relationship should end?''

''It *will* end. And you'll be one bauble richer.'' Exasperated, Graham nodded toward the box. ''Open it, and let's go on.''

She bit her lip. ''It *is* a lovely gesture on your part.''

''Don't make it more than it is. I saw it, and thought of you. Nothing more.''

''That is a great deal.'' Julia raised her face to his, and the open gratitude in her expression humbled him. ''To think of me, when most times...well, let's simply say I was not missed greatly when I left Avalanche for the States.''

''No one is missed for long.'' Graham had learned as much, himself. Sometimes painfully.

Her gaze met his. Suddenly, it was as though she could read the truth of his wandering days. Cold beds. Strange faces. Always, *always* keeping his back to the wall. Somehow, Julia saw inside him...and he wanted to confide in her further.

But then she looked away, and their connection was lost.

''I know,'' she said. ''And I thank you for wanting to make me feel better. But soon I'll be gone again, and none of that will matter. Getting away from here will be my salvation.''

Determinedly, Julia squared her shoulders. She

squinted at the box. Then she drew in a deep breath, and visibly battled with herself over opening it.

"As a drifting man yourself, you of all people must understand how freeing it is to rely only upon yourself," she went on. "To surround yourself with only those who have no part in the running of your life."

"Yes," Graham said. But here in this cozy, warm space, with Julia by his side and the promise of more time together to come, his reply felt strangely false. He'd struck to the trail apurpose, time and time again, yet now...now his wandering life had lost its luster. "And to surround myself with those who won't open a simple gift."

She smiled. "Clearly, it would be a greater social sin to make a friend unhappy than to accept an improper gift. Wouldn't you say so?"

Graham couldn't answer. His mind—his heart—was stuck on the word *friend,* and the soft, sincere way she'd said it. When was the last time a woman had called him friend? Not since Frankie, and she'd known him from childhood.

But an answer wasn't needed. A moment later, Julia opened the box with a little jiggle of anticipation, and looked inside.

"A hatpin!" Smiling, she lifted the delicate spun-metal creation from its place in the box. "Thank you! It's beautiful."

Not so beautiful as you, when you smile at me that way, Graham thought, watching as she fiddled with the pin's placement through her hat. But all he could muster aloud was a gruff, "You needed something to keep those monstrosities on your head. 'Tis a stiff wind that blows from the mountains to this town."

She clasped his hand in both of hers. The warmth of

her skin could be felt even through her gloves, and her grasp was excitedly firm. Julia's eyes shined a bright, happy blue.

"You are a kinder man than you let on, Mr. Corley," she said quietly.

He muttered a denial.

"It's true." She skimmed her hand over his jaw, briefly cupping his face in her gloved hand. "And I swear that before this is done, I'll prove it to you."

"Hmmph." With a smile to hide his uneasy feelings, Graham turned to the book-laden table to begin their lessons. "I doubt it."

The trouble was, he realized as Julia joined him across the table and opened a book, she already had begun to prove his kinder side to him. And he feared he was already far past the point of refusing her anything else she wished.

Their days together continued, taking on a predictable pattern. They met at the abandoned shed in the mornings, practicing pronunciation and reading over selections from the McGuffey's reader. In the afternoons, Julia helped Isabel at the soda fountain in the Emporium. Mr. Corley, she suspected, spent that same time conducting business at various establishments in town, looking for word of a new bounty-hunting engagement, for when their "betrothal" was finished.

And in the evenings, he would come to call on her. Those were the times she began to look forward to most...for it was then, seated side by side with Graham, that Julia allowed herself to believe their affection for each other was real.

She allowed herself, for a single precious hour each night, to believe that he really did care for her. That he truly meant the lingering looks he gave her. That he listened avidly to everything she said because he wanted to, not because she'd promised to tutor him in return.

And it was not only his conversation that enthralled her. It was the whole of the man himself. He was powerful and sure, loyal and mysterious, with a continually easy laugh and a love of all things ribald and improper. Graham exerted a pull upon her unlike anything she'd ever experienced, and Julia knew that if she had not chosen wisely for her false fiancé, she had at least chosen thrillingly.

His attentions kept her in a state of anticipation-filled excitement. Julia took to reciting portions of her behavior books, silently, just to keep her head when the bounty hunter smiled. On one occasion, Mr. Corley reached across her skirts to take a sweet from Alice's platter, and the careless brush of his forearm over her knees required recitation of all the proper cutlery for a formal meal, just to avoid an unladylike exclamation…or worse.

She wasn't sure what was happening to her, but she was certain Mr. Corley was at fault. He charmed her, wooed her, and continued to bring her unsuitably permanent gifts. It was almost as though he intended to surround her with mementos of their time together, so that after he was gone, she would remember him.

As though she could possibly forget.

He was an excellent learner, with an ability to concentrate that astounded her. Once he'd set his mind to something, Julia discovered, Graham Corley could not be deterred. 'Twas likely a quality that helped him in his bounty hunting, but she found it unnerving to think he may have applied that skill to his courtship of her, as well. How would she ever separate sham from genuine, when he proved so adept at both?

It wasn't that he was dishonest. It was merely that he'd agreed to help her, and doing so required a certain quantity of...embellishment. Julia had the sense that under ordinary circumstances, it would have been impossible to coax so much as a well-meant, polite-society fib from Graham—and it was that, most of all, which concerned her.

Why had he agreed to compromise himself...*for her?* Surely he could have received reading instruction from any number of tutors during his travels. It seemed unlikely that an interest in reading alone was enough to motivate such a decision. Bedeviled by the question, Julia told herself Mr. Corley was simply an honorable man helping a lady in need, and tried to leave it at that.

She was, unfortunately, not very successful. She never had been terribly skilled at leaving an unanswered question well enough alone.

But as the days drew on and became nearly two weeks in Graham's company, Julia had to admit that her scheme was, at least, successful. Even her father, whose insistence she find a loving husband to accompany her East had begun it all—seemed to enjoy the bounty hunter's company. With her papa's approval so nearly in hand, Julia decided it was time to move forward to the next step.

Never mind that she'd originally thought the demands her father had placed on her leaving would be impossible to fill. Never mind that finding a man to love her wholeheartedly, bookish ways and all, had seemed as achievable as finding a real-life knight in shining armor. With Graham she had found a man willing to pretend those things were true, and that would have to be good enough for now.

With that assurance in mind, Julia made ready to begin the next part of her plan to leave Avalanche: turning Graham Corley into the ideal suitor.

In the private salon of a clothier's establishment at the edge of Avalanche, Graham stared into the looking glass and frowned. Reflected beyond his image were those of Julia and the tailor, Georges, a Frenchman who'd come to the Territory hoping to strike it rich in Tombstone. He'd eventually retired to the north after several unsuccessful digs. If his mining equipment had been as froufrou as the gentleman's suit Georges had outfitted Graham with…well, he was surprised the man had made it out alive at all.

''What do you think?'' Julia asked, clasping her gloved hands together and giving him an expectant look. ''Georges assures me it's the latest style.''

''*Oui,*'' Georges said. ''The fancy plaid wool cassimere is *très elegant.* It becomes you, *monsieur.*''

Doubtfully, Graham stared down at the gray suit with red-and-black checks interwoven into the fabric. The coat buttoned halfway to his knees, the pants rode high on his boots, and the shoulders constricted his movement so much that he felt nigh shackled. He squinted into the looking glass again. Oddly enough, the whole effect looked familiar, somehow.

And then it struck him. He'd once seen something very much like it on an embezzling vaudevillian actor he'd tracked down in New Mexico Territory. Quite possibly, this was the same ugly suit.

''How long have you been a tailor, Georges?'' he asked.

"Oh, many years now. *Oui.* It was my first love, before the gold fever struck me. I must say, I—"

"The truth."

"*Monsieur!* I tell you truly, I—"

Graham shifted subtly. He looked over his shoulder, and waited.

"—six months," Georges admitted reluctantly. He gave an eloquent Gallic sigh. "Before I tried my hand at mining, I was a...a chimney sweep in Baltimore."

Julia gasped. "You assured me you'd trained in Paris! Sir, I am positively shocked."

She stared in openmouthed amazement from the tailor to Graham, and back again. Georges shrugged.

How did you know? she mouthed to Graham. Then, as though she'd grasped the reality of their situation, Julia pressed her lips together and straightened.

"Well, since Avalanche has no other tailor, you will have to do," she announced. With a businesslike air, she approached Graham, her pale blue skirts rustling. "We have calls to pay later this week, and Mr. Corley simply must be outfitted properly."

He raised an eyebrow. "You call this proper?"

"With a few adjustments, certainly."

Graham snorted. "Do you plan to adjust the suit or me? Because if it's me...I like my legs the length they are."

"We shan't hack them off at the ankle, just to make the trousers fit," Georges said with a twitter. "Although if you were a tad less muscular, it might help. Also—"

"Stay out of this, chimney sweep."

The man closed his mouth, and developed a sudden interest in a bolt of fabric on the nearby worktable.

"Mr. Corley, please," Julia said, touching his upper

arm, "there's no need for surliness. Be reasonable. I think you look quite handsome in a suit."

Gazing down into her face, he softened. Already he felt closer to Julia than he had to anyone in his life, save Frankie. The weeks they'd spent together had given Graham a risk-free glimpse into the life he might have had, had he chosen a wife and neighbors instead of his wandering ways. He was grateful to her for that. And if wearing the ugly suit would make her happy....

"I'll think about it," he said halfheartedly.

"Excellent! You won't be sorry," she told him, smiling. "A gentleman should always be well-dressed, and his dress should never be noticeable."

"That doesn't make sense."

She made a dismissive sound. "Of course it does. It's from my latest work, *Miss Julia's Behavior Book, volume three.* I'm sure you're not suggesting I'm not knowledgeable about my own field of expertise."

Given the number of little girls carrying pet chickens Graham had glimpsed this morning—and the fact that he'd learned the local etiquette instructress was behind the entire sodas-with-chickens craze—Graham wasn't so sure about that. But he remained silent. Better that, than embark on the nonsensical poultry discussion that was sure to follow.

His inattention cost him, for a moment later, Julia raised up on tiptoes and slipped something over his head. Graham was too busy savoring the inadvertent press of her bosom against his chest as she balanced herself to notice what it was at first. And then, realization struck.

"A necktie?"

"Certainly," she replied, looking pleased. She grasped the dangling ends as though preparing to knot it herself, and Graham nearly—dangerously—allowed her to. "I adore a gentleman in a necktie. Every proper man needs one, you know."

He stopped her hands with his. "Not this man."

"But—but—"

"No. I won't wear a necktie. Nor a suit. Not for making calls, not for doing business, and not even for being buried in." Graham's boots clomped as he released her and strode closer to the mirror to take a final, savage glance. "I won't do it."

He wrenched off the necktie and flung it away.

"Please, Mr. Corley! Let's not be hasty. I truly think that with a few minor alterations—"

Decisively, Graham unbuttoned the coat and tossed it aside.

Julia gawked.

He set to work on the shirt, wrenching the cuffs open. He shucked his boots and kicked them across the clothier's glossy parquet floor, watching them come to a stop beneath the shop window. At the heavy thud they made, Julia jerked. Her gaze whipped back to him, and he could see her gathering her determination as he took off his shirt.

"Wait. With a few alterations, we could certainly—"

His shirt landed atop a dressmaker's dummy in the corner. "Miss Julia, unless you want to *alter* your sense of maidenly innocence," Graham said, "I suggest you take your leave now. I'm about to remove my pants."

He reached for his fly. She shrieked. By the time the hideous gray, red-and-black-checked mass of wool hit the floor, Julia had fled for the safety of the shop's front yard.

Clad only in his drawers and a pair of socks, Graham listened to the clank of the door shutting behind her and couldn't help but grin. It seemed he and Miss Hoity-Toity had made progress together...if the dead-on interest in her face had been anything to go by.

After all, she'd stayed until two-thirds of his clothes were off. Given another few days, who knew what could happen?

The barber shop in Mulligan's hotel was the most elegant, most modern establishment in all of Avalanche. The windows looking onto Main Street were plate glass. The barber chairs were ornately carved mahogany, with red velvet padded cushions, tilted head- and foot-rests, and fully adjustable reclining capabilities. One entire wall was lined with ornate shaving mugs, their tidy arrangement in floor-to-ceiling cubicles a testament to the resident barbers' skills.

Another wall boasted green-and-rose floral wallpaper, mostly obscured by advertisements for hair tonics and straight razors. In the back room, hot baths were sold for twenty-five cents—soap and towel included. For ten cents and two bits more, any man in town could enjoy a fresh shave and a haircut. Many of Julia's gentleman acquaintances and neighbors availed themselves of the services regularly.

Graham Corley, however, looked askance at the entire operation. When they arrived late after a reading lesson one morning, he scrutinized the waiting barbers in their matching white coats, neckties, close-clipped haircuts and waxed mustaches. Then, making a sour face, the bounty hunter immediately turned to leave.

Fortunately, Julia had anticipated just such a development. She'd convinced her father to come along for a fresh *toilette,* as well. Unless Graham wanted to tread upon Asa Bennett in his haste to leave, he was stuck.

He realized as much when he all but barreled into the older man, and was forced to stop a few feet from the exit.

He pivoted slowly. "Miss Julia," he said, and there was a definite speculative glimmer in his midnight eyes. "You've tricked me."

She felt the considerable force of his attention directed solely upon her. Swallowing hard, Julia blustered onward anyway. "Sir, I would never presume to—"

"You've tricked me."

At the warning tone in his voice, she remembered poor Georges, the fraudulent tailor, and how he'd so readily confessed to the bounty hunter. She was likely to fare no better. Perhaps it would be best to desist, Julia decided.

"I merely failed to mention this small detour," she told him, examining her kid gloves for spots. "Nothing more."

Graham spoke through his teeth. "You said we were taking your father to lunch at the hotel dining room. This, unless I've mistaken shaving mugs for soup bowls, is not the dining room."

Boldly, Julia took his arm and steered him toward the first barber's chair. Her father followed, and settled into his usual place. The comforting sounds of the other barber greeting her papa, retrieving his mug from the rack, and shaking out a towel for his face filled the shop.

"Well, it's just that I so *adore* a man with a nice close shave," she said in a low voice. "And I thought we could stop here before lunch, just in case you felt in need of one. You, quite naturally, look *very* handsome as you are. However, if things are to take their natural course between us..." Julia cleared her throat delicately, raising her eyebrows to achieve the desired intimation. "Well, I think you understand what I mean?"

What she meant was that Julia Bennett could not possibly allow herself to become betrothed—even falsely—to an unkempt, unfashionable, and most of all unshaven, fiancé. No one would *ever* believe their ruse, in that case.

Amazingly enough, Graham nodded.

"I do." His grin was surprisingly broad. And for some reason, the rogue waggled his eyebrows, too. "I guess a shave won't kill me."

The barber, a thin man who hadn't removed his gaze from the bounty hunter's gun belt since they'd arrived, swallowed hard. "Indeed, sir. I assure you it will not."

Graham settled into the nearest chair, watching with narrowed eyes as the barber drew the razor over the strop. Then he settled back and folded his hands over his chest. His eyes drifted peaceably shut.

This was proceeding even more smoothly than Julia had dared hope! With a final glance at her soon-to-be "fiancé," she gathered her reticule in her hands and prepared to leave.

"I have some errands, but I'll be back in an hour or so," she said. "Do take advantage of the facilities here, Mr. Corley. I understand the bathing room has been recently installed, and is said to be most pleasurable."

Suddenly, an image assailed her—one of the bounty hunter lounging in an enormous galvanized tub, with soap bubbles surrounding him and steam wreathing his clean-shaven face. She imagined the gleam of water against his skin, the scandalous length of his dark hair streaming in wet hanks as it clung to his neck and shoulders. She saw, as though it was happening at this very moment, the flex and play of Graham's muscles as he soaped his sinewy arms and muscular chest...and cursed that glimpse of his partly naked self she'd had at the clothier's. It had made her occasional wonderings that much more vivid.

That much more difficult to ignore.

Swathed in shaving lather, Graham cracked open one eye. He seemed puzzled to find her still there. "Fine. I might try a bath, although I can buy the same for five cents less at Mrs. Harrington's boardinghouse."

The barber sniffed in offense. Mr. Corley ignored him.

Julia blinked, attempting valiantly to throw off her new vision. This one featured an outrageously unclad Graham, dripping water as he extended his arm to invite *her* into the tub with him. In fascination, she allowed her gaze to drift to his forearm...his hand...his fingers. Would it really be so unforgivable to explore the *romantic* side of her nature, while she carried out this *faux* marriage scheme? Certainly the free thinkers at Vassar hadn't believed so. And honestly...

Miss Julia's Behavior Book, volume two: Let all women remember that to be pure and to seem pure at all times and in all places, is to establish a character which is armor proof against debauchery, malice and slander. One must guard against the temptations of indulgence, in all forms.

Drat that book! Volume two, three and all the rest! In frustration, Julia clenched her reticule and stammered awkwardly to Mr. Corley.

"Yes, well. Perhaps you'll enjoy this, as well. I must be going. *Immediately.*"

She made her escape just in time to avoid embarrassing herself with yet another fanciful imagining...but too late to avoid the very knowing, very seductive grin on the bounty hunter's half-lathered face. *Oh, my.*

Chapter Nine

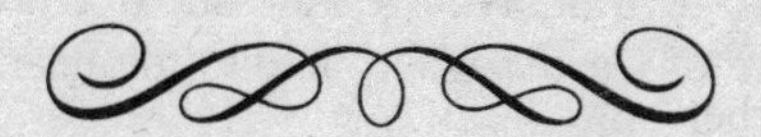

A shadow fell across the barbershop floor. Graham looked up from his newspaper, and spied Julia standing there.

Her arms were laden with packages—so many that they nearly obscured her purple-flowered gown. Her hat, a straw creation embellished with satin ribbons and miniature wax rabbits, stretched from one side of the door frame to the other. It was that hat, he suspected, which had blocked out the early-afternoon sunlight.

She looked surprised. And beautiful. No sight could have pleased him more than that of his pretend beloved, with her upswept dark hair and wispy tendrils, pert nose and lively eyes. Playing the part of a lover to Julia had been scarcely a hardship at all.

Save the ugly suit and necktie, of course.

Clenching his lighted cheroot more tightly between his teeth, Graham smiled up at her. No new clients had arrived to claim his barber's chair, nor the other chair. He and Asa Bennett had passed an enjoyable hour or so being shaved and seen to. After what Julia had said earlier...about things taking their natural course between the two of them...no force on earth could have kept Graham from receiving the full treatment.

After all, what else could she have meant, except that she'd been too offended by his growth of beard to kiss him until now? It seemed a reasonable explanation, once she'd put it to him the way she had. Her skin was far more delicate than that of the painted ladies he'd known on the trail. No wonder she'd clobbered him with a cake of Castile when he'd come near enough to injure it.

Yes, it was all clear to him now. And with the reward of Julia's affections dangling before him, Graham had never been more eager for a barber's services in his life.

"Good heavens!" she said, breaking into his thoughts. "What on earth has happened here?"

"Ah, Julia!" Asa Bennett said, looking up from his newspaper with a bland expression. "You've returned. Good. I see by the look on your face that you're surprised by our transformations."

"Surprised? That's the least of it!" She dropped her packages at her feet, still staring at the men. "Papa, you've hair hanging all around your face. Hasn't the barber had a chance to see to it yet?"

Asa laughed. "It's my new style. Very like Mr. Corley's, don't you think so? Makes me look younger. Indeed."

"Younger? You look—you look—" Julia stopped, examining her father's appearance with obvious befuddlement. "Well, mere words can hardly do it justice, I'm afraid."

The older man preened. "Wait until Geneva has a look. She'll be amazed."

"At the least."

"'Bout time I had a change, I decided. And with Mr.

Corley here as inspiration—'' Asa nodded toward Graham. The movement sent the unsnipped lengths of his graying hair flopping forward over his angled cheekbones ''—there was no time like the present.''

Julia's mouth opened and closed several times. She blinked. 'Twas true, Graham thought, that Asa looked different with his hair left to hang free. Ordinarily, the man combed the whole mass toward the back of his head and brilliantined it.

''No man ought to have to put grease in his hair, and spend his mornings staring into a looking glass,'' Graham said. ''Life holds better things. I pointed that out to Asa.''

His words seemed to remind Julia of his presence there. She turned toward him, shaking her head.

''And *you.* I thought you would at least trim that mountain-man hair of yours! But, no—you've elected to corrupt my father, instead!''

''He did not corrupt me, daughter. He inspired me.''

She rolled her eyes.

''I had a shave,'' Graham protested. He plucked the cheroot from his teeth and held it at arm's length while he tilted his jaw upward, the better for Julia to admire its new smoothness. ''And a bath. As you suggested.''

At the mention of a bath, the interest he'd seen before flared again in her eyes. Julia, being Julia, immediately tamped it down.

''This will not do,'' she said, crossing her arms.

''Why not? I did everything you asked me to.'' Graham crushed out his cheroot and set his newspaper aside. Slowly, he got to his feet.

''I'd hoped you'd be inspired to do more.'' Julia's gaze followed him upward. Steadfastly, she held her ground, though his advance should have forced her to retreat a few paces. "You must have known that."

"Why?"

"Well, well—because any reasonable person would!" Julia said. "You can hardly expect me to spell out my every request in plain language. It would be rude."

"It would be sensible." Smiling, Graham gazed down at her, fighting an urge to forcibly unclamp her arms from her middle and wrap them around him, instead. Even fired up with feminine annoyance she was bewitching. But if he told her so, she would doubtless brain him with a bottle of pomade, and so he did not. "That's probably why a woman can't do it. Because it's sensible."

"*What?* Now you're insulting my entire sex?" Julia unfolded her arms, and gestured wildly with them as she moved closer. "I'll have you know, sir, that any woman would have understood what a barber's services were for, and would have availed herself of them. Completely."

"She'd have a bit of trouble getting a shave, I'll wager," Asa commented mildly, rising from his chair. "Unless she was one of those peculiarly hairy women, with a dark little mustache above her lip. Then, I suppose—"

"Papa, please."

He looked at her, and winked. "I'll just go find us a table at the hotel restaurant."

Asa retrieved his hat from the rack and put it on. He grabbed Graham's, and tossed it to him. Then, giving a chuckle, he left the shop.

Graham was left standing with Julia. She glared up at him.

"I can't believe you've influenced my father this way. He'll be a laughingstock." She bent to retrieve her packages, and began filling her arms with the wrapped bundles. "I suppose this is all very amusing to a drifter like you. You don't know how it hurts to have your friends and neighbors ridicule you."

She gave a choked exclamation that pierced Graham deeply. He tugged on his hat and then hunkered down beside her to gather up twine-wrapped boxes. In the back of the shop, the sounds of the two barbers having lunch punctuated their conversation.

With everything from the floor retrieved, Graham took several packages from Julia's arms. As he did, he saw her lower lip wobble. The knowledge that he'd caused her to worry made him gather the rest of her purchases, too.

"No one will ridicule your father," he said sternly, rising with his arms filled. "I won't allow it."

A hoarse laugh burst from her. "And how do you propose to accomplish that?" She straightened, brushing her skirts. "No, he'll be mocked by half the town by tonight, and the other half tomorrow, and no amount of blustering on your part will change it. It's too late."

Graham looked at her. Although she busily fussed with her dress and gloves, Julia was clearly avoiding his eyes. And although she held herself firmly, the catch in her voice told him this bothered her far more than she'd admitted.

"Have they mocked you, too?" he asked quietly. "Is that why you—"

"I'll not hear this." Raising her head, Julia cast him a scathing look. "You can read a book passing well these days, Mr. Corley. But you cannot read me. You know nothing about me, and since our association is

temporary, you likely never will. Now—'' She took a deep breath, and forced a smile. ''Papa is waiting and we must go.''

''Wait.'' Graham touched her arm, and she stiffened with her back partway toward him. 'Twas a bit of progress, though, and he was grateful for it. ''You must know I would spare no mercy for anyone who hurt you.''

She swallowed hard. For a moment, Julia's haunted gaze met his over her shoulder, and he spied a jumble of emotions in her face that he could not name. A fierce protectiveness welled inside him, and Graham swore it was true. He would punish anyone who hurt this woman, and give no leniency in the task.

A ghost of a smile passed over her lips. ''Then you must begin with the whole town, from schoolhouse to saloon,'' she said. ''From the churchyard where the minister's wife wouldn't allow me to join in the sociable picnics because I'd bested her son in mathematics and recitation and geography, to the book depot man who refused to order the volumes I wanted because I corrected his French pronunciation.''

''I swear it,'' Graham said. ''I—''

''And you'll have to continue with my father,'' Julia went on, a quaver in her voice. ''Because it is he who is keeping me here. He, who's forced me to take a bogus fiancé in order to leave, when all I want is to put this town behind me, and go on. Can you do all that, Mr. Corley?'' she challenged, and her voice shook with emotion. '''Tis not a big place, Avalanche, but it is filled with people.''

And so many of them, he thought, *resentful of the uniqueness in their midst.* It was not right. But it was believable. And Graham had no notion how to set it straight.

Julia mistook his silence for defeat.

"I thought not," she said, and for a moment he saw hope fading from her eyes. "So let's go on with our plan, and have done with it. Over lunch, I shall announce our engagement to my father."

"I'm telling you truly, Isabel," Julia said the following day. She stood behind the soda fountain counter at the Emporium, infusing a sarsaparilla syrup-filled glass with fizzy soda water. "I never expected my papa to react that way. Never."

Beside her, her friend sighed. She wiped clean the glass of pear cider soda she'd just prepared, then slid it across the counter to a waiting customer. Frowning, Isabel took up a corner of her apron and began polishing the fountain's ornate spigots.

"So your father is making you wait for his decision," she said, her accent reminiscent of the Mexico of her childhood. "It's really not surprising. You've only been seeing the bounty hunter for a little over two weeks."

"Yes—and I have less than two weeks before I need to travel East!" Julia said. "He likes Mr. Corley, he told me so himself. And a short engagement is desirable, in case either party changes its mind. Hearts can be fickle, you know."

"Is that from volume one, two or three?"

"*Miss Julia's Behavior Book, volume two.*"

Isabel grinned. "Still…a week's engagement is *very* short."

"Nonsense." Deliberately, Julia kept her tone light, trying not to show how much this setback had affected her. "It's perfectly adequate. Especially when accompanied by strong emotions—like true love, for instance. But when I suggested as much to my father, he would only say that he needed to consider the situation before giving his approval.''

Julia served the soda she'd been making, then checked the amount of ice in the fountain's receptacle. Regular visits from the Avalanche ice man were a necessity to ensure the success of the drinks they served. With the recent popularity of Libbie's pet-chicken-and-sodas routine, they'd frequently been running low.

''What did the bounty hunter say?''

''About waiting for an answer from my father?'' Julia raised her eyebrow, and at Isabel's nod, clanked shut the ice receptacle's lid. She picked up a box of assorted notions that a traveling drummer had delivered. ''He was too busy trying to give the impression that the engagement was *his* idea to put up much of a battle over the delay.''

''Well, it *is* customary for the gentleman to announce the betrothal,'' Isabel said. ''And perhaps he really *is* taken with you. After all, you have said his courtship seems authentic.''

''Seeming and being are two different things,'' Julia told her firmly. ''For instance, I may *seem* composed and patient right now, but in truth—''

''You've just squirted mocha coffee syrup into that box of notions.''

''—in truth, I'm all in a muddle!'' With a wail, Julia snatched out a gloopy mess of sticky grosgrain ribbons from the box. She dropped them onto the marble counter and leaned over them, burying her face in her hands. The rich scent of coffee syrup rose to meet her. ''*Why* is everything going wrong? Why, why, why? I don't have time to find another man now. Mr. Corley simply *must* do!"

"Oh, it will be all right. Truly!" Making sympathetic sounds, Isabel hugged her. "It can't be easy. You told me how the bounty hunter refused new clothes. Refused to cut his hair. Refused to print calling cards, stop smoking cigars and refrain from telling ribald jokes. Faced with all that, it's no wonder you're upset."

"I am." Julia sniffed. "I don't see how any of this can possibly work now. And it seemed so simple, in theory. An excellent plan! I just don't see where I've gone wrong."

Isabel patted her back, murmuring reassurances.

"Usually, things go so well for me," Julia went on. "Sensible things, I mean. Things I can plan for and study and learn about. This tangle with Mr. Corley should be no different. I arrive at a plan, implement the plan, and then—"

"And then, some knuck from far afield comes along," interrupted a deep, masculine voice. "And follows the plan not a'tall."

Julia jerked her head up. "Mr. Corley!"

"In the flesh." He tipped his hat to her and Isabel. How they had missed the jangle of the apothecary door's bell and the sturdy thud of his boots across the Emporium's floor, she didn't know. "Come to disrupt your life still further. With this, for a start."

Grinning, the bounty hunter lifted the covered basket in his hand. He cradled it against his chest, atop his big spread palms. The width of it nearly obscured his dark shirt.

Trailing her gaze lower, Julia took in his equally dark rough trousers and boots. Realizing the blatant way she'd been examining him, she whipped her attention quickly to his face…just in time to glimpse the knowing look in his eyes.

Beneath his flat-brimmed black hat, Graham's hair was still long, flowing to his collar in rugged brown locks. His jaw was still hard-edged, his dark eyes still mysterious, his features still as strong as ever. Somehow, though, despite all that, Julia couldn't seem to look her fill of him.

When he smiled, her heart filled with unreasonable cheer. When he advanced closer, her senses danced with anticipation.

Alarmed, she began cleaning up the soiled ribbon mass with quick jerks of the cloth from her apron pocket. All the while, she sensed his gaze upon her, steady and alert. Perhaps, if she kept busy, the bounty hunter wouldn't realize how he affected her. Perhaps, if she remained diligently proper, he would never know that—

"The sun from the window makes your hair shine like spun silk," he said, his voice gravelly.

His hands, still holding the wicker basket, came into view, and as she tucked the soiled cloth and ribbons beneath the counter, Julia dared to send a glance up the length of his arms and shoulders to his face.

"*You* look beautiful."

—never know that she found him too irresistible for her own good. What was the matter with her? Graham Corley was supposed to be a mere pretend fiancé. Nothing more. It would not do to turn spoony over him now.

Not when she was leaving soon. And not when *he* would turn to the trail again soon, as well. Only a ninny would give her heart to a drifting man…surely she was wiser than that?

"Thank you," she said, grinning like a loon. Her

throat felt suddenly parched. She filled a glass with undiluted, purportedly medicinal soda water, and rapidly drank it. Could the fancy water, Julia wondered wildly, cure an inappropriate infatuation? ''You look nice, as well.''

Good manners made her say it. The silly smile she felt on her face as she spoke made her believe it. Something was happening to her, and Julia felt fairly certain she would never have deliberately planned something so absolutely befuddling.

''I'm beholden to you, if I do,'' Graham said, still watching her. His smile broadened. '''Tis a wonder what a simple shave can do. Or so I've heard.''

He winked. Isabel tittered. And Julia melted. How could a simple roguish wink—the variety that ordinarily would have made her issue a lecture on the inadvisability of over-familiarity between the sexes—make her instead feel like giggling? Somehow, on Mr. Corley the gesture seemed charming, although she couldn't quite explain why. It was downright unaccountable.

''Yes, well.'' Julia straightened her apron and attempted to seem as though she weren't on the verge of abandoning all her work, simply to gaze, starry-eyed, at the bounty hunter. ''No doubt every woman you've met has appreciated the civilizing effects of your visit to the barber yesterday.''

''I'm interested in only one woman. *You.*''

A gusty sigh came from Isabel. Julia and Mr. Corley stared at her.

She seemed abashed. ''Well, it *is* romantic, you know!'' Leaning closer to Julia, she added, ''Him, interested in only you. It's enough to make a lady swoon.''

''It's a charade, silly,'' Julia whispered back. She

raised her voice a bit, not quite enough for her papa to hear from his druggist's counter. "Tell her, Mr. Corley. Tell her you're only pretending."

He pressed his lips together. Above them, his eyes sparkled with humor.

"Tell her!"

When the bounty hunter remained aggravatingly silent, Julia answered for him. "He is," she assured Isabel with a chastening glower for Graham. "Aside from his obvious talent for provocation, our Mr. Corley has turned out to be an excellent actor, as well."

Isabel peered at him. Then she looked at Julia. "I don't think he's acting. I think he's fond of you."

"He's *fond* of plum tarts. Me, he delights in tormenting."

Graham laughed. "Never. If you're bothered by our charade, it's only your own making." He raised the wicker basket, drawing their attention to it. "I've simply come to take you on a picnic. Can you come?"

A picnic. An outing befitting a courting couple. It was perfect, and yet... "I'm not sure. Isabel, can you accompany us?"

"Me?" She looked startled, nearly dropping the strawberry soda she was preparing. "Why me?"

"To chaperone, silly. I can't possibly go with Mr. Corley alone, especially outside the boundaries of town."

Miss Julia's Behavior Book, volume three: A true lady never offers herself for untoward speculation. Instead, she minds her manners, seeing nothing she ought not to see, hearing nothing she ought not to hear, and doing nothing she ought not to do. To behave otherwise renders her claims to ladyhood false, and invites any number of scandalous consequences.

All the same...*how* she wanted to go!

"I'm sorry, Julia," Isabel said, collecting the coins for the soda she'd finished. "I'm helping my mother with the sewing this afternoon. After today, our turn with the new Singer machine is over with."

Julia nodded. Several families had pooled their money to buy the expensive high-arm treadle machine, something none of them could have afforded on their own. Making use of a turn with it was an unbreakable commitment. Otherwise, Isabel and her mother would have more than twice the work to clothe their family.

"Come alone," Mr. Corley urged Julia. "Please. I promise to behave."

His smile utterly contradicted his statement. It was, Julia saw, downright wicked...and completely, curiously, undeniably stimulating.

Why could she not resist him? Her mind, usually so reliable, seemed to have failed her. Instead of communicating to her heart that picnicking alone with the bounty hunter was impossibly risky, it told her that doing so would be thrilling. Unforgettable. Even worthwhile.

Did she dare?

She wanted to, Julia realized. Being alone with Mr. Corley, outside the boundaries of their student-tutor relationship, would give her a chance to discover more about him. To learn who he was, beyond his wandering ways.

It would also allow her to solidify her bond with him, Julia realized. In the face of her father's refusal to approve of their betrothal—at least for now—it was more important than ever that she and Graham work together. Her plan simply *had* to succeed!

"I truly can't," she said reluctantly. "However—"

Julia darted a glance toward the druggist's counter, ensuring that her papa was safely at work "—I do plan to take a walk this afternoon. Right along the..."

She raised her eyebrows meaningfully toward Mr. Corley. The bounty hunter looked confused for a moment, then caught on.

"Along the trail that winds up the mountainside?" he asked.

"Indeed." A secret excitement made her feel fairly giddy inside. With difficulty, Julia effected a serene demeanor. "If we should happen to meet along the way, perfectly by chance, of course...well, there could hardly be any fault in that, now could there?"

"No." With exaggerated seriousness, Mr. Corley shook his head. "I'd think not. Especially if this accidental meeting happened at around..."

"Two o'clock?"

He nodded. They shared a conspiratorial grin.

Julia rose on her tiptoes, filled with a delicious sense of daring. "I shan't be surprised if we meet," she said, and then prepared to make it happen for certain.

Chapter Ten

The mountains of northern Arizona Territory were as different from the rocky deserts to the south as they could possibly be. Looking like some giant had mislaid them amidst sudden juniper-studded hills, they jutted out of the landscape for miles around Avalanche. It was as though their rocky oak-and-pine-studded angles could not be contained, and demanded to be seen.

Within the mountains' craggy hideaways, elk and deer flourished, jays squawked, and a constant cool breeze kept the evergreen branches in motion overhead. Tumbled boulders offered seating. In the spring, fragrant wildflowers carpeted the grassy spots and added their scent to the tang of fir and the earthy scrub of soil. When people visited, as they often did, conversations carried far. Voices rose, despite the grandeur the surroundings provided. Laughter could be heard.

But none so loud, nor so joyous, as the laughter that Graham and Julia shared, on the day they happened upon one another on the lowest mountain trail…and sat to share a picnic in the shade of a twisted oak.

For Graham, it was a revelation unlike anything he'd ever known. He'd opened his borrowed basket—and his heart—to a lady whose smile made him happier than his own. And although the picnic lunch he'd bartered for was simple, he and Julia had a splendid time.

Usually, picnics were nothing he indulged in. Girlish, over-civilized affairs where citified people pretended to be on the trail for an afternoon struck him as ridiculous. But Asa Bennett had confided in him his daughter's love of a meal out-of-doors while they'd taken their turns at the barber's, and once inspired, Graham had been unable to resist.

And so he found himself stretched atop a clean saddle blanket at the end of a long afternoon, head propped in his hand, listening to Julia chatter on about books she'd read and people she'd met at Vassar. She flung her arms wide as she spoke, nodding and laughing, freer than he'd ever seen her.

Occasionally she'd seem to realize her lapse of decorum, and would return to sitting primly with her hands folded atop her pale pink skirts. But those times never lasted for long. Something about the fresh air, and the fact that Avalanche was out of sight even though it lay over the next rise of trees, seemed to ease her. And Graham was glad for it.

"You seem happier here," he said when her latest story was told and they'd eaten their fill of the meal he'd brought. He gestured toward the pines surrounding them, and the expanse of rocky forest rising beyond. "I begin to believe you really want to leave Avalanche, after this."

She paused with a cupful of cider halfway to her mouth. Her surprised blue-eyed gaze met his. "You did not believe me before?"

Something in her face, something instantly guarded, warned him away. Graham shrugged. "While you were so busy beginning a craze for pet-chickens-and-sodas, and setting the newest fashions in outlandish headwear? Pshaw."

He nodded toward her latest hat, a tightly woven creation embellished with pink ribbons and colorful wax birds with real tail feathers. He smiled at the sight of it, so thoroughly Julia. "I didn't believe it for a minute."

At his words, she touched her hat. Beneath her gloved fingers, he glimpsed the metalwork of the hatpin he'd given her. Happy as he was to see Julia wearing his gift, he was happier still to see her expression brighten again.

"Say what you will," she declared proudly, "Libbie is much happier now. She has more friends than ever before. And my hats *are* popular. It's strange...I can't imagine why the same people who used to—"

She broke off, looking alarmed.

"Used to?"

"It's nothing. Never mind."

Julia waved her arm, and busied herself with repacking the things he'd brought for their picnic. With a mighty frown of concentration that the foodstuffs surely did not deserve, she wrapped the leftover beef jerky, biscuits and tinned peaches.

"The same people who used to ridicule you?" Graham asked. "The people who mocked you for your mind, the way you feared they'd mock your father for his hairstyle?"

She crammed the checkered napkins he'd borrowed from his landlady into the basket. "I don't know what you mean. Really, the afternoon is drawing on, and I—"

"Julia, *tell me,*" he urged. Swiftly, he levered himself upward and captured her arm, stopping her movements. Ignoring her indrawn breath, Graham used his other hand to turn her face toward him. "Tell me, and I'll make it right. I swear it."

Her rueful smile made him twice as helpless.

"It's too late," Julia said. "What's done is done."

He shook his head. "The lawmen tell me it's too late to find the desperadoes I trail. I always track them anyway. I've never missed one yet."

"Then you're ahead of me." Her lips quirked upward, but her eyes did not join the joke. "Because I miss *you* already, and you haven't even left yet."

Graham gawked at her. Of its own volition, his hand lowered, releasing her. The soft sound of her unbelievable admission still swirled in his head, befuddling him all over again. She would miss him?

No one had missed him.

Not even Frankie, not much. Not once she moved on with her new life.

In astonishment, Graham stared at the woman who was his pretend fiancé, in all but her father's approval. "What did you say?"

"Nothing. It's getting late, and I—I—" Julia worked more rapidly, shaking out crumbs from the biscuit box and setting it into the basket with a clatter. She drew in a deep breath, but did not look at him. "I'm saying things I do not mean. It's polite behavior, nothing more. I sensed that you felt your efforts today hadn't been properly appreciated, and I wanted you to know, most assuredly, that I—"

"Stop. Chattering won't change this."

"What will?"

His mind locked. Her expression, half hopeful and

half fearful, made him yearn for a future he could not give.

"Uhh," Graham began. "You—" He broke off, shaking his head to clear it. Only one thought persisted. "You'll miss me?"

Panic swept her face. "I have to leave."

She scrambled to her feet, skirts swishing. He caught a glimpse of high-buttoned boots, lacy petticoats and Julia's trembling hands before she set out for the trail. Graham followed her, unwilling to let her go.

He caught up within three strides, beneath the spreading branches of a pine. "Don't go," he said. "First it was me, now you, leaving. If we keep at this, we'll never be together long enough to gain your father's word."

The words were meant as a jest. The hoarse edge to his voice doubtless spoiled the effect.

Nevertheless, they worked. Julia stopped, and faced him.

"I must have it!" she said. "He must approve, so I can leave. I'll not rusticate here, in Avalanche—" Her outflung arm indicated the town they couldn't see, more than the mountainous forest surrounding them. "—if there is a way out. *You* must understand. Oh, Mr. Corley!" Julia exclaimed, her eyes bright. "You've done everything *I* could only dream of. You've traveled, you've seen the world—"

"Only the meanest parts of it."

"—you've had adventures, all on your own. It must have been marvelous to be so free. To *still* be so free."

So alone, he thought instantly, but said nothing.

She wrapped her arm 'round the thick-barked pine beside her and hugged herself toward it, looking outward. In the direction they faced, miles of open land could be seen. "*How* I envy you the exciting life you've lived."

With a sigh, she looked over her shoulder at him. All the longing he'd sensed in her before was surely, suddenly, there in her eyes. Graham had thought he'd glimpsed passion in her weeks earlier, when he'd nearly held her...but that was paltry compared with the emotion he sensed in Julia now.

"That's how I knew you were perfect for this scheme," she went on. "A man like you can understand why I need to get away from this place. A man like you won't try to keep me tethered by his side."

"But why not stay here?" Graham asked her, driven to the question by an unease on her behalf he couldn't name...and a caring he didn't want to admit. "Avalanche is a good town." *For those suited to such a life.* "And you can be happy here. Life afoot...can be lonely."

At his grave admission, she looked up. Some of the exhilaration left her half-shadowed expression. "You don't understand, Mr. Corley," Julia said, resting her temple against the tree trunk as she gazed outward again. *"I'm lonely here."*

He was stricken. Driven to do something—anything—to help her, Graham moved forward. Only Julia's narrow back was visible to him now, and all at once she seemed impossibly delicate...dangerously vulnerable. He raised his arms to hold her.

Inches from her body, he stopped. He flexed his hands, desperate to act correctly. Would a touch from him now be welcome? Or would it only promise more than he, a drifting man, could give?

Graham stiffened. "I ache for you, Julia."

"You should not call me that." Her voice was muffled, as though with unshed tears. "It's not prop—"

"Damn what's proper. I care what's right." His palms lightly touched her shoulders, skimmed outward to the tops of her arms. *"I care about you."*

"Don't. Don't say that."

He felt too strongly to heed her. "If leaving here is what you want, I'll make it happen," Graham said urgently. "Come away with me. Tonight. I have all we need, and—"

"No. Shhh." Abruptly, Julia turned. The movement ended their tenuous contact, but in the next moment she lay her gloved fingers over his mouth, stopping his words. "My plan can work, and it will. I know it. So long as you don't, for my sake, pretend to be someone you're not."

He removed her hand. "I mean what I say."

"That you'll take me away, like a fairy-tale hero spiriting his ladylove away in the night?" A smile crossed her face, making her more beautiful than any mere bonnet or dress ever could. "I don't doubt your sincerity, Mr. Corley. Truly. But to burden a wandering man with obligations—to saddle him with *me*—would be very unfair."

She rolled her eyes, making a jest of the whole idea. He should have been relieved by her quick thinking, Graham knew. He was not.

"We have a bargain," he said stubbornly. "I'll meet it."

Julia wrinkled her nose. "Our bargain calls for you, in return for my tutoring, to court me, to become engaged to me, and even to wed me. With an annulment to follow, once we leave town, of course. It does not require utter self-sacrifice."

He frowned.

"Oh, I can see that you want to take action," she said, "and we do seem stymied now. But Papa is merely being mulish. He'll come 'round. As I see it, if he can change his hairstyle *and* laugh over dinner, all in the same month, then anything is possible."

She smiled, and patted his hand. How had it come to pass that *Julia* was comforting *him?* 'Twas a muddle, to be sure, and Graham couldn't make heads nor tails of any of it. Her moods were mercurial, with smiles coming as often as near-tears. It was enough to turn a man nearly loony.

Or enough to keep him interested for all his days.

"Honestly," Julia said. She clasped his hand between hers, and held it as she spoke. "Have faith. And do *not* say more about taking me away with you, please. If I thought you'd changed from anything but a drifting man, especially for my sake, I couldn't bear it."

Uncomfortably, Graham remembered the happiness he'd taken in being welcomed at the Bennetts' table during so many past evenings. He recalled the camaraderie he'd discovered at the Avalanche livery stable, and the enjoyment he'd found in tipping his hat to a host of familiar faces on the streets of town...all because of Julia, and the bargain he'd made with her.

He cleared his throat. Still, his voice was gruff when he spoke. "All right. I'll say no more about sneaking you away."

Graham closed his fingers around hers, treasuring the warmth of her touch. From somewhere inside, he managed a grin with which to lighten the mood between them. It was the least he could do, given her attempts to cheer him.

"I'll do this as you wish," he told her. "No matter how you might tempt me to end this charade *my* way."

His teasing worked. Julia glanced up, batting her lashes coquettishly.

"Your way?" she asked. "And what, pray tell, would that be?"

Graham lowered his gaze to their joined hands. "'Tis simple." He stroked his thumb over her wrist, teasing the pearl buttons on her glove, remembering the way he'd unbuttoned them once before. "I would compromise you, quite possibly in the woods—" with a speculative air, he examined the deep drifts of fallen pine needles surrounding them "—and most definitely pleasurably. And then you would be forced to wed me, approval or no. Immediately."

She gasped. A sharp tug yanked her hand from his.

"Sir! You would not!"

Graham raised his eyebrows and gave them a roguish waggle. Julia jumped. Openmouthed, she looked around.

"In a bed of pine needles?"

He shrugged.

"I don't believe it!"

For several minutes, Julia gawked at him. More than likely, Graham guessed, she was deciding how heavy an oak branch to use to wallop him with, for his impertinence. 'Twas possible he'd gone too far with her again. But it felt good to have things in the open between them, and he could not regret it.

"I am a man who solves problems," he told her. "Problems that sometimes range across several states and territories. I did not earn my reputation by throwing up my hands and surrendering at the first difficulty."

"Yes, but—"

"In this, with you, I've kept my solutions to myself for too long," Graham went on, frowning as he thrust his arm downward for emphasis. "You'd be wrong to think that means I'm an overly amiable man."

At his warning, Julia seemed to suppress a grin. "Oh, I doubt very much that I—"

"Because I am not. Not amiable, not settled—"

"Will you let me say a word edgewise?" she asked suddenly. Looking exasperated, Julia spread her arms wide. "I believe you, and everything you've said. It's only that I meant to tell you before...."

She stopped. Bit her lip.

Now *this* interested him. Her hesitancy intrigued him, far more than up-and-down moods and near-constant talking. Graham edged closer. "Hmmm? To tell me what?"

"Well, I meant to ask you...." Her voice grew very small. "Wouldn't the pine needles poke?"

The bounty hunter stared at her. Then he began to laugh. Uproariously. Julia heard the hearty sound of his laughter circle the hills and mountains surrounding them, as loud as though it echoed off the pine boughs and oak branches and was redoubled by the action. He bent over, clutching his middle.

She considered kicking him. Her shoes were pointy. His shins were within reach. She felt fairly certain an indignant jab would gain his attention and restore his sobriety.

But then Julia remembered she was a well-mannered woman. And, more importantly, she'd brought all this upon herself with her dratted curiosity. It would not be right to assault Mr. Corley for the sake of it.

"It's not that funny!" she said.

"Oh, yes." His chuckles subsided, long enough for Graham to sweep a mirthful glance over her person. "It is."

"It's not. And it's *very* ungentlemanly of you to laugh."

"It's unladylike of *you* to contemplate bedding down with me on a pile of pine needles," he pointed out, his smile revealing a dimple at the edge of his mouth. "But I'm happy you did...or are." His smile widened. "I knew you had passion."

She was stymied. As discourteous as the ideas behind them were, the words *sounded* complimentary coming from him.

"That's, er, irrelevant," Julia said, trying desperately to regain the propriety she'd lost. "It was mere intellectual curiosity that made me ask. Nothing more."

"It was much more."

He was right. She was as curious as any woman—possibly more so. As a girl, the boys had been more interested in copying from her slate than in stealing kisses in the schoolyard. As a grown woman, the Avalanche men had tried courting her...until she'd begun discussing politics, philosophy and literature.

The best of them had tried debating in their turn, but it seemed nothing discouraged the average man like being proved mistaken in his notion of Darwin's theories, or some other subject. In the end, Julia had realized she would either need to bury her intellect for the sake of pleasing a man, or forever wonder what a true kiss felt like.

She'd chosen wondering.

And now, for the first time in quite a while, she found herself regretting that decision. Perhaps if she'd pretended ignorance a bit more often, she would have gained the experience to meet Mr. Corley on more equal footing now.

But that couldn't be helped. She'd simply have to forge onward, Julia decided, and extricate herself from this mess some other way.

"You're right," she admitted, not looking at him. She lay her hand on the trunk of the pine tree beside them, and offhandedly examined the thick layers of bark. "But only because I felt close to you just then, and knew you would not judge me."

Graham tilted his head, watching her closely. Waiting. "You're right. I'm no one to judge you, or anyone."

Julia took a deep breath. Glancing at him from beneath her lashes, she said, "These are called strawberry pine trees. Do you know why?"

If the bounty hunter was befuddled by her sudden change in topic, he didn't show it. He shook his head.

"Because someone—I don't know who—discovered that if you get very close to one of these trees…" Julia captured his hand in hers again, and pulled him closer. "And if you close your eyes and inhale, very carefully…"

Gently, she demonstrated. Angling her head so her wide hat brim didn't interfere, she leaned near enough that her nose almost touched the rough bark. "The bark smells exactly like strawberries. Strawberry pine. See?"

Silence. Julia opened one eye, to glimpse Mr. Corley watching her with a bemused expression. *You're daft,* his reluctance to follow suit said. But the tenderness in his gaze told another, more captivating story.

"Why aren't you trying it?"

Graham shifted. Looked downward. "I'm not a fanciful man."

"It doesn't require fancy. Only willingness."

"I'm short on that, too."

"You're not!" Laughing at his obstinacy, she squeezed his hand in hers. "You were willing to contemplate pine needles. Try this, too."

"'Tis girlish." He squinted at the pine tree, as though the bark might somehow contaminate him with skirts, bustles and high-swept hair if he came any closer. "I'm not—"

"Please. For me?"

That seemed to settle it. Casting her a silly face, Graham closed his eyes and then leaned nearer. In encouragement, Julia leaned closer, as well. His actions—however silly the bounty hunter thought they were—touched her heart.

"Do you smell it?" she asked. "Like a giant strawberry?"

He grunted.

Resting her forehead against the rich-scented bark, Julia looked at him fondly. "I declare. With your eyes screwed shut and your forehead scrunched up like that as you concentrate, you make quite a picture, Mr. Corley. It's charming."

"Shhh. I think I'm getting it." He waved his hand for silence and inhaled deeply. "If I can only—"

"You've done enough," Julia said. "More than you can ever know."

Her heart filled with gratitude. That, and something more. Something she would never have thought herself capable of expressing, and yet...an idea occurred to her, and for once in her life, cautious Miss Julia Bennett decided to act on impulse.

She ducked beneath Graham's arm, placing herself between him and the tree. She lay her hand against his cheek, to steady herself. And then, then…she kissed him.

Chapter Eleven

What surprised her most, Julia thought wildly, was his warmth. The bounty hunter fairly burned with heat. And although all she did was quickly press her lips to his clean-shaven cheek, a great deal of that heat seemed to be transferred to her, right away.

Graham held utterly still, one hand braced on the bark above his head, the other wrapped partway around her middle—a placement accidentally arranged by the way she'd stepped up to him with their hands joined. His big body seemed to go rigid beside her. It was as though some magic swirled in the air between them, and could only be felt if they stood very, very close together.

Julia wanted that magic. She wanted his warmth, and she wanted...*something* more. Rapidly, before she could come to her senses and change her mind, she levered herself on tiptoes and kissed him again.

''Julia,'' he began. ''You—''

''Oh! Of course you must think me terribly rude.'' Some sort of intoxicating sensation burbled inside her. It was as though she'd drank gallons of the Emporium's fizzy soda waters, all at once, and they'd somehow filled every inch of her body. "I'm sorry, but I was simply overcome by the—"

"That's not what I—"

"—moment." Giddily, she squeezed his hand, still united with hers within her skirts. "Please, Mr. Corley. I hope you won't think me unpardonably forward when I ask this, but...may I kiss you again?"

His grin was like sunshine, warming her all over. "You don't have to ask."

"Oh, but I must! I don't think it would be proper to simply *assault* you, whenever I wished. Do you?"

"Proper? You're asking the wrong man."

"Of course I'm not." His eyes drew her in, deep blue and intent. His jaw intrigued her, solid and square beneath her palm. His mouth fascinated, compelling her to... "I'm sorry. I've quite forgotten what we were talking about."

Julia glanced upward, puzzled.

"Assault by kissing," Graham supplied helpfully.

"Oh, yes." With a sigh, she remembered. Wrinkling her brow, she contemplated her next move. More than anything, she wanted to be truly daring and kiss him on the mouth. "That's right."

As though guessing her thoughts, Graham spoke. "You can move a little further east on that kiss next time, if you want."

Julia frowned. East? Which way was...? Determined to play along, she lowered her arm and pointed left. She raised her eyebrows.

He shook his head.

She pointed right, and he nodded.

Encouraged, Julia raised up and kissed him again, an inch to the right. Pleased, she lowered again, keeping her gaze fastened on that place on his cheek, so she could better gauge the next kiss.

"Further east," he suggested.

She complied.

"Further." His voice sounded tight, strung with some emotion she couldn't name, and did not ease with the next kiss.

"Further."

Julia hesitated. "I'm running out of cheek to kiss."

"I know."

"I'll—I'll have to kiss your lips. I hope that's all right." She stared at his mouth, wondering how it would feel against hers. Excitement filled her. "I wouldn't presume to—"

"Presume anything you want," Graham said, his voice a rasp of emotion. "I'm at your mercy."

What an interesting notion! A burly, mysterious man like the bounty hunter, wholly at her disposal. Filled with courage at the thought of it, Julia edged upward.

Their breath mingled. His gaze met hers, and she thought she glimpsed a needful depth to his expression. Slowly, she inhaled, prolonging the silent union between them. And then, simply because she couldn't wait any longer, Julia kissed him.

Their lips met, and Graham's whole body tightened. His hand grasped hers more firmly. Swept away by the thrill of the moment, Julia closed her eyes and savored the press of his mouth on hers. His lips were firm, warm. His rumble of pleasure vibrated between them, setting her senses atingle. 'Twas wondrous to be kissing him, she discovered. And it was over with much too quickly.

Breathless, Julia lowered. Her heart pounded wildly, and her breath quickened. Doubtless, she'd been too bold. But the impulse to touch him had been too strong not to heed. Once Graham had agreed to smell a pine tree, for her sake alone, she'd truly been lost. It was daft, but true.

She gazed upward. As she watched, Graham opened his eyes. In their depths, all the wonder she'd felt was reflected, redoubled, renewed. Her heart gave a little skip, and Julia knew that things would never be the same between them.

Whatever happened now, there would be no going back.

The realization should have scared her—would have, most likely, before the time she'd spent with Graham. But being with him so often during the past weeks had made her feel…braver, somehow. Actions that Julia had shied away from in the past suddenly seemed open to her. Remarkably so.

Graham looked at her. Seriously. "You'd better take off your hat."

She touched it, and frowned. "Why? I'm quite sure I angled my head properly, so I wouldn't jab you in the eye with the brim. With some practice, it's likely I'll master the technique even more perfectly."

At her mention of "practice" he grinned. Leisurely.

"I don't want it to get crushed," he explained.

"It won't." Now that she knew how this kissing business worked, Julia felt much more confident. "Don't worry."

"I'm not so delicate at kissing as you." With an air of warning wholly befitting a man like him—a wandering man she could never give her heart to—Graham came nearer. "I'll try not to be too rough, but I can make no promises once I've touched you. Take it off."

His movements, steady and sure, fairly pinned her

against the tree trunk at her back. At her front, the bounty hunter spread his hands on her hips and held her possessively in place. He nodded toward her hat.

His bossiness should have summoned up miles of etiquette rules from her head. His arrogance should have pricked her temper. Instead, insanely, Julia found that neither of those things happened. In this, she didn't mind that the bounty hunter took the upper hand.

Quite likely, that was because of the smoldering, wickedly intense look he'd given her while doing so.

With an arch of her brow to show him she wouldn't be commanded except by her own choosing, she plucked out her hatpin. She removed her hat and thrust the pin into its crown. Feeling exposed and a little vulnerable, Julia tossed the pair onto the saddle blanket a few feet away. They landed with a breezy spin that brightened her mood, and made her impromptu assignation with Mr. Corley feel downright fun.

"Thank you," he said politely, sweeping off his own flat-brimmed hat.

Then he tilted his hips forward, pinning her more firmly to the tree behind her. He raised his hands, touching her upswept hair for the first time. He lowered them slightly, cradling her cheeks with an expression so loving it made her sigh.

Slowly, Graham angled her face, gently preparing her for what came next.

It was, Julia discovered, a kiss. One unlike any other. It began slowly, chastely, with their lips brushing only faintly. It built with tender little nips, all along the fullness of her lower lip. It intensified with a nudge of Graham's tongue at the seam of her lips, became sweetly intimate when she opened to him. Their bodies pressed closer as their mouths angled and delved deeper, and it was all Julia could do to grasp Graham's shoulders and hang on.

Kissing him called forth every bit of longing she'd ever known, every ounce of need she'd ever felt when he'd looked at her. It united them in a way Julia could scarcely describe. It was tender and fierce by turns, heartfelt and wicked in equal measure. It was all that she needed and not quite enough, and when Graham finally drew away, she couldn't suppress a sigh.

"Oh! Oh, my!" she whispered.

He smiled. *The rogue.*

She touched her lips, somehow feeling as though they'd changed...right along with the rest of her. Her mouth *felt* the same, but being kissed by the bounty hunter had transformed her nonetheless, Julia was certain. It had turned her into a woman, with a woman's wants and a woman's needs—and they did *not,* to her surprise, center around leaving Avalanche as quickly as possible. Instead, they focused on Graham Corley...and how best to convince him that what lay between them deserved greater exploration.

New love was like that, Julia supposed wistfully. Deserving investigation and attention and—*oh, something more,* she told herself hazily as Graham leaned closer and smiled again. *Something that mattered little when he looked at her that way.*

"Too rough?" he asked.

"Rough? Oh, no." She felt a wide, silly smile spread across her face. "That was...perfect. Just perfect."

"'Tis a shame Asa wasn't here to see it," Graham went on. "He'd have believed our betrothal was real, for certain."

Julia's heart sank, just a little.

"My father?" She choked out the words, trying desperately to recover from their kiss as fully as Graham seemed to have done. "More than likely, he would have been appalled at my behavior."

"Why? Surely he was in love, once." The bounty hunter studied the fallen pine needles beneath their feet. "Wasn't he?"

"Madly. With my mother, of course. They came to the Territory together, determined to begin a new life here." Julia leaned her head against the tree trunk behind her, wishing Graham would put his arms around her again. Their kiss had been so stirring, so...*brief.* Conversation was all well and good, but when compared with a kiss, it turned up decidedly lacking, she decided.

Nevertheless, she continued: "She believed in him, and he cherished her. That is why my papa insists I find a man who loves me to take me East. He says it's impossible to be truly happy without love."

Graham looked up. His shrewd expression put her instantly on guard.

"And what do you say?" he asked.

I say I believed him the instant your lips met mine, Julia thought. *I say I never knew what it was to need someone, until now.* But she could not bring herself to say the words aloud.

"I say we'd better head back," she told him instead, moving briskly to retrieve her hat from their picnic blanket. "It's getting late."

As she settled her hat atop her head and pinned it in place through the knot of her upswept hair, she felt the bounty hunter's gaze on her. His scrutiny continued for so long, in fact, that Julia began to believe Graham had guessed the truth—she'd fallen in love with him, however unwisely, in the space between one kiss and the next. Between one sniff of a strawberry pine and the determined silliness that had engendered it in the first place.

Ducking her head, Julia darted a glance toward him. Would he challenge her? Ask her to speak of her feelings? She didn't think she could. A lifetime of hiding her emotions had schooled her against anything so reckless as that.

Graham's face was impassive. If he did know how she felt about him now, in the wake of their kiss, it wasn't revealed in his expression...nor in his voice, when he spoke.

"I'll walk you to the edge of town," was all he said.

After helping to gather their things, Julia accompanied him. She kept herself calm, and even managed to carry on a spirited discussion with Graham about the various people he'd met in town. But all the while, Julia's mind was spinning.

The spinster of Avalanche had fallen in love—wildly, madly, improbably in love. And in this, as in all things, she had no intention whatsoever of letting chance have its way. Somehow, someway, she would find the courage to tell Graham what was in her heart, charade or no. And, heaven help her, she would do it soon.

At the edge of the mountainous forest, Graham stood in the shadow of a towering strawberry pine and watched Julia step from the rocky path onto the grassy yard that bordered the church. It was the first building at this edge of Avalanche, and the civilizing effects of town could already be seen in the flowers and clipped bushes bordering the church steps. From there, the road leading inward wound directly past the white clapboard building and made its way into the heart of town, where businesses faced it on both sides.

With her feet safely on the grass, Julia paused. She looked over her shoulder at him, her expression lost to the distance separating them. Graham fancied he saw sadness there, and a reluctance to leave him...but in truth, he had no better luck guessing what Julia was thinking from afar than he did when they were a hairsbreadth apart.

She raised her arm and waved. Solemnly, Graham raised his palm to her, his salute feeling more a goodbye than any had before. More than ever, their limited time together weighed on his mind, and he was not a man who easily pretended anything he did not feel.

That was...perfect. Just perfect.

It had been. Julia lowered her arm. With a final smile, she turned and walked away.

No, not away, Graham reminded himself. Toward town. Julia walked toward town and not specifically away from him, but the time would come soon enough when she would leave...and then where would they be?

Where would *he* be?

He'd nearly revealed himself to her. Earlier, when she'd trembled in his arms and had moaned beneath his kiss, he'd been ready to declare himself to her and have the charade between them finished. Julia had thought he'd been teasing when he'd spoken of compromising her in the forest—

Wouldn't the pine needles poke?

—but he hadn't been. Not in truth. Being with her made him forget his bounty hunter's past, made him yearn for something...more. Their kiss had felt *real,* and to Graham's smitten heart, it had meant an end to the loneliness he felt. If only for a while.

He'd nearly confessed, Graham remembered as he watched Julia's distant form disappear around the corner toward Mulligan's hotel. Had nearly told her he'd wanted her from the start, wanted her still, wanted her in spite of their pretend courtship, and not because of it.

But then he'd come to his senses.

Just as he was learning the appeal of a settled life in town, Julia wanted to be away. Just as he discovered the uncertainty of loving someone in secret, Julia strove to improve their charade. With her quick mind and her determination, it seemed likely to Graham that her kisses today had simply been a part of the plan...and at the last moment, he'd thrown away his chance to end the deception, with a question designed to make her believe she meant no more to him than he did to her.

'Tis a shame Asa wasn't here to see it. He'd have believed our betrothal was real, for certain.

Instantly, he'd thought he'd glimpsed disappointment in her face. But by then it had been too late. The words were said.

Still, that disappointment gave him hope. It showed he meant *something* to Julia, something more than a man to practice kisses on.

Graham smiled at the remembrance. Julia kissed like a woman held in darkness too long, and then allowed outside to turn her face to the sun. 'Course, with her the experience was measured and sampled and tested, tried in small, ever-eastward movements. If Miss Julia Bennett were in charge of the sunrise, it would happen maddeningly slowly, over the course of an entire morning instead of the space of a few minutes.

And if she were left in charge of their "courtship," Graham realized, it would take a similar course. He'd be an old man, pining for a woman in faraway New York state, by the time Julia understood that he cared for her.

She saw him as an aid to her scheme. As a student to be tutored. As a temporary fiancé, to be molded as she saw fit. Whatever else he did, Graham vowed as he hefted the bundled-up saddle blanket and supplies and started into town, he would make Julia see him as he was.

As a man.

And he would do it, beginning *now.*

Chapter Twelve

The following morning, Julia suggested that she and Mr. Corley take their lessons outside, to the Avalanche Municipal Park where they'd met. The late-spring weather was balmy and the air was crisp with the scents of pine and newly grown grass, and although she presented the outing as an opportunity to practice reading in a more challenging setting, the truth was simpler.

She did not trust herself to be alone with Graham. Not in the shed-turned-schoolroom behind the Emporium. Not since their kiss. And not since she'd discovered her feelings for him.

Oblivious to all that, the bounty hunter had agreed. And so they found themselves seated on a bench beneath a spreading cottonwood tree, Julia with a stack of paper propped on her knees...Graham with a McGuffey reader spread in his hands. She sat properly, taking up as little space on the bench as possible. He sprawled comfortably, his brawny body sideways with his feet just a few inches from her green-flowered skirts.

He read aloud, most words coming easily to him now. The sound of his voice soothed Julia into a state of dreamy contemplation, and she let her mind—and pencil—wander as Graham continued in his practice.

When he faltered, she glanced up, and found Graham frowning fiercely at the printed pages before him.

"What's wrong?" she asked. "You look as though you'd tear the meanings from those words forcibly, and crush them if they didn't cooperate."

"McGuffey is as goody-goody as a preacher, and twice as long-winded," he grumbled, staring down at the pages in his hands. "This story about the little boy and the turtle—"

"Illustrates some very important virtues," Julia told him. "Honesty, industry, courtesy and obedience are—"

"Boring. I've had enough." With an air of finality, Graham closed the book. "What are you writing?"

Obviously seeking a more interesting entertainment, he leaned nearer and peered at the pages on her lap. Julia looked down, too, and was appalled at what she saw.

"Mrs. Julia Cor—" Graham read, squinting at the ornate loops of her handwriting. "Corley? *Mrs. Corley?*"

She slapped her hands over the careless doodles she'd made.

The bounty hunter grinned. "Indulging in flights of fancy today?"

"Of course not." Her face heated. Sitting up straighter, Julia endeavored to seem more composed than she felt. *What* had possessed her to script row upon row of variations on Mrs. Graham Corley, Julia Corley, Mrs. Julia Corley, Mr. and Mrs. Graham Corley…? "These are ah, um, a series of examples—for my latest etiquette book."

He looked skeptical. "Examples?"

"Indeed. Examples of proper address. For calling cards, greeting cards and other personal correspondence." *My, that was close.* "It's a subject of enduring interest to my readers."

His smile dared her to elaborate on her lie.

Julia saw no choice but to do so. The alternative—admitting that she'd been daydreaming, filled with hopes of making their upcoming engagement real—was unthinkable.

"In fact," she went on, "that's one of the reasons I'm writing a fourth book at all. The editor at *Beadle's* suggested it."

"What will it be called?" Graham folded his hands across his middle, looking as though he believed her not at all—and as though he was enjoying her tall-tale-spinning immensely. "*More Manners To Make Life No Fun? One Thousand And One Ways To Wear A Necktie? Castile Soap: A Guide For Ladies With Passionate Suitors?*"

"Very amusing." Casting him a sideways glance, Julia gathered up her papers. "As it happens, I'm currently deliberating between *The Gentleman and Lady's Book Of Politeness and Propriety In All Situations* and *The Lady's Guide To Perfect Gentility, In Manners, Dress, Conversation, And In The Family, On The Street, At Table, In Company At The Piano Forte, And In Gentleman's Society.* Which do you prefer?"

"I'm not sure. In my mind, the title should take up fewer pages than the actual book."

She made a face. "Well, there's always *Miss Julia's Behavior Book, Volume Four.* The format has worked nicely for me until now. The success of the first few books is the reason why I've been offered an interview for the etiquette columnist position at *Beadle's Magazine,* you know.''

Why she felt compelled to brag about that fact, Julia couldn't imagine. She only knew that she wanted Mr. Corley to think well of her...and so far, he didn't appear to.

''In New York City?''

''Yes.'' Julia looked down at her gloved fingers, feeling the breeze stir the colored ostrich plumes on her hat. ''Lucinda Druiry, from Avalanche, is hoping for the position as well. We were at Vassar together.''

''Ahhh. Competition.'' Graham ran a hand over his clean-shaven jaw. His sharp-eyed gaze pierced her. ''So that's why this is so important to you. You want to win.''

''Of course not!'' Julia said. ''Winning has nothing to do with this. I feel as though I can make a difference for people, people who are hungry for guidance. More and more members of the merchant class are entering the highest parts of society, and there's a demand for—''

''You're lying.''

''I'm not!''

Graham leaned closer, and grasped her chin gently in his hand. With a rueful shake of his head, he regarded her. ''You are. I've tracked too many liars not to recognize one when she's right in front of me. No matter how pretty she is.''

He winked, and released her.

She might have known the bounty hunter would see through her tale. He'd sensed so many other things about her.

''Very well,'' Julia said, surrendering to the inevitable. ''Do you want to know the truth?''

His nod set her insides atumble. Did she dare? She'd never confided in anyone before. It was strange that she felt compelled to, now. Perhaps it was because she had less at risk with a drifting man, a man who likely wouldn't remain in Avalanche long enough to reveal her secret.

"Fine," Julia announced. "I'll tell you."

Graham folded his arms again, and leaned back. The wrought-iron edge of the scrollwork bench jabbed into his shoulder blades, and he shifted to be more comfortable. It wasn't easy. In an effort to impress Julia, he'd asked his landlady to add more starch to his laundry, and his shirt collar poked at his neck. His pants were so stiff, he feared for his manhood every time a strong breeze came along.

"I'm waiting," he prompted.

"I know." Visibly flustered, Julia fussed with her papers and pencil. Her skirts were lifted in the current from a passing freight wagon, and she wrinkled her nose at the dust the vehicle raised. "It's just that...well, I've never confided in anyone before. I suppose I'm not very good at it."

"Don't worry," Graham said. "I'm trustworthy. Ask anyone who's hired me."

"It's not your ability to keep your employer a secret that I'm worried about. It's your ability to..."

"To?"

"...to not make fun of me."

Her voice was very small. She kept her head ducked, and her monstrosity of a hat shielded all but the tip of her nose from view. Still, Graham spied the tense set to her shoulders, and the slight trembling of her hands, and knew that Julia had meant what she said.

He didn't move, lest he scare her away. "I'll not make fun of you."

"Good." She drew a shuddering breath, and looked at him. "Thank you. You're a fine man, Mr. Corley. Have I told you that before?"

Graham shook his head, and said nothing. Patient waiting was the way with this woman, he'd learned.

"Well, I'm sure I have." An uneasy smile quivered on her lips, then vanished. Julia ducked her head again. "I may as well simply come out with this, and stop being such a ninny."

She paused, as though waiting for him to agree. Because he wasn't a fool, Graham did not.

Another deep breath. "As you know, I've...not always been welcomed in town." From beneath her hat brim, she gazed at the buildings surrounding them, and the people who milled past on the distant street. "For as long as I can remember, I've not been a part of things. I've never quite fit in. Not really. And oh, Mr. Corley...*how I wanted to.*"

Her voice shook with emotion. As though working to suppress it, Julia shook her head. "I wanted to belong. To have dozens of friends, to share whispered secrets in the schoolyard and laugh over a jest, like everyone else did. But somehow, that never happened for me."

Graham swallowed hard, and looked away. Her tale of being apart from everyone else was much like his. It hurt him to hear it told, and hurt even more to know how she must have felt.

A jay squawked past, coming to perch in the cottonwood tree over their heads. Another freight wagon rumbled by, followed by the morning stage. When they'd both passed, Julia spoke again.

"I wanted to belong. I knew I could figure out how, if only I had the means." A rueful expression touched her face, half-shadowed by her hat. "I was intelligent. I only lacked the proper insight. When I enrolled at Vassar and discovered my roommate's cache of etiquette instruction guides, I reasoned that I had found exactly what I needed: a foolproof means to finally doing the right thing. To finally being accepted."

At the longing in her voice, Graham felt a lump rise in his throat. He swallowed past it, and regarded her seriously.

"You read them?"

"Of course!" Her disbelieving gaze met his, then moved swiftly away. "I knew that when I was done, when I'd learned all they had to teach me, I would know exactly what to do. At all times, with all people."

"And no one would turn you away?"

A tear trickled down her cheek, and Julia impatiently brushed it away. She nodded. "That was the notion I had, yes. To solidify my knowledge, I began taking notes, and my books were born. But they were only a tangential result. My real goal was—is—to make sure I didn't give anyone a reason to…to reject me again. I knew that if I was perfect, just as perfect as possible—"

"Ahhh, Julia." Leaning closer, Graham covered her hand with his. The delicate fabric of her skirts tickled his wrist, and served to heighten the differences between them. "Don't you know? You don't have to be perfect…to be loved."

"It's worked!" she said fiercely, jerking her hand away. "Hasn't it? You've seen how it's been since I returned to town. Everyone wears hats like mine. The ladies in Avalanche hang on my every word, buy my guides at the book depot, copy my dress styles and mimic my calling cards! Even Papa's hairstyle wasn't ridiculed as it might have been. It's worked, it has!"

"Anyone who cares only for those things is not worth having for a friend."

The sound of disagreement she made bordered on rudeness.

"You simply don't want to admit that etiquette has its place," Julia argued. "You'd rather believe—"

"I'd rather believe the people in this town have come to their senses, and taken you to their hearts because of who you are." *As I have,* Graham countered silently. "Not because you've studied which fork to use when."

"That's daft. And oversimplified." Her voice raised, and her grasp on her paper and pencil tightened. "I'll have you know, Mr. Corley, that—"

"You can't admit you're wrong," he interrupted, and realized even as he said it that he believed it to be true beyond a doubt. "You won't admit you're wrong."

Julia pressed her lips together. A moment ticked past. "*If* I was wrong," she said grudgingly, "then perhaps—"

"Aha! I'm right. It's true."

"It's not!"

"So long as you close your eyes to it, it will continue to be true," Graham said. "You are not always right, Miss Bennett. No one is."

"I am right in this," she insisted. "And you're a fine one to talk, Mr. Corley, with your wandering ways and your disdain of a settled life! How could you know how I feel? You've never stayed in one place long enough to be turned away."

He gaped at her. A sudden anger simmered inside him, and Graham swung himself 'round to sit straight.

The motion released some of his feelings, but the renewed tightness in his shoulders remained.

"Perhaps that's why you head for the trail," Julia went on, gesturing wildly toward the road with her pencil. "After all, no one can turn from you if you've already gone."

"Enough." Graham sent her a warning look. "I have your secret, and I'll keep it. Do not try to guess mine."

"I already have!"

Abruptly, he got to his feet. "This lesson is finished."

She said nothing, only glared at him furiously from her place on the bench. She tapped her pencil against her stack of papers, making the carefully scripted joining of their names skitter across her lap.

"I'm not wrong," she finally grumbled.

"And I'm not staying." Clenching his McGuffey reader tightly, Graham turned to leave. Julia's voice followed him.

"Running again, Mr. Corley? I should have known."

He stopped. "You know nothing about me."

"I know that you're mistaken about my being wrong." The playful edge to her voice was unexpected. So was the touch of her hand on his arm, waylaying his escape. "I know that you'll probably never admit it." Her tone softened, and she squeezed his forearm gently. "I know that I'm sorry for speaking so unkindly to you before. I want you to stay."

I want you to stay. How many times had he wished to hear those words? Too many to count, if he were honest with himself. And yet…

"You know I won't stay," he told her gruffly. "'Tis the reason you chose me."

"Do you think so?" she mused. "I begin to believe

it was the challenge of learning about you that drew me. You're beyond mysterious, Mr. Corley. And you know it's a rare woman who can resist a puzzling man."

Graham laughed, and looked over his shoulder to see her do the same. "Another jest? Miss Bennett, you amaze me."

"I'm not without humor," she informed him.

"I'm not without mystery. Or so you say."

"It's true." Julia tugged him toward her. "Please, don't go. Here we are, very nearly misleadingly engaged, and I know next to nothing about you."

She had dimples when she smiled, Graham noticed. Dimples, and an enchanting openness in her expression. Whatever had made her call an end to their disagreement, it must have been powerful, indeed.

Like love.

Or maybe 'twas merely the growing feelings he had for her that made him wish it were so. Either way, Graham let her pull him back beside her on the bench.

"What do you want to—" He paused, seeking the correct words—something he'd found himself doing more and more often these days, in an attempt to impress Julia. "What do you wish to know?"

"Everything."

She folded her hands atop her lap with an air of absolute expectancy, and cocked her head. Graham balked.

"No."

"All right, then...." Her gaze traveled over him, finally coming to rest on the sheaf of folded paper sticking partway from his duster coat pocket. "Tell me about Frankie. I've helped you read two of her letters now. I'm curious."

Automatically, he put his hand on the latest letter. It rested against his heart, as always, and would join the others he'd saved in his saddlebags as soon as he returned to his boardinghouse room. Carrying Frankie's letters was like carrying a smile in his pocket. They were always there for him.

"There's not much to tell," he said, at a loss to describe his friend of more than twenty years. "Frankie is...Frankie. A lady, like you."

"Named Frankie? She must be unconventional, to be sure."

"She is." Graham smiled in remembrance. "Francesca Maria Bailoni is unlike anyone else. She was the skinniest, stubbornest, *luckiest* girl to ever come to the Sisters of Mercy home."

Julia gawked. "Lucky? How could she be, when she grew up in such a...such a..." Belatedly, she seemed to remember what Graham had revealed of his childhood. "Place?"

"Frankie's family came for her," he said simply. "In the end, her relatives found her, and took her away from Boston to live. That was the kind of luck we all wished for."

"Oh." Compassionately, Julia covered his hand with hers and gave a little squeeze. "You must have been happy for her."

"I was." *And miserable, for myself.* "After she left, she always wrote me. But by then I'd started working at the wharves, and didn't have the time—" *or the strength, as a boy of eight years doing a man's full day of work* "—to learn to properly write her back. I started paying to have her letters read to me, and to have someone write the replies I sent. And it's been that way, ever since."

"That's why you never learned to read," Julia said. "You were working." Her expression was sympathetic. "Well, we simply *must* begin your handwriting lessons right away. Think how wonderful it will be to write a letter to Frankie yourself!"

Her eyes shined with anticipation. Graham didn't have the heart to remind her of the truth—that he'd likely be gone from Avalanche, having played his part as her "fiancé," long before such a thing came to pass.

Julia leaned nearer. "I think you must love her a little bit, your Frankie," she said. "Your eyes turn all wistful when you speak of her, and you lose that grouchy expression of yours."

Graham grunted. "I'm not a man given to love. 'Tis the foolishness of poets. And drummers wanting to sell perfume."

"Oh, Mr. Corley." Julia sighed. "You have a solitary soul, I'm afraid."

Her pronouncement made him feel twice as alone. And her next words didn't help matters any.

"Haven't you *ever* wanted to fall in love?" Julia asked. "To have a wife and children and a family of your own?"

He saw the way she held her breath to await an answer. The way she watched, unblinking, as he hesitated. And knew that he would disappoint her again, when he told her the truth.

"I have no desire for those things," Graham said gruffly. "As I am, I'm bound to no one. I like it that way."

Or at least, he always had.

"But—"

"Enough talk." He rose, unaccountably uneasy, and extended his hand to her. "There's something I want to show you."

Chapter Thirteen

Holding her manuscript paper and pencil against her chest, Julia hurried down the Main Street boardwalk after Mr. Corley. She had to take twice the steps to keep up with his lengthy strides, and before long her breath was coming in rapid pants.

Dratted stays! Julia wouldn't have dreamed of appearing in public without being properly corseted—what true lady would? But the blasted garment definitely had a way of restricting a person's movement. By the time she and Graham were midway down the street, she was nearly ready to join with the dress reformers and become truly radical.

But then they walked farther, and she realized where he was headed, and all thoughts of fashion became unimportant.

"The livery stable?" Swallowing a gasp, Julia pulled at Mr. Corley's coat. "I can't go back to the livery stable! You saw what happened last time. Of course, the men only wanted to make it clear that Tom's stables are the usual province of the men in town, and it's my own fault for forgetting how downright surly they can become when they're disturbed, but—"

"No one will bother you this time."

"You don't know them," Julia disagreed. "Naturally, the men in town are perfectly cordial to me when we pass on the street, or if we meet while paying a call. But at the livery stable...well, I only went there in the first place because I was interested in tracking you down."

"Tracking me down?" He raised an eyebrow. "Why, Miss Bennett. I didn't know you cared."

The teasing tone to his voice only served to put her dander up. "No caring in the world would be sufficient to convince me to make an appearance at the livery stables again." Julia stopped on the boardwalk and raised her chin. "Please, let's go pay some calls, instead. Several of my acquaintances are interested in meeting you, and—"

"I want you to see this." Graham grasped her hands in his. Gently, he pulled her toward him. His face was shadowed by his hat, his smile a white slash within the darkness. "Please."

"But I—" Hesitating, Julia bit her lip. She didn't want to return to the stables. But she also didn't want to disappoint Mr. Corley. Not when he smiled at her, and gazed at her with such palpable hopefulness. "Very well."

"Thank you," he said, and tugged her down the street. "Don't worry. You can trust me."

Julia only hoped he was right. For wasn't that what she had done, all along?

At the livery stables, Julia's worries multiplied. But to her relief, she and Mr. Corley didn't go within. Instead, they approached the building from the side, Graham gesturing for her to follow his lead as he stopped beside an open window.

"Stand here," he said, "and listen."

Julia did, cocking her head to one side. At first, she heard mostly the sounds of stabled horses shifting in their stalls, and then the scrape of the stable boy's shovel as he cleaned up. Finally, the sound of a voice speaking could be heard—faintly at first, and strangely halting.

Curious, she held on to the bounty hunter's shoulder for balance and raised herself on tiptoes to peer inside the window. The sight that greeted her was amazing.

At least twelve men gathered around the stables' pot-bellied stove. Some stood. Some sat on overturned barrels or bales of hay. And one man stood in front of them all, his hands filled with an open book. Julia recognized him as Wilson Richards, a lawyer who kept his offices next door to the mercantile.

"The judge and the widow went to law to get the court to take me away from him and let one of them be my guardian," Wilson read from the book he held, "but it was a new judge that had just come, and he didn't know the old man; so he said courts mustn't interfere and separate families if they could help it."

She looked at Graham. "*Huckleberry Finn,*" she whispered in surprise. "*The Adventures of Huckleberry Finn,* by Mark Twain. I recognize it!"

"'—said he'd druther not take a child away from its father," Wilson went on as the assembled men listened carefully. "So Judge Thatcher and the widow had to quit on the business."

As Wilson continued to read, Julia lowered herself again. Still holding on to Graham's shoulder, she urged him downward until they were face-to-face. "I can't believe it!'' she said, keeping her voice low. ''So *this* is what the men in town come here to do?''

''Some of the time.''

''And *this* is their big secret, that they don't want the women to find out about?''

''More'n likely,'' the bounty hunter agreed. He tipped up a finger and closed her doubtlessly gaping jaw. ''If they keep the ladies away all the time, then they'll never be around during the reading hour.''

''Very clever.'' With reluctant admiration, Julia shook her head. ''I'd never have guessed it. But why don't they simply read at home?''

Graham shrugged. ''Books are expensive. Most of those men are farmers and small-town merchants. I doubt many of them could afford a copy of that book on their own.''

Julia frowned. Books were one of the great pleasures of her life. She couldn't imagine what it would be like not to have access to them.

''By doing it this way—'' Mr. Corley nodded toward Wilson Richards, whose voice could be heard as he continued reading to the group ''—they can share a single book.''

''At Mr. Richards's leisure,'' she pointed out, nettled by the unfairness of it. ''Knowing him, I presume he's reading aloud so that no one else will touch his property!''

Graham gave a wry chuckle. ''You've pegged him. Nobody's allowed to touch that book.'' He took her arm. Together, they walked from the livery stables, headed in the direction of the Emporium. ''And here I am, nearly ready to read parts of it myself for the first time.''

This last was said in an undertone, nearly too low for

Julia to make out. Having heard it, though, she glanced at the bounty hunter. "You're becoming an excellent reader," she assured him. "I have no doubt you could read much of *Huckleberry Finn* by now."

He tugged his hat lower, and said nothing.

"In fact, you must have had at least some schooling," she went on, enjoying the solid feel of his muscular arm beneath her hand as he guided her onto the boardwalk. "You already knew the alphabet and some of the letter sounds when we started. That's probably why you've made such speedy progress."

"'Twas my tutor." His grin warmed her, all the way to her toes. "She has a knack for inspiring me."

Julia couldn't help but grin back at him. At the private moment they shared, a giddy feeling enveloped her.

"Thank you, kind sir," she said, inclining her head toward Mr. Corley. "I'm most indebted to you for your generosity. However...what of your schooling at the sisters' home in Boston?"

He made a face, and gazed at the ice man's ornately painted wagon as it passed by them.

"I was not the most cooperative student," Graham allowed, grudgingly. "Particularly on the days when we had visitors to the home—people looking for a child to add to their family. What little I mastered was done mostly in the corner, by myself, while being punished for one thing or another."

Julia paused, stricken by the notion of a small and vulnerable Graham as a boy...alone. Alone like her, and with no one else to turn to. The thought was enough to break her heart, and she struggled for something to say that might ease the hurt he surely still carried, somewhere deep inside.

As though confused by her stopping, Mr. Corley looked down. Instantly, comprehension swept over his rugged features.

"'Twas not so bad as all that," he said, setting her into motion again. "Frankie helped me some. I got by. So save your long faces for someone who needs them, Miss Mush-Hearted Bennett. I'm fine."

Fiercely, she hugged his arm close to her. In obvious surprise—probably at her utterly improper show of emotion—Graham looked down.

If she could have, Julia vowed, she would have gathered his whole big body close, right there on the street, and squeezed all the love she could into him. Then, he'd have some warmth to keep close on those lonely trails he loved so well...and she would have the memory of having cared for him.

"And that's not what I brought you out here to talk about, either," Graham continued. Determinedly, he frowned. "I wanted you to see the way things are, so you would understand."

"Understand what?"

He cleared his throat, as though he were about to say something difficult. "Understand what I want to do. Before leaving Avalanche."

They reached the Emporium, and passed beneath its bright show globe, which swung in the breeze to designate the pharmacy inside. Julia smiled up at the ornate, multi-chambered fixture. Her mother had selected the show globe years earlier, when she and Asa Bennett had begun their business. And her father was rightly proud of his expertise in using his apothecary chemicals to mix up exactly the correct shade of colored water for it.

It was a brilliant deep blue. Precisely the color, her papa always said, of her mother's wedding dress.

Shaking off the nostalgia that threatened, Julia concentrated her attention on her conversation with Graham. She didn't like to think about the day when the bounty hunter would leave Avalanche, but now he'd forced her to.

"Before you leave?" she asked. "What is it you'd like to do?"

Buy one of those fancy cigars at Thompson's mercantile, she expected him to say. Or, *see the showgirls perform at Cole Morgan's saloon.* Men typically loved the wilder things in life, she'd learned. Why should a wandering man like Graham Corley prove any different?

But instead of expressing a long-felt yearning for imported cigarillos and scantily dressed hussies, he only looked at her squarely and said something completely unexpected:

"I want to open a public lending library."

Julia gawped at him. "But there won't be any cigars or loose women at a lending library!"

He grinned, some of the discomfort leaving his expression.

"No?" Graham's eyebrows rose in mock surprise. "Blast it! Somebody should have told me about that before I went making plans."

"You're teasing me."

"I'm not." He put his hand, faintly scarred and strong, over his heart. "I want to start a library in this town. So the men at the livery stables can get a book whenever they want one. So a drifter like me, passing through, can have a place to go that's quiet, where nobody will look at him funny for wanting a book."

"Oh, Mr. Corley." At his generous idea, Julia couldn't help but feel impressed. "That's very noble of you. But libraries cost money, and book collections take time, and I'm very afraid that in your case, neither are—"

He held up a palm. "Just say you believe I can do it."

Helplessly, Julia gazed up at him. Emporium shoppers milled around them, and signs for various patent remedies and tonics glared their messages from the walls in vibrant ink. The fizz of the soda fountain levers being worked to produce yet another cherry soda punctuated the conversations surrounding them...but the only sound that seemed to matter to the bounty hunter was the answer he waited to hear.

She didn't want to mislead him. His was a serious undertaking, requiring a commitment that a drifter like him shouldn't have been able to muster. Even a modest lending library would need funding, and workers to shelve the volumes, and a place to house them to begin with. So far as she knew, Graham didn't have any of those things.

But then she took in his determined stance, and the steadiness in his expression, and knew that she would have to tell him what was in her heart. In this, she had no other choice.

Julia raised her hand, heedless of the people moving past them. She cradled his cheek in her gloved palm, and nodded.

"I believe in you," she said.

"That's all I need to know," Graham replied, and when he captured her hand in his and squeezed, a pact was born between them.

* * *

It only took three visits for Graham to decide that paying social calls was torturous. The chairs were too small, the chatter was too loud, and the entire endeavor felt false to him. Formally paying calls, on friends? He'd asked Julia why the women didn't just agree to meet in a particular place—Bennett's Apothecary and Soda Fountain Emporium, for instance—and avoid all this house-to-house nonsense. But her only reply had been a smiling shake of her head that verified just one thing: he would never truly understand women.

Now, a day after revealing his library plans to her, he stood with Julia on the front porch of yet another household, waiting for the maid to tell them if her mistress was "at home."

"I don't see how she can't know already, if your friend is at home," Graham grumbled, tugging at his shirt collar. He'd put on a suit furnished by the chimney-sweep-turned-tailor, and although Julia had assured him he looked "remarkably handsome," he felt like an idiot. "They live in the same house, don't they? Spend all their time within fifty feet of—"

"Really, Mr. Corley," Julia said. "This is the way it's done. A person would think you're advocating raw honesty!" She gave him a half-teasing, mock-horror-stricken look. "If that were true, I would be required to tell you how absolutely delicious you look in your new suit."

He felt his jaw drop open. She tipped it shut with a gloved fingertip, and smiled coquettishly. "I declare, a person would think you'd never been told what a wickedly appealing man you are."

Wickedly appealing—huh? Frowning, Graham stared down at her. In her pink-sprigged gown, wide, flower-trimmed hat, and ruffled parasol, Julia *seemed* the same as ever. But the sparkle in her eyes was new...and befuddling...and the sultry edge to her voice set his senses reeling. Could this truly be Miss Julia Bennett, the hoity-toity etiquette instructress he'd come to know?

She raised herself on tiptoes and did something to his hair, rearranging it at his collar to suit her. The fragrance of oranges wafted toward him, and her bosom faintly brushed against his jacket front. Instantly, Graham felt his blood stir.

Her body was warm and intimate, and Julia almost seemed to offer herself to him with her closeness. Her dress delivered a surprising glimpse of gently curved bosom, and her smile, when she glanced up after having settled his hair to her satisfaction, promised things he had hardly dared to hope for.

I believe in you.

Confused, but nonetheless willing to play along with her game, Graham put his arm around her. Julia jumped at the contact. He splayed his fingers at the small of her back, enjoying the suppleness of her body beneath his hand, and tried out some teasing of his own.

This, he decided, could truly enliven the boring social calls that lay ahead.

"If you had told me all that," he said, lowering his head so their conversation would remain private, "I'd have had to tell you how much I've been wanting to kiss you again. The taste I had amongst the pines will never be enough to satisfy me. Not when you felt so soft and warm and amazing in my arms."

She cast her gaze downward, obviously surprised that he'd joined in her outrageous talk. Her lips moved, parting and then closing as Julia struggled to recover. When she had, Graham knew it immediately. An answering challenge was in her eyes when she looked up at him again.

"Nor will *I* be satisfied with so small a taste," she said, her voice even huskier. "Not when you hold me like this now, and—and tempt me to kiss you again."

At the invitation in her words, he wanted to groan with need. Instead, Graham let his palm stroke up and down her back. Like a cat, Julia arched slightly beneath his touch.

This was a dangerous game they played. Graham could scarcely believe they'd begun it. But now that they had...he could no more stop than he could change his days as a trail-bound man.

"I wish you would kiss me again," he said, hearing the hoarse need in his own voice as he spoke low against her ear. "Here. *Now.* Long and slow, with all the passion I know is inside you."

She drew in a sharp breath. "Again? H-here? *Now?*"

At the nape of his neck, her fingers began an uncertain patter. Julia gazed upward, and he found himself loving the sassy tilt of her nose, the scattered freckles on her cheeks, the luscious bow of her mouth. She looked beautiful, uniquely herself. Graham knew he'd remember her face as he had no one else's, long after he'd gone from here.

Her brows drew together in thought. Seeing the movement, he braced himself for the inevitable.

"Of course you know I can't kiss you here, on Maybelle Marchant's front porch," she said briskly, clearly having only just now realized the need to clarify things between them. A fine line appeared between her brows. "Don't you?"

"Do I?"

"I—I—" Her fingers stilled. Her eyes widened. "I don't think you do!"

She drew back in alarm. Graham hauled her closer again, and gave her a carefree smile. The lady deserved at least that much, he reasoned, for playing with fire the way she had.

"I'm a drifting man," he reminded her. "Beholden to no one. With no boundaries but those I choose. If I decide to kiss you, I will, and no power on earth will stop me."

"No power at all?" Julia gulped. "Truly?"

"None save a refusal from the woman in my arms. I would not force myself on a lady who didn't want me." Graham paused, deliberately resuming his long, careful strokes up and down her narrow back. "But since that's not the case here—"

"Um—" Panic lighted her eyes. Julia bit her lip, looking wildly from his face to the quiet porch, and the front door that still remained closed while the maid consulted her mistress. "Mr. Corley, I do believe—"

"Since that's not the case here," Graham said again, "since you do want me—and I want you—then what's to stop us from indulging ourselves?"

"Propriety!" she said. "Plain common sense!" Her voice took on a pleading edge. "Over-familiarity between the sexes, especially in public, is entirely vulgar, and is—is—is always avoided by ladies and gentlemen of delicacy and refinement."

"It is?" He cupped her chin in his free hand, and stroked his thumb over her lower lip. Julia shivered at the contact. "Is that from *Miss Julia's Behavior Book, volume one*?"

She gave him a blank look.

"Your book?" he prompted. "Volume one?"

''Oh!'' A nervous laugh escaped her. ''Er, v-volume three. I think.''

Julia looked as though she weren't thinking at all. She looked, he thought with pleasure, as though she were only feeling...feeling, and coming alive.

''Ahhh. I see.'' Smiling, Graham regretfully lowered his hand. He had no intention of compromising her, especially here, of all places. Despite the hanging swing in the corner, an open porch would hardly be the place to show Julia how much he wanted her. ''Volume three.''

''Yes.'' She darted a nervous glance toward the door, where the maid could re-emerge at any moment. ''I've only been so bold as I have because I knew I was protected by the rules of etiquette. Don't you see? Teasing you was safe, because I knew the proper social boundaries would prevent things from going too far between us.''

Her flirtatiousness suddenly made sense to him. *How like her,* Graham thought, *to place so much faith in a bunch of ''do's'' and ''don't''s.* 'Twas unfounded, he knew. But Julia believed, and that was what mattered.

''You've forgotten one thing,'' he said.

''What's that?''

Before answering, he removed his arm from around her waist. A current of cool air swept between them, and Julia sighed. With relief? Or disappointment?

''I'm not versed in society rules,'' Graham told her. ''And those I do know...I mostly ignore.''

She gasped. ''Impossible! Even *you* must—''

''Very possible,'' he assured her. Hearing a sound from behind the door, Graham straightened. He swiftly examined Julia to make sure she wasn't embarrassingly rumpled, and then adjusted his hat. ''Look, the door is opening. With any luck, your friend has decided she's in. I'll have another chance to try to remember my manners."

"Try?" The word emerged, partly strangled. Julia's eyes bugged. "*Try* to remember your manners?"

"Mm-hm." Graham winked. "And you can try to keep your hands to yourself. I know 'twill be difficult, given how 'wickedly appealing' you find me."

He'd have sworn she turned purple. Graham felt his grin widen.

In front of them, the door swung within—revealing not the maid, but another woman. She looked at them both, gave a muffled sob, and then pushed past.

Julia gaped after her in astonishment. Before she could say a word, though, the maid reappeared.

"Mrs. Marchant will see you now," she said.

And just when Graham had resigned himself to yet another session of miniature cakes, overly sweetened tea, and giggling conversations about the latest fashions, he earned an unexpected reprieve. Julia took one look at the disheveled woman who'd hurried past them. She paused with a shrewd expression on her face, and then straightened to address the maid.

"We won't be calling after all," she said. "And please don't bother to give Mrs. Marchant our regrets. As of this moment, I don't believe we have any."

Then Julia lifted her parasol, and followed the woman.

Chapter Fourteen

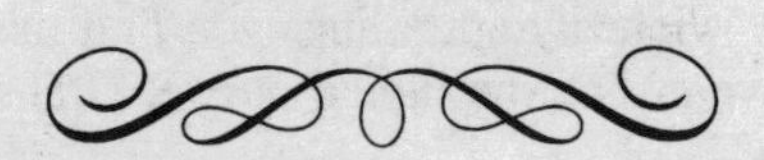

"Wait!" Julia said, shoving aside thoughts of the scandalous banter and enticing closeness she and the bounty hunter had just shared. She hurried down the porch steps in pursuit of the woman, with Mr. Corley following in her wake. "Mrs. Farmer? Is that you?"

The woman stopped. Beneath the plain calico of her day dress, her shoulders slumped. She wore no hat, nor gloves. Wiping a raw-knuckled hand across her face, she reluctantly turned.

"Yes, it's me. Abbie Farmer," she said. "I suppose *you* don't want to be seen talking with me, neither."

"Oh, no, that's not true! Although I—" Julia paused. Strong emotions weren't discussed in polite society, and yet…Abbie's plight struck a chord with her. *Pish posh,* she decided. *Rules could be bent, if not broken.* "You seem to be upset. Is there something I can do to help?"

"I—well…" Before she could get another word out, Abbie burst into renewed tears. Turning away in embarrassment, she hid her face in her hands.

Oh, dear. Grasping her parasol firmly, Julia hurried to include Abbie beneath its shielding ruffles. From up close, the woman's blotchy, tear-streaked cheeks were plainly visible, and her pale hair straggled from its chignon.

Julia wrenched at the drawstring closure of her reticule, searching for a handkerchief. Before she could locate one, though, Mr. Corley reached over her shoulder and, with a rumbled word of kindness, offered his.

Abbie accepted it, and dabbed her eyes. She looked at Graham gratefully, insensible of the way Julia beamed at him. The gallant gesture, however small, only proved what she'd begun to believe of him. Despite his rough ways, the bounty hunter truly was a gentleman—on the inside.

"I'm awful sorry," Abbie said, speaking between stifled sobs. She blew her nose with gusto, and then held out the wadded-up handkerchief toward Graham.

"Please keep it," he said, remarkably straight-faced.

"Thank you." Abbie clenched the handkerchief in her hand and drew in a deep breath. She stared at her work-roughened fingers, kneading the handkerchief as she spoke.

"I—I'm not usually so emotional, but...you see, I been calling on Mrs. Marchant for more'n a week straight now. And she never would see me. But today—today her girl told me she was in, and showed me to the parlor."

"See now?" Although she was still unsure as to what was amiss, Julia did her best to be soothing. "That's progress, isn't it?"

She put a comforting arm around Abbie's thin shoulders, and glanced past her parasol's edge toward the three-story redbrick Marchant home. In an upstairs window, a lacy curtain fluttered back into place, as though someone had been watching them. Frowning, Julia slowly walked Abbie away from the house.

"I thought so, too," Abbie said, sniffling. "She's an important woman in this town—no offense to you, Miss Bennett. Of course I heard of *you!* I heard your books were right fine."

Julia smiled and patted the woman's shoulder.

"I'm saving up egg money to buy me one," Abbie continued. "But it'll take a while. My Jonas, he turned out to be a good husband," she explained in an aside to Julia and Graham, "but he don't make a lot of money working at the freight office."

At that, Julia remembered what she knew of Abbie Farmer. Aunt Geneva had written to say that the woman had come to Avalanche shortly after Julia had left for her final year at Vassar. A mail-order bride, Abbie had been a stranger to Jonas Farmer at first, but Aunt Geneva had made it sound as though things had turned out fine in the end.

Looking at poor Abbie now, Julia had her doubts.

She'd only met Abbie once or twice, in passing at the mercantile or during a brief hello after church. But the misery in her face was all too familiar to Julia. She couldn't bear to see anyone suffer...especially at the hands of Maybelle Marchant, one of Avalanche's most high-and-mighty residents.

The three of them walked farther, passing by other houses as they left the Marchant residence in the distance. Mr. Corley remained with them, silently offering his protection as he strode on the trafficked side of the street.

Julia was grateful for his presence. If she were honest with herself, she'd have to admit that it was his example which had inspired her to help Abbie in the first place. In the old days—the days before the bounty hunter had come to town and accepted her betrothal bargain—Julia knew she would have been too paralyzed with indecision to act in time. She would have been too fearful of doing the wrong thing, of stepping outside propriety's boundaries and giving anyone cause to reject her, to do what needed to be done.

But now, inspired by the way Graham always followed his own path, Julia felt strong enough to take a chance.

"From what I recall," she said, returning to her conversation with Abbie, "your husband has a claim in the mountains near here. Someday, when Jonas Farmer strikes it rich, Maybelle Marchant will be begging you to call on her."

Abbie gave a faint smile. "You really think so?"

"I do."

"Maybe." Looking doubtful, Abbie pushed tendrils of blond hair away from her cheeks. "But until then, I'm not to call on Mrs. Marchant at all. Or even address her in the street."

Julia stopped. *"No."*

"Yes." Abbie nodded, pausing beside her. She did not look up. "That's what she called me into her parlor to talk about today. She said she'd got so tired of turnin' me away, she figured she ought to just tell me straight."

"She didn't!" Disbelief mingled with fury. At Abbie's affirming nod, Julia shook her head. She pressed her lips tightly together. "How *dare* she?"

"I—I guess she didn't think nobody would care." Abbie sniffled again. "I probably shouldn't tell you, only...only you seemed so nice, and all. Nicer than I heard you were."

A sudden sense of shame filled her. Julia closed her eyes against it, but there was no escaping the truth. Was it possible she had let her quest to be accepted in town blind her to common kindness?

As though sensing her dismay, Graham laid his hand on her shoulder. The comforting weight of his touch did ease her, but it was his next words that truly humbled her.

"Miss Bennett is a fine woman," he told Abbie. "Anybody who says differently doesn't really know her. Not like I do."

Abbie swabbed her eyes again. When she looked up, she wore a wobbly smile. Her gaze swept over Julia and Graham both, and her smile widened still further.

"I reckon you're right." She cleared her throat, and addressed the bounty hunter directly. "We haven't been prop'ly introduced, but I recognize you, Mr. Corley. The whole town's heard of you nabbing that outlaw you brung into Avalanche a few weeks ago."

He nodded, acknowledging her compliment.

"And maybe it isn't my place to say so," Abbie continued, "but you two make a right fine pair." Her gaze settled tellingly on Graham's hand, which still rested on Julia's shoulder. "Sometimes the unlikeliest matches work best, you know. Me and my Jonas are proof of that."

Suddenly, at the mention of her husband, Abbie grew unaccountably somber.

"Abbie, what's wrong?" Julia asked.

She waved her hand, as though whatever troubled her were inconsequential. Julia didn't believe it for a moment.

"Well, Jonas..." Taking a quavery breath, Abbie confided in them. "He noticed how I don't have many lady friends here in Avalanche. 'Most a year since I come here, and nobody but one or two of the teamsters' wives will speak to me. I don't know why! I try to be kind and all, and I know I don't have much time for callin', what with all my housework to do. But anyway, Jonas wants me to be happy, and he told me to leave my work for a while to make some friends. He'll be—''

Her face crumpled again, and she swabbed at her eyes with a clean edge of the handkerchief, visibly struggling for control.

''It's all right,'' Julia said. She patted Abbie's forearm, hardly knowing how to cope with so much unrestrained emotion, all at once. It was beyond her experience. ''You don't have to go on, if you don't want to.''

''Might help, if you do.'' Gruffly, Graham tugged down his hat and looked away. He shrugged. ''Women seem to like jawing about their troubles. We'll listen.''

At their combined efforts, Abbie seemed encouraged.

''Well,'' she said bravely, ''it's just that Jonas will be so disappointed if I don't find some friends! He's been so nice about encouragin' me—even said I could order a new dress from the Bloomingdale Brothers' catalog, if I thought it would help. But now, after Maybelle saying all that…I don't know what to do! All the ladies in town follow her lead, you know.''

''I know,'' Julia said. It was true. She'd been shunned by their clique herself, before returning to Avalanche with her etiquette-book fame stamped on her like a seal of approval. ''But you don't need a new dress, nice as the Bloomingdale's catalog is,'' she went on firmly. ''And you don't need Maybelle Marchant, either. *I* will be your champion!''

Overcome with the drama of the moment, she thrust her parasol into the air, the gesture mimicking the rise of a legendary knight's sword. Brandishing the pink-ruffled instrument, Julia pretended to skewer an imaginary foe.

Abbie laughed. Graham gawked.

Julia came to her senses.

What a spectacle she was making of herself! Feeling her face heat, Julia lowered her parasol. A quick glance told her no one on the street or in the passing wagons and carriages was looking their way, but she still couldn't believe she'd acted so rashly. What had gotten into her?

Hurriedly, she began walking again. Perhaps if she kept moving, Abbie and Mr. Corley would forget what had just happened. Like some sort of motion-induced amnesia.

A lady could hope, couldn't she?

When Abbie addressed her again—barely suppressing her laughter to do so—Julia knew she'd been too optimistic. Still, there was a new hopefulness in the woman's face, and Julia was glad for it.

"Do you really think it will work?" Abbie asked as they continued down the street. "Do you really think you can make the women in town be friends with me?"

"Yes. I shall," Julia announced. Already, plans tumbled through her mind, moving with the same rapidity she applied to arithmetic problems and philosophical puzzles. "Beginning today."

"Today?" Abbie looked from her newfound benefactress to Graham, and pulled a mostly pretend worried face. "Can she truly do that?"

Mr. Corley simply laughed. Apparently he'd walked off all of his chivalry during their stroll.

"Never doubt Miss Bennett's determination," he said. "When she puts her mind to a task, obstacles leap out of the way in dead fright. 'Tis an awesome thing."

Julia only grumbled, and surreptitiously gave him a pinch. Graham would see the good she could do. She'd make sure of it.

The rest of the afternoon rolled past quickly. Graham discovered that small gilded chairs didn't feel quite so tiny—nor quite so prissy—if he were seated in one to watch Julia work her social hocus-pocus. He found it fascinating.

In a confusing, otherworldly, *female* sort of way, of course.

It seemed, Graham learned, that those etiquette rules of hers could be applied any number of ways. 'Twas like a game of poker, with high stakes, varied players, and plenty of bluffing. With each new household they visited, Julia varied her game just enough to suit. And as he watched her now, Graham had to admit that he'd underestimated her skill.

Without seeming to do so, Julia deftly gathered Abbie Farmer into every visit, every conversation. She finagled invitations for her newfound friend, and convinced everyone they visited that the freight man's mail-order wife had to be included in every town event from church socials to Sunday dinners. She encouraged Abbie, in a gentle and thoughtful way, to fully participate in the calls they made, and no one who hadn't seen Julia brandishing an imaginary pink-ruffled sword would have known anything was afoot.

For the first time, Graham was glad he wasn't in Avalanche now for professional reasons. If he'd had call to bring in Julia Bennett for a bounty hunting job, he wasn't altogether sure he'd have been able to capture her. 'Twas an elusive thing, this ability of hers—to influence, without seeming to hold any power at all.

She was all smiles as they visited. Even now, with the sun moving low in the sky beyond the parlor windows, barely able to penetrate the heavy drapes, Julia talked and laughed and made plans on behalf of Abbie. She was seemingly tireless, and surprisingly generous.

It seemed that Avalanche's primmest etiquette instructress carried a much softer side...a side that championed for the underdog, and couldn't bear to see anyone else turned away.

''It's all in the timing,'' she'd confided in him earlier, as they'd walked as a trio between houses. ''If I strike now, it won't matter what Maybelle Marchant says or does later. Abbie will already be established. She'll have every necessary invitation, and all the friends she needs.''

Looking at the three women opposite him now, Graham had to agree. They chattered away, cozy as desperadoes sharing bank-robbing plans. Anyone who saw them would have believed them steadfast and longtime friends.

Abbie laughed at something their hostess said. Happiness lit her careworn face, making her seem almost beautiful in her plain clothes and hastily fixed hair. Julia glanced at her, and smiled. A surprising tenderness filled her expression, replacing the look of fierce determination she'd worn earlier.

Briefly, she squeezed Abbie's hand in hers. They shared a triumphant, joyful look. For Graham, witnessing that moment of feminine camaraderie roused a passel of mush-hearted feelings inside him, better left untouched...and did something else, aside. It brought to mind everything Julia had shared with him during their picnic.

In Avalanche, Graham remembered, Julia had been

turned away, time and again. She'd had no parasol-wielding champion to smooth her path, no expert on her side to help. From childhood onward, she'd been alone, save her family.

You don't understand, Mr. Corley. I'm lonely here.

'Twas why she wanted to leave. Why she needed to return to the East. Why she hoped so desperately that her father would approve of her sham engagement.

His sympathy for her grew. The emotion felt strange to him, uncomfortably soft and defenseless, but there it was. Graham couldn't help it. He felt for Julia, and her determination to put behind her all the people who'd made her feel on the outside looking in. He had to help her.

Even if it meant letting her go?

As though she'd guessed the turn of his thoughts, Julia paused in the midst of pouring more tea. She glanced up at him. Her contented expression changed to one of puzzlement.

Even if it meant letting her go?

Graham frowned, still feeling her gaze upon him. He'd been too long in this domesticated place. 'Twas almost like Avalanche and its people had wound roots around his ankles, and he was beginning to feel comfortable in their hold. The notion didn't sit well with him. If he didn't strike the trail soon, it might be too late.

He might not be able to ever let go.

Spooked by the thought, he sat up and grabbed his hat from the chair beside him. Julia cocked her head and raised a teacup toward him.

"More tea?" she mouthed.

He lifted a hand in refusal. Something was happening to him. Something rough and unfamiliar. Graham wasn't ready to lie down and surrender to it. He wasn't a quitting kind of man, and gallons of sweet tea wouldn't be enough to make him forget that.

Amidst the chatter of the ladies' ongoing conversation, he stood. Julia's face fell. She quickly ducked her head and went on pouring the tea, but Graham could feel her watching him as he strode to the parlor window.

She wanted something from him. He sensed it. 'Twas not about the teasing talk they'd shared earlier, enjoyable as that had been. And it could not be about the social calls they'd paid, because he'd surely done his duty in a whole afternoon of visiting. No, Julia wanted something…*more.*

Torn, Graham parted the drapes at the parlor's bay window. He looked outside into an ever-darkening late afternoon, feeling only a fragment of the belly-tightening anticipation that usually struck him when he gazed at the mountains beyond, where the trail leading away from Avalanche wound into the distance.

Today, Graham thought, it hadn't been Abbie alone who'd been welcomed into a dozen parlors. It had been him, too. Thanks to Julia, he'd been received into home after home, an experience both unsettling…and painfully glad. Not since his days as an unwanted boy had he found himself standing on so many doorsteps.

Not since then had he wanted so much to be admitted.

The difference was, today he had been. And this time, once admitted, he'd actually *stayed.*

Memories rushed at him, memories of his boyhood and all those things he'd foolishly yearned for then. Graham gripped the drapes more tightly and stared resolutely outside, determined to hold against the grim feelings those memories roused.

Always before, striking out for someplace new had

forced those remembrances into hiding. Spending nights beneath the stars and days on horseback putting miles behind him had made everything feel like it should. But now...now he was committed to staying, at least for a while.

It wouldn't be easy. Even with his boots planted comfortably atop a posh carpet and his belly filled with delicacies the likes of which he'd rarely sampled, Graham's every instinct urged him away. The pull of it was still strong enough, he reckoned, to unwind those roots from his ankles.

But despite all that, Graham meant to keep his word. For Julia's sake, he could.

Or maybe, the unsettling thought occurred to him... 'twas for his own sake, too.

Biting her lip in consternation, Julia raised the silver sugar-cube tongs and carefully measured out the desired amount of sweetness into each cup on the table before her. *Don't look,* she ordered herself. *Don't look at the window. Pretend nothing is happening.*

But it was no use. She glanced upward to see Graham still standing there, one hand braced on the painted wood frame above his head to keep the drapes aside. Partly silhouetted by the orange-and-pink glow of the sky beyond him, the bounty hunter almost seemed a part of the outdoors himself.

Uncontainable. That's what Graham Corley was. He carried a sense of unqualified freedom, of pure motion, with him. No parlor, however respectable, could have restrained it completely.

As he had for the past several minutes, Graham gazed through the glass, looking as though he'd like nothing better than to lift the sash and step right out into the gathering sunset. Watching him, Julia's spirits sank.

Her efforts hadn't been enough. However much she'd tried to make him feel welcome among her friends and acquaintances, she obviously hadn't...although she, surprisingly, had enjoyed herself a great deal. Until now, at least.

However much she'd tried to please him—for that's what her awkward attempts at coquettish flirting and repartee had been—she clearly had not. However much she'd hoped Graham might, in some small way, come to enjoy their time together, he very plainly wasn't. Not really.

The rigid line of his shoulders, stark against the sun's setting rays, told her that much. Dispirited, Julia passed the filled teacups one by one to Abbie and their hostess. She put on a smile and tried to continue their conversation, but inside she knew her heart wasn't in it.

She wanted to go to Graham. To hold him in her arms and rest her head against his chest, to feel his heart beat. To savor the strength and the sureness inherent in him, and keep him close to her for as long as she could.

It wouldn't be long, Julia knew. Already he yearned to be away; she could see it. The bounty hunter had spent the whole day politely visiting and talking and smiling, charming everyone they saw, but he must have reached his limit of mannered society. Everything in his stance bespoke a need to strike the trail.

She had only to see the melancholy edge to his profile when he turned to watch a passing rider through the opposite bay window to understand that. Graham Corley was a man who needed to be free. And it was wrong of her to deny him that.

He entered this bargain of his own free will, a part

of her reminded. *He wanted tutoring in exchange for his pretend courtship, and he's been getting it.* But no matter how she tried to reason away what she knew was true, Julia could not. Her feelings denied all logic.

She wanted him with her.

It was as simple, and as impossible, as that. For she was leaving and he would be gone, with the both of them headed in their separate ways. A future between her and Graham could not work, and something inside her warned that their current pretense was untenable, too. But what could she do?

Let him go, her heart whispered. *He'll be happier for it.*

Abruptly, as though he'd come to a decision of some sort, Graham pivoted from the window. He crossed the fancy furniture- and knickknack-filled room, carrying his hat in his hands. Julia watched him, hoping against hope he was coming to her. It was a foolish wish, she knew. But she couldn't help it.

If you let him go, another part of her argued, *it will mean sacrificing everything. You'll be lonely forever.*

Julia stilled, her teacup raised halfway to her mouth. The cheerful conversation she'd only half-participated in for the past few minutes swirled around her, but she paid it no mind.

Her thoughts raced, foretelling a future where she had no fiancé—sham or otherwise—and could not leave Avalanche. A future where no other man stepped forward to claim the druggist's ''uppity'' bluestocking of a daughter. A future where the columnist's position at *Beadle's* was denied her. Where she lived amongst people who didn't truly understand her or care for her…and the only man she'd ever loved spent his days wandering.

"My goodness, Julia!" her hostess suddenly cried. "You've spilled your tea!"

Julia started, coming out of her downhearted reverie to find both her companions dabbing at her skirts with napkins and carrying on about how badly Earl Grey stained fabric. Graham lowered into the chair nearest her, and regarded her through knowing dark eyes.

"It's fine. I'm fine," she said, blinking as she looked away. She set aside her teacup and its tea-filled saucer, and did her best not to succumb to the despair that crept in on her. "I'm very sorry for all this trouble."

She looked at Graham again. "Very, very sorry."

Their gazes held. Her apology stretched between them, meager, yet heartfelt. Doubtless the two women believed it was meant for the spilled tea, but Graham knew better. After a long moment, he nodded once.

It was his nod that convinced her, that assuaged her misgivings long enough to keep Julia on the path she'd set. With Graham's understanding, she could continue onward. For now.

She had another plan in mind, something that might leave the bounty hunter feeling as though his days in Avalanche had been time well-spent. With any luck, Julia would be able to carry it off. And if fortune smiled and everything went very, very well...in the end Graham would be glad.

Chapter Fifteen

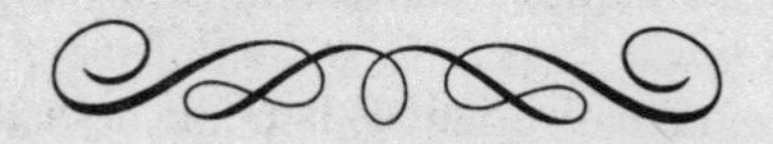

Bea Harrington's boardinghouse was two stories high, thirty-six feet wide, and exactly disreputable enough to attract a half-dozen very diverse boarders. From drummers hawking newfangled gadgets to the newest saloon girl in Avalanche, people of all kinds found a temporary home beneath Mrs. Harrington's shake-shingled roof. All were welcome, if they had the seven dollars a week to pay.

Among those boarders was Graham Corley. As Julia went to collect him late in the day three weeks into their *faux* courtship, she smoothed her skirts and checked the bustle on her lavender-flowered dress, and tried to prepare herself mentally for what was to come.

Facts and figures swirled in her head, information regarding outlaw captures and well-known lawmen that Julia had gleaned from old editions of the Avalanche newspaper. She hoped to regale Mr. Corley with stories he would enjoy, on the way to their destination. If that failed, she'd gone so far as to copy down and memorize a ribald joke she'd overheard the ice man telling her father. Graham was a man who took pleasure in bawdy humor, she'd reasoned. There was no reason why she couldn't provide him with some. If it came to that.

She hoped it wouldn't come to that.

Suddenly nervous, Julia slipped the copied-down jest from her reticule and reread it. The ending was the most difficult part to remember. "And that's why frogs don't have lips," she mouthed to herself, refolding the paper as she hurried across Main Street. "That's why *frogs* don't have *lips.*"

Several muttered variations later, she thought she had it down as well as could be expected. She paused on the threshold of the boardinghouse and looked down at herself one last time.

Mr. Corley admired lavender, hence her choice of dress. He turned absentminded when he smelled her perfume, so Julia had made sure to apply plenty of her specially mixed, orange-scented fragrance. He made faces at her beloved hats, so she'd visited the milliner and requested a smaller, more modest *chapeau.* And she'd taken special care with her hair, as well, rinsing it twice with a rosemary brew Aunt Geneva had assured her guaranteed glossiness and a becoming softness.

Despite her preparations, though, now that the time to unveil her surprise had come, Julia felt all undone. Her heart was aflutter. Her palms were damp beneath her gloves. If anything happened between now and her arrival with Mr. Corley at the Emporium…well, she felt honestly certain any hindrance could bring on her first full-fledged nervous disorder.

She *so* wanted things to go well.

She feared awfully they would not.

If the bounty hunter laughed at her efforts—or worse, ignored them altogether—Julia didn't think she could bear it. But she'd never been one to shirk from a challenge. So she girded her courage, lifted her head and her skirts, and stepped into the boardinghouse for the first time since she'd paid Mr. Corley's bill in a last-ditch attempt to make him discuss their bargain.

Ten minutes later found Julia seated in Mrs. Harrington's miniscule front parlor, sipping tea and gazing at a ghastly print of a quail-carrying hunting dog. It wasn't easy to carry on a conversation without revealing her ever-growing certainty that the bounty hunter would laugh the moment he saw her. Self-consciously, Julia touched her small, plain hat.

"That's a delightful bonnet, Miss Bennett," Mrs. Harrington said, noticing the gesture. "I don't fancy those modern styles myself—too small to offer the proper protection for a lady's delicate complexion, don't you know. But it looks lovely on—"

She stopped, angling her head toward the stairs just beyond them in the foyer. Julia listened too, her heart gone suddenly still.

Mrs. Harrington waved her hand. "I'm sorry, dear. I thought I heard your Mr. Corley coming downstairs. I did tell him you're here, so..."

She let the statement linger tellingly, or so it seemed to Julia. Was the bounty hunter not coming? They'd made arrangements for this yesterday. Surely he wouldn't leave her waiting for him to no purpose?

Fifteen minutes' conversation later, Julia feared mightily that he had. What else? A man had nothing to do to prepare for an outing, save toss on a suit coat and hat! He couldn't possibly—

A creak on the stair stopped her in mid-thought. Drawing in a deep breath, Julia fixed her gaze on the landing just visible through the parlor door...and waited.

* * *

Three steps down the stairs, Graham paused. He patted his pockets, checked inside his hat, ran a hand over his jaw, and still remained befuddled as to what was wrong. Swearing beneath his breath, he pounded up the stairs to his room.

There, he confronted himself in the mirror.

"What's the matter with you?" he demanded to know, issuing himself his most fearsome look. "You've got the suit—" Graham peered critically at the brown tweed coat and pants he'd bought from the Frenchman, Georges. He had a sneaking suspicion the clothes may have originally been prepared for a desk-bound clerk of some sort, judging by how damned uncomfortable they were, but they would have to do.

"You've had the bath, the shave and the haircut—" He'd revisited the barber, but still hadn't been able to part ways completely with his long hair, which now grazed the bottom of his suit collar. "And you've got the necktie." He tugged at the offending garment, deliberately *not* looking at the discarded mound of gaudy possible choices which he'd borrowed from his boardinghouse neighbor—a traveling musician—and which now littered his room's narrow bed.

"So why aren't you down there with Julia?"

Clenching his hands on the edges of the looking glass, Graham stared himself in the eye. What he saw there shocked him.

'Twas fear that had kept him in this room the past twenty minutes or more. Fear that had made him spend more time preparing for a woman than he ever had in his life. Fear that she'd not like what she found when she saw him, and fear that she'd turn away from him if that were true.

With a scowl, Graham pushed away from the mirror. He rotated his head to loosen the tight muscles in his neck, and worked his jaw. This was madness. He'd even gone so far as to surreptitiously consider colognes at the mercantile this morning, before he'd come to his senses.

Graham Corley smelled like Bay Rum for no woman.

He strode across his ten-by-twelve room, now rolling his shoulders. He lit a cheroot, puffed once, and stubbed it out. The motion knocked aside the stack of *Godey's Lady's Book* periodicals he'd collected from another of his boardinghouse neighbors, a military wife awaiting her husband's return from Fort Lowell in Tucson. Frowning as the magazines slid to the floor in a waterfall of illustrated dress patterns, maudlin stories, and poetry, Graham gathered the heap and laid it on the bed. They'd been of little use to him, as it turned out, in making sense of the mystery that was Miss Julia Bennett.

She was indecipherable.

Whip-smart, damnably determined, secretly softhearted and prettier than any woman in ridiculous headwear had a right to be, she was unlike anyone he'd ever known. He wanted to understand her, and to please her—which explained *Godey's,* and the shave, and especially the necktie. But more and more, Graham feared his efforts would come to nothing.

He was not a man who knew about settling down. Nor was he a man who courted the way ladies seemed to want to be wooed, with sugared words, ten-dollar compliments and false promises. If he were wise, Graham knew, he'd pull foot from Avalanche right now, and go back to the trail. There, things were familiar.

Lonely, but familiar.

"Awww, the hell with this," Graham muttered. "Only a crazy man talks to the mirror."

Then he gave himself a nod, pulled his hat back on, and headed downstairs. This time, he didn't stop once.

Together, Julia and Graham said their goodbyes to Mrs. Harrington. Together, they left the boardinghouse and descended the few steps to the gritty boardwalk beyond. Neither said much; each avoided the other's eyes, as though stricken suddenly shy.

Twilight cast shadows along Main Street as Julia let Mr. Corley take her arm to guide her. They always seemed to be together in the half-light, she mused as his fingers wrapped familiarly around her elbow. Just after dawn, just before sunset, just as night fell, or in the shade...forever between one state and the other.

The bounty hunter cleared his throat. She glanced up at him. Now seemed the perfect time to bring out her new knowledge about his business, so Julia drew in a breath.

"I've been reading about Sheriff Shibell, down in Tucson," she began, awkwardly.

"I reckon the, uh, new smaller bustle is a good idea," Graham said at the same time. He rubbed the back of his neck, and cast her an inquiring look.

"I'm sorry, do go on."

"I understand calico is an enduring favorite," he rumbled on, looking supremely uncomfortable. And oddly determined.

"Yes." *Dressmaking? From the bounty hunter?* "As was Charles Shibell. As sheriff from 1877 to 1880, he had a terrible time with those desperadoes who were menacing travelers on the stage, though. Perhaps you've heard about it?"

Graham frowned. "Don't think so."

Their footsteps echoed from the buildings and shops they passed. At this hour, shortly after dinnertime, businesses were closed and most people were home.

"Well." Julia hesitated, groping for something else. "Then surely you've heard of the lawman who came into office after him." She went on to describe the sheriff's efforts against a series of robberies that had begun when the railroad first came into Tucson in 1880. "He must be a very popular figure amongst your colleagues."

"I'm a bounty hunter, Julia. It's not a social club."

"No. No, of course not. How silly of me." *Drat! What was she going to discuss now?* Well, politics always seemed of interest to men. "Um, President Cleveland's position on Civil War veterans' pensions is quite controversial, isn't it?"

Graham rotated his neck and made an agreeable, if somewhat preoccupied, sound. "Nearly so controversial as the practice of substituting combinations for a chemise and knickers. They might be a novelty now, but—"

"Mr. Corley!" Aghast, Julia stopped to stare at him. She prayed he could not tell she'd adopted the scandalously modern combinations herself, and found them quite comfortable. "Dis—discussing ladies' undergarments is simply not done!"

He paused. Pulled at his necktie, as though it were strangling him. "Then what do you think of needlepoint?"

She was at a loss for words. Gamely, she dredged up a reply. "I—I think it's nearly as excellent a pastime as enjoying a fine cigar." Julia gave him a quizzical look and began walking beside him again. "In fact, I was talking with Mr. Thompson at the mercantile about the newest varieties, and—''

''*You* were discussing cigars?''

''Yes.''

The bounty hunter shook his head. He seemed taken aback by the whole idea. But he blew out a gusty breath and proceeded to continue their conversation, all the same.

'''Tis no stranger than me poring over German cologne and brilliantine, I reckon,'' Graham mused, inexplicably.

Near as she could tell, he wore neither cologne nor the oily hair tonic so favored by dandies. Instead, he smelled of soap and clean clothes, tobacco and leather. And his clipped hair brushed his collar in an attractive way that had Julia fairly yearning to touch it. She still remembered the silky, intimate feel of those strands between her fingers.

However, she had to admit—his comment was no stranger than anything else he'd said tonight.

As though sharing her befuddlement over the turn their meeting had taken, Mr. Corley fell silent. Slowly, he slid his hand from her elbow to her wrist, then clasped their hands together. The gesture was companionable...and something more.

Somehow, as they walked Julia felt the gentle abrasion of their palms rubbing together all the way up her arm. The sensation spread, until it seemed her whole body were rhythmically joined with his. The feeling was nearly thrilling enough to make her forget her mission altogether.

She sighed with pleasure. And, newly motivated, tried again to please him. Gathering her courage, she asked, ''Do you know why a frog doesn't have lips?''

He burst out laughing. "Julia, now I know something's afoot. What has you telling bawdy jokes?"

"I haven't told it yet!" she huffed. Frustration welled up, and Julia could restrain herself no longer. "How am I to please you, if you won't begin to let me?"

"You?" The bounty hunter gawped at her. He stopped in front of the express office, pulling her nearer. "How am I to please *you,* if you won't let *me?*"

"But you… My dress… I—I wanted—" Awash in confusion, Julia resorted to the first tangible, explainable thing she thought of. Gesturing with her free hand toward her lavender skirts, she said, "I only wore this dress in the first place because you—"

"'Tis beautiful," he interrupted quietly. "It couldn't be anything else, so long as you're wearing it." Graham lowered his head so their foreheads nearly touched, and he carefully stroked her cheek with his thumb. "I must have been too bedazzled to tell you so before now."

"Oh." The word escaped her on another sigh. Gazing up at him, Julia allowed herself to abandon her mental checklist of lawmen, desperadoes, cigars and politics, just for a moment. "Thank you."

He nodded, shifting into a strangely stiffened position beside her. His hat shadowed his face, its rugged, flat-brimmed style only a little at odds with his new suit. Graham cleared his throat and looked up past the express office's sign at the sky, where streaks of orange and gold marked the place where the sun had recently set.

Angling his head, he went on staring skyward. Raptly.

"Mmmmmph," he rumbled.

"Pardon me?"

"Do you mmmmph?"

Julia frowned. First, a downright perplexing interest in ladies' fashions. Now, an inability to speak without sounding as though he had a mouthful of rocks. What next? she wondered.

"Perhaps we'd better carry onward," she suggested gently. Now that the time to unveil her surprise had nearly arrived, she was beginning to experience a bit of excitement, mingled with her nervousness. "Everyone will be waiting for us."

"Do you like my suit?" Graham bit out. His gaze met hers, unexpectedly vulnerable, then quickly whipped skyward again. "Do you like it?"

Why, *he* was nervous, as well! Julia realized with amazement. The same brawny, fearless man who hauled in dangerous criminals to face justice stood before her now with his Adam's apple bobbing with apprehension. His fingers fairly crushed hers as he waited for her reply.

"Yes! Yes, I do like it," she said.

She stepped nearer, close enough that her skirts brushed against his dark pants legs. A sense of overwhelming tenderness filled her as she gazed up at him, knowing that her opinion mattered as much to him as...as his did to her.

"I think you look very handsome," Julia told him, quite seriously. "Like a man to be reckoned with. Strong and certain and very, very masculine. Any woman would be proud to be with you tonight. I know I—"

"Julia—" His interruption was gravelly, and a wealth of emotion could be heard in that single word.

"I," she continued doggedly as she squeezed his hand, "am proud to be with you tonight. Very proud, and happy."

Graham's sudden interest in sunsets vanished. He cleared his throat and set them both into motion again. "You're right," he said abruptly. "We've lingered here too long."

They strode together, hand in hand. More at ease now, Julia recalled Mr. Corley's approval of the dress she'd chosen especially for him, and savored her remembrance of the heated look in his eyes when he'd told her of it. That was a moment she'd remember forever.

Amidst her musings, she glanced up. In place of his frequent dangerous glower, Graham now wore an expression of unfocused delight. He smiled, smiled more widely, and smiled wider still, the farther they walked. Before long, his stride was downright jaunty.

Bennett's Apothecary and Soda Fountain Emporium loomed at the turn in the street, a mere fifty yards distant. The windows glowed from within, thanks to the newfangled, frightfully expensive gaslights Asa Bennett had installed earlier in the year. Officially, her family's establishment was closed for the evening...but Julia knew better.

Mr. Corley's attention was not for their destination, however, Julia saw when she ducked her head to surreptitiously gauge his reaction. His attention, instead, was for *her*.

As though prompted in the moment when their eyes met, he spoke suddenly.

"Ahhh, Julia. I don't think this can work."

"What?"

"I thought I could see this through the way you wanted." Graham glanced around them, as though seeking something, then looked back at her. "I thought the damned suit would make for chivalry to spare. That, or the necktie would strangle any wayward impulses I had.''

Impossible, Julia thought, *for a rogue like him.* But she only remained silent, and did her best not to pucker her brow in confusion while he spoke—however befuddling his words were.

Aunt Geneva insisted extreme facial expressions were unflattering. If there was anything Julia hoped to accomplish this evening, it was to win over her pretend beau's affections, and make them more real than their ''engagement'' was. She would not accomplish *that* with unbecoming wrinkles and puckers.

''That has not happened,'' Graham continued. ''Instead—'' He paused. Peered at her. ''Are you all right? You look like you've swallowed a bad-tasting bug.''

So much for attractive serenity. ''I'm fine.''

''I'm not.'' The bounty hunter's dark-eyed gaze swept over her. ''I need you, Julia. And I'm not waiting anymore.''

Before she could take another step, Julia found herself whirled sideways. The tall building-sides of an alleyway rose up around her, and with a surety she might have expected from him but had not, Mr. Corley fairly danced her up against the clapboard side of one of them. Its chill penetrated her lightweight gown, and made her shiver.

His hands flattened against the wall and caged her in. His stance, bold and masterful, ensured that escape would not work—unless he wished for it to. One look up into his dark-shadowed face, and Julia knew he did not.

His heat enveloped her. Slowly, and with an air of complete absorption, the bounty hunter leaned nearer.

His lips brushed hers, so softly she fancied she'd imagined it.

The hammering of her heart told her she had not.

"Kiss me," Graham demanded. He cupped his hand at the back of her neck, and tilted her face upward. "Kiss me, and I'll know this confusion was worth it."

Julia didn't ask what he meant. She didn't need to. She'd felt the same confusion...and now, the same need.

"Yes," she whispered.

His mouth met hers, a kiss almost savage and entirely sweet. Trembling with the force of it, Julia gave herself to him like a wanton, wrapping her arms around his neck and drawing him closer as though she meant to never let him leave her again. She couldn't help but feel, all at once, as though she'd waited a lifetime for this joining.

Again and again, Graham took all she had to offer, and gave as much in return. His lips stroked, his tongue delved to sweep against hers, his moan vibrated against her chest. His hands cupped and stroked her, pressing new heat into her hips, her derrière, her waist. Shamelessly, Julia arched against him, and when it was over and he began to pull away, she was having none of it.

She grabbed his necktie and tugged. "Not yet," she begged, and lost herself in his arms all over again.

Finally, finally, he raised his head. His tender expression soothed her, as did his fingers against the nape of her neck. Coming to herself, Julia looked around.

"Someday," she said, languidly unable to move, "we really must try this in another position."

He raised an eyebrow.

"My knees feel near too wobbly to hold me," she explained.

His smile turned devilish, and wholly male. "Another position? I think that could be arranged. Purely for the sake of your knees, of course."

"Of course."

He kissed her again. "*Soon.*"

The anticipatory gleam in his eyes weakened her knees still further. Feeling short of breath, she let herself sag a little against the building behind her. Really, Julia mused, the bounty hunter had the most exciting effect on her. It was almost as though he sensed what would thrill her most…and then delivered it.

"You must think me frightfully bold," she said as she looked down, interlocking her spread fingers to re-align her gloves. "And terribly forward, even for a 'fiancée.'"

Graham shook his head. "If you cared so much what anyone else thought of you, you would not have lassoed me just now, the way you did."

His words struck something inside her. Was it true? Was she coming to rely on her own judgment, rather than making herself daft with wanting to be perfect for those around her?

If so, it was an unprecedented thing, and all the more unsettling because of it. She wasn't quite sure her new-found bravery extended so far as that.

Mr. Corley raised a hand to his necktie, askew from her efforts to tug him nearer. He winked. "I like this free side of you. The side that's cut loose from your etiquette books, and is bold enough to touch me."

"You don't think it's…strange of me?" Always before when she'd indulged herself—to read a weighty book, to walk by herself on the mountain trails, to work mathematical theories for the pleasure of discovery alone—someone had ridiculed her. "Unappealing? Unfeminine?"

Those were words that had been applied to her, however she'd tried to ignore them. Those, and more.

"Did you want to do it?" he asked, his voice low. "Did you want to touch me?"

"Truly?"

He nodded.

A flush warmed her face. "Yes," Julia whispered.

"Then I find it very appealing. And completely feminine." Giving her a long look, Graham shook his head. Then he gathered her in his arms and held her close. His chin nestled against the top of her head. Inexplicably he sighed, his chest expanding and releasing against her. "To be sure, I don't understand you a'tall. But I wish you could be happy as you are, and not question things this way."

She closed her eyes. All the same, tears prickled there. *I want that, too,* Julia yearned to say. But it seemed impossible, especially for someone like her. She knew the facts of things too well. And so she only relaxed in his arms and let him hold her, and imagined this security and warmth could be hers forever.

Graham's tweed coat rustled as he snuggled her more closely against him. Bravely, Julia raised her arms and embraced him, too. Their breathing slowed, combining to a steady rhythm that was both reassuring and intimate. She smelled the lingering astringency of his soap, felt the smooth crispness of his ironed shirt against her cheek.

With a tender gesture, the bounty hunter stroked his thumb over her temple. His hold felt strong and sure, anchored by broad shoulders and a caring soul. With each passing heartbeat, Julia began to imagine that Graham meant to keep her with him ...no matter their differences.

The alleyway around them seemed to fade away. The rumble of passing wagons grew quiet. All the world narrowed to her, and Mr. Corley, and the togetherness they shared. The sweetest dream could have been no better—nor could it have ended more abruptly.

''Miss Julia, your pa sent me to bring you to the Emporium,'' said a childish voice. ''He said to quit spoonin' with Mr. Corley, and come right quick, before your surprise gets ruin't.''

Julia and Graham jerked apart. The delivery boy, Patrick O'Halloran, stood but a few feet away, giving them the impish grin of a child who knew he'd caught his elders at something scandalous. When he spied them looking, he squelched the amusement in his fresh-scrubbed face, but it was too late.

''Um, thank you, Patrick.'' It was impossible to add starch to an acknowledgement when you'd been shamelessly cuddling a moment before, Julia discovered. ''We'll be along directly.''

She wanted to sink into the ground, to disappear without a trace. If her father had sent Patrick for them, then surely he'd seen everything that had transpired—or at least a goodly portion of it. What would he say?

Even worse were the more immediate consequences, Julia soon discovered, when Graham turned to her and raised an eyebrow.

''Surprise?'' he asked as the boy trotted off. ''What surprise?''

Chapter Sixteen

'Twas passing hard to walk when blindfolded and led by a person wearing high-heeled shoes, Graham discovered. Julia had produced a long silky scarf from her reticule—the thing was seemingly bottomless, so numerous were the items she'd pulled from it since their acquaintance—and had tied it securely around his head to cover his eyes. Then she'd caught hold of his hand and led him across the street.

Their wobbly progress was slow. It felt as though, in her fancy shoes, Julia walked about as gracefully as a swan on a rutted road—when Graham knew that wasn't true. He'd watched her ladylike movements long enough to appreciate the elegance she possessed. He'd also glimpsed the seductiveness that lay beneath her propriety, and it was that which drove him near wild as he tried to match his steps to hers.

"Almost there," she assured him, sounding breathless. "Remember, no peeking. I want this to be a true surprise for you."

"It already is." This giddy side to her had been a revelation to him, more akin as it was to sheer pleasure-loving woman than rules-abiding etiquette instructress.

''And I'll not peek. Else you might take out an eye, with tying this thing even more tightly than you did.''

Scoffing, she adjusted the length of red fabric. Another surprise. Who would have guessed demure Miss Julia held a hidden fondness for bordello-red silk?

''Nonsense.'' Several more steps, and they halted. ''And I know you peeked, because I saw you step around those horse leavings in our path.''

He grinned. ''Well and truly caught. But I never claimed to be anything but a bounty hunter, rogue and drifter.''

''Rogue, first and foremost,'' she teased.

Graham shrugged, surreptitiously trying to detect what was going on around them. She'd led him seventy-two steps to the west. Onto the boardwalk, judging by the hollow clank of his boots hitting gritty lumber. Gaslights were on nearby, because he heard their hiss and felt their warmth to his right. And Julia hadn't needed a key to open the door to the building he felt with his outstretched hand. It had to be Bennett's Apothecary and Soda Fountain Emporium, as the boy had mentioned.

But why?

''Stay here,'' Julia said. Her gloved hands pressed on his shoulders, as though he were a sapling to be planted in a spring-thawed dirt mound. ''I'll be right back.''

Graham nodded, stifling a grin. If she thought anything but his own desire kept him there, she was mistaken. But the seriousness in her tone as she sowed his place on the boardwalk kept him silent.

Shuffling feet moved nearby. One pair, two. Several more. This felt like a trap. And he felt like a fool. He was dying to snatch the covering from his eyes. If any of the desperadoes he'd tracked discovered him like this—trussed up like a clerk on his wedding day, hair combed and whiskers gone, wearing a necktie and preparing to submit to a mysterious surprise—they would shoot first and laugh themselves silly later.

Then suddenly, Julia was there.

Her hands touched his jaw, lingered a bit more than necessary as she made her way up on tiptoes to relieve him of his blindfold. "Ready?" she whispered.

Her body pressed against the length of him as she worked at the knot she'd made, leaving him aching for more. "More ready than you know."

"Good. And—" hesitating, she stilled her arms over his shoulders and brought her mouth near his ear "—please remember. I did this because I care for you."

Silk whisked over his face, fluttering before his vision in the gaslight until Julia swept it aside and hurried away. Graham registered the bright expanse of the Emporium before him, recognized that he was standing alone in the doorway facing the inside…and then all hell broke loose.

"Surprise!" yelled dozens of voices. "Surprise!"

Neighbors, friends, Julia's family…they all filled the room. He spotted Asa and Aunt Geneva, Isabel Deevers, Lizzie with her rooster, Patrick the delivery boy, Abbie and Jonas Farmer. The men from the livery stable beamed from their places in front of the soda fountain counter, their arms wrapped around their smiling wives. Mayor Westley raised a palm in greeting, as did the sheriff. Everywhere he looked, Graham saw familiar faces.

'Twas festive. Friendly. And so unlike the life he'd led 'til now that it brought a lump to his throat. Awash in emotions he'd scarcely felt before, Graham stood fixed to the floor. He hardly knew what to do. Suddenly his smile felt strange, his posture uncertain.

Julia took charge, and in the process, saved him.

"Ahem!" she said.

A distance to his right, she cleared her throat, quieting the hubbub. She stood straight and tall, a wide smile on her face, and raised the thing in her hands. 'Twas a tall frosted cake, Graham saw, and it held a single burning candle amidst the swirls of sugary icing.

"Ready everyone?" she asked, nodding toward the cake.

A roar of yeses filled the room.

"All right, then...one, two, three. *Happy birthday!*"

The combination of dozens of voices was deafening. And heartening. To his amazement, Graham found himself surrounded by friends wishing him well. Hands grasped his, palms slapped him jovially on the shoulders. He was buried in "happy birthdays" from all sides. From somewhere near the druggist's counter, the members of Avalanche's city band struck up a rollicking tune. And through it all, Julia kept advancing toward him, balancing a cake the likes of which he'd never seen.

"I hope this day agrees with you," she said when she reached him. "It's too long now that you've gone without a birthday, and you deserve better. I thought this day might do."

Her face glowed in the light from the candle, burnished with affection and flushed with excitement. Her hopeful blue-eyed gaze captured his, and in her eyes he glimpsed a sort of caring he'd never dreamed of finding. She raised the cake on its stoneware platter.

"Make a wish," Julia urged. "Make a wish, and

blow out the candle, and we'll all hope that it comes true for you."

The lump in his throat rose all over again. Graham couldn't quite clear it away.

"I could not wish for anything more than this," he said. The hoarseness in his voice would betray all he felt, he knew. But he could not help it. "I've never had so much. Nor known a night like this one."

Understanding softened Julia's features. "Then wish for something for later," she said softly. "Please. It's your birthday, if you'll have it. There must be something you want."

Hearing their exchange, neighbors pressed closer. Their encouragement was rowdy, often ribald, and always warm-hearted. It touched Graham to the core, and lent him a lightness he sorely needed...before he blubbered like a babe over this surprise of hers.

He held up a palm. "There is something I want," he announced to the crowd. His gaze met Julia's, and held. "'Tis unlikely I'll get it, but a man can hope."

"Hear, hear!" Aunt Geneva shouted, raising her glass.

"Yes, go on!" Asa Bennett called. "Make your wish, and we'll share a toast."

Graham tilted his head toward Julia. "A man can hope," he repeated in a low voice. "However unlikely his wish may be."

She understood what he asked. The knowledge was there in her eyes, in the quaver that briefly tilted her smile.

"Indeed," she said, "I doubt there's a soul here without a secret wish, or two. Even me."

Her admission heartened him. If her wish were anything near his own, his future looked bright. Graham closed his eyes.

I wish for Julia, he thought, and blew out the candle in a single breath.

Cheers rose to the rafters. Grinning, Graham opened his eyes and found a mug of ale being pushed in his hand. He drank as the women clustered around Julia to help serve the cake.

The birthday cake.

For him.

The notion made him fair giddy, like a boy with a new plaything, or a man recently visited by the bordello's finest lady. He laughed aloud with every jest, made many of his own, raised his ale in toast more times than he cared count. 'Twas his *birthday,* thanks to Julia—the first he'd ever had.

How had she known he'd want this? He hadn't known himself, had done all he could to discourage even the smallest talk of it. That night at the Bennett's house, when he'd revealed his past as a foundling child in Boston, Graham had never meant to arouse such an impulse in Julia. In truth, he'd hoped she would forget what she knew of his past...the same way he forgot what he'd left behind, when he struck the trail each time.

But this...'twas far beyond hoped-for. And all the sweeter for it.

"Are you having a good time?" Julia appeared beside him, flushed and eager and bearing a piece of white cake on a plate. She took the ale mug from his hand, set it aside, and replaced it with the sweet. "Were you surprised? You're not angry, are you? Some people don't like surprises, and a man like you—"

"A man like me needs them twice as much, I think."

Her smile was gentle. "Oh, Graham. I'm so glad you don't mind. After Papa remarked that we should simply choose a birthday for you, I couldn't stop thinking about it. I decided there was no earthly reason not to designate a day."

"'Tis the nicest thing anyone has done for me," he admitted. "And by far the most surprising."

He speared a bite of cake with his fork. Julia squeezed his arm, gazing up at him with palpable hopefulness.

"You look as though heaven depends on my tasting of this cake," Graham told her, hiding a smile. "Did you make it yourself?"

"Yes. Well, I had some help from Alice." She went on watching his fork, pinning the morsel of cake with an anxious look. "Aunt Geneva is helpless, you know, at anything involving domestic skills, and naturally, Papa doesn't know anything more about the kitchen except how to retrieve just-baked cookies from the sideboard."

He nodded, and slipped the bite into his mouth.

She watched, wringing her gloved hands, as he chewed. "That's part of what I was doing while paying all those calls with you," she chattered. "Collecting recipes and hints from every lady I knew. I thought surely you'd guess what I was up to, with so many inquiries about frosting versus glaze, egg yolks and butter versus egg whites and sugar—"

"Aaagh!" Graham clutched his throat and rocked backward. "The cake! It's…it's…."

With a little cry, Julia grabbed him. "Mr. Corley! Graham! Are you all right?" She looked desperately around them. "Oh, dear—someone help! I've poisoned him with my cake!"

"...it's delicious." Grinning broadly, Graham levered himself upward. He dragged her to him and kissed the surprise from her face. Their friends shouted their approval, even as the woman in his arms realized what he was about and surrendered to his kiss—but not before a muffled protest.

He couldn't help but laugh as he thumbed a smear of frosting from the corner of her lips, and tongued the sweetness into his mouth. "Thank you. I may never get enough."

"You rogue!" Julia pushed away and swatted his shoulder, red-faced and laughing as she recognized his ruse. "You were teasing me!"

He shrugged. "I had to make you quit chattering somehow. You were drowning out the music."

"Ooooh!"

Graham grinned and finished his cake. It was the best he'd ever eaten...maybe the only he'd ever eaten. The fact that it sucked moisture from his mouth like hardtack, sat in his stomach like a buttered brick, and made his teeth ache with sugary sweetness didn't matter. Not so long as Julia watched him fondly, and stayed there by his side.

She delivered two more pieces at his request, looking all the while as though the sight of a fully grown man cradling a plate of sweets was the most amusing she'd ever seen. And looking proud, very proud, of her part in this day.

They exhausted themselves with dancing, the men in town having helped Asa move aside the store's furnishings 'til they stood against the walls and revealed a small square of floor space. They ate and drank, Julia turning rosy-faced and tipsy with the quantity of wine her aunt Geneva pressed upon her.

Graham reveled in the gathering, in the closeness, storing up memories of this day. If he could have, he'd have stowed them in his saddlebags beside his letters from Frankie, and taken them out later. He'd want them, when an empty sky pressed upon his shoulders and miles stretched long between him and a friendly face.

Suddenly downhearted, Graham separated himself from the crowd of boisterous men around him. Across the room, Aunt Geneva waved. The delivery boy, Patrick, chased his sister and five of her rooster-toting friends. Abbie Farmer, clad in a dress Graham would have bet his last ten dollars came from the Bloomingdale Brothers' catalog, danced with her husband to the music that continued to play.

Julia stood speaking earnestly with her father, her hat discarded and one glove missing. He watched her for a minute, but did not go to her. If he were wise, he'd stay away while she felt the effects of the wine. Already she'd pressed against him much more freely than ever before, and he wanted nothing she would regret to happen between them.

She spied him, all the same. Just as he turned his back, Graham heard her high-pitched exclamation. An instant later, she'd clasped his arm and was beaming up at him.

"Graham Corley, you rascal." Momentarily distracted, she slipped off her remaining glove and tossed it over her shoulder. She smiled. "A very happy birthday to you!"

"Thank you."

Friends slipped past them, some offering renewed birthday greetings. As it turned out, Julia had not revealed to the townspeople that he'd had no birthday until now. Instead, she'd merely arranged the surprise celebration as though Graham had been having birthday parties all his life, thereby safeguarding his past—and his pride. He was grateful to her for that. For that, and more.

"But you look as though you're sneaking away!" Julia said. She puckered her lips in a crooked tsk-tsk. "We can't have that. Not before you've had your gift."

"There can't be more."

She nodded. "Oh, yes! There is more. Come with me."

Tugging at his arm, Julia weaved her way toward the Emporium's front door. At the threshold, she snatched up a lighted lantern someone had left there and carried it, swinging cheerfully, in her free hand. They stepped together into the chilly, pine-scented night. As they passed beneath the show globe and walked through the squares of light spilling from the windows onto the boardwalk, Julia chattered about how she ought to consider bringing everyone outside to reveal his gift.

"But I can't do that," she told him, lowering her voice conspiratorially. She leaned tipsily nearer, making the last of the gaslight shine on her dark hair. "Then I'd have to share you with them, and I don't want to. At least for now, you're mine to keep."

She nodded in emphasis, her tone firm. Graham grinned. 'Twas passing strange to be claimed by a woman who held every opinion tight as a nailed-on horseshoe. Strange, but wonderful.

"In that case, I'll not try to sneak away," he said.

"Oh, you can't! What of your wish? I'm fairly certain that escaping your own birthday party invalidates your wish."

"And this doesn't count?"

"Seeing your gift is a part of the party," Julia announced after a moment's serious deliberation. "I'm certain this is fine."

They rounded the corner. Buildings loomed nearby, huddled shapes against a starry sky. In the distance, the sounds of the party could still be heard—music, laughter, conversation, feet stomping in rhythm to some new dance. The air held a hint of woodsmoke, and it mingled with Julia's citrus perfume to create a homey scent that Graham deliberately lay aside in his memory. The lantern light swung ahead of them in jerky ovals, illuminating plain dirt, patches of grass and the rutted path 'round the side of the Emporium.

Avalanche was the same as a hundred western towns he'd seen, Graham mused. Made of the same buildings, the same necessities, the same kinds of people. How then, he wondered, could it feel so different, suddenly?

So *welcome?*

"Ahh, here we are."

With a satisfied air, Julia plunked the lantern down on a set of plank steps leading to a doorway. 'Twas the shed where they'd taken their reading lessons, Graham realized. Now that he looked, its narrow lumber sides, sloped roof and small chimney could be seen straight ahead. He turned to Julia.

"My birthday gift is an extra reading lesson?" he asked, unable to resist teasing her. "Damnation, but you're a strict teacher, Miss Bennett. Some might be tempted to indulge the guest of honor, but you—"

She laughed, and gave him a nudge forward. "No! Look closer. In the lamplight."

Graham began at the steps and sent his gaze upward. Three steps, a scrap of windblown paper, the bottom edge of the shed's door, the door's lower surface. He made it all the way to the doorknob before he paused, giving Julia a sideways glance.

"You're jumping around fit to rival a pair of dice in a saloon drunk's hand," he said. She'd hugged herself, he saw, and was making little side-to-side skips as she waited for him to discover this new surprise. "Are you sure you don't want to just tell me what my gift is?"

"Look! Look!" she cried. "Keep going!"

He grinned, and hesitated apurpose. "So, let me get this straight...I'm supposed to look higher?"

Her muffled exclamation made him laugh. "Yes! Yes!"

"All right."

She was beyond easy to rile up. 'Twas part of what made being with Miss Julia enjoyable, he decided. Obediently, though, Graham tilted his head. He focused on the doorknob, the middle section of the door, the top of the door. Skimmed to the roofline, past the...the hand-painted sign? *That hadn't been there before.* Graham squinted.

"The Graham Corley Public Lending Library!" Julia read aloud, obviously unable to remain silent a moment longer. She clutched his arm as she gestured wildly toward it with her other hand. "Surprise!"

Not waiting for his reaction, she took his hand and scurried up the steps, pausing to retrieve the lamp on the way. She flung open the door and hurried within, hauling Graham inside in her wake.

"See?" Happily, she raised the lantern.

Its wobbly glow illuminated a room far different than the one he remembered. Beneath the unfinished eaves, unlighted lanterns hung at the ready in wall holders, each aligned over a small table and chair. Graham counted eight in all. Between the lanterns and spanning the perimeter of the room, shelves had been fixed to fill the space between the wall studs. Atop the shelves, beneath carefully lettered signs designating different letters of the alphabet, were....

"Books!" Graham said. He reached to touch the nearest volume, a copy of *Moby Dick* shelved beneath *M*. "You've found books, and tables and chairs, and—ahhh, Julia. 'Tis a lending library for sure, just as I wanted. How did you do all this?"

I believe in you, he remembered her saying, and saw the same in her face as she watched him.

She rocked up on tiptoes. "The volumes are donated," she told him. "When we went calling, I wasn't only searching out the very best birthday cake recipes. I was also asking for book donations, from nearly everyone in town. 'Graham Corley is starting a free lending library,' I said, and it seemed everyone else shared my opinion of that particular notion."

"And that was?"

"That it's a fine, noble idea." Julia set down the lantern and came to him, clasping his hands in both of hers. "That it's a rare man who would think of so generous a thing, especially for a town he's shared less than a month. That it's proud I am, to know such a man, and to call him mine, even for just a little while. I hope—I truly hope you like it."

The sincerity in her voice shook him. Honored him. Overwhelmed by all this night had brought, Graham swallowed against the lump that rose again to his throat, and gazed out through the shed's—no, the *library's*—still-open door, afraid he'd unman himself if he so much as tried to speak. He squeezed Julia's hands instead, and concentrated on the soft feel of her skin against his until he found his voice.

"It's exactly as I imagined it," he said gruffly. "Thank you."

He lowered his head and touched his mouth to hers, driven to express all he felt the best way he knew how. Through action. Through touch. Through the wondrous meeting of their lips, their breath, their heat. Graham angled his head and kissed her fully, and although no mere taste could deliver all he needed to say, it was the best he could do. It would have to be enough.

Again and again their lips met. Their mouths angled, seeking more…their tongues touched, danced, retreated. 'Twas heady stuff, kissing Julia. By the time they drew apart, Graham was breathless, with a pounding heart. He'd wager, upon seeing her pink cheeks and bright eyes, that she felt much the same.

"I'll never forget this," he told her, lowering his forehead to touch hers. "Never."

Her smile turned wistful. "Not even after you leave?"

"Not even then. Nothing could—"

"What's this?" a masculine voice interrupted. "Leaving? Ho, Geneva. The man thinks he's leaving here, and this with Julia in his arms even now."

They jerked. Asa Bennett stood in the open doorway, flanked by Aunt Geneva to his right. Hastily, Julia stepped away from Graham, her flush deepening guiltily.

No sooner had she done so than Asa entered the room all the way. With an indulgent smile, he used both hands to gently steer his daughter back into Graham's arms.

"Look there, Asa," Aunt Geneva said, following her brother-in-law inside. She waved her fan flirtatiously, her eyes dancing with good humor. "Julia wants to undo all the good work we've done."

"I see that." Asa cast an exaggeratedly speculative look toward Graham and Julia both. "It's beyond my understanding. Nearly so much as that talk of Mr. Corley leaving they were doing when we followed them here."

Geneva tsk-tsked. Beside Graham, Julia boggled.

Both elder people shared a conspiratorial smile. "I told you they'd suit perfectly," Geneva informed Asa. "I know you were skeptical at first, Asa, but I knew eventually our Julia would be smitten. After that, she only needed a helping hand."

"You're right," Asa agreed. "Fine work, we've done."

"You—*you've* done?" Julia choked out. "Whatever do you mean?"

This time their shared smile was indulgent.

"We might as well tell you," Asa said, gesturing toward Graham and Julia alike. "We've...well, we've been scheming to bring the two of you together. Since the day Mr. Corley first came to dinner at our home." He thrust his thumbs into his waistcoat and puffed up his chest. "Dinners, calls, outings. Frankly, it's worked even better than I expected."

"Not better than *I* expected," Geneva put in, fanning herself.

"Papa! Aunt Geneva!" Julia looked dumbstruck. "You don't mean—"

"We had to do something, child," Geneva said gently, smiling fondly at her niece. "You've always had more interest in mathematics than in finding a man to care for you. That's why your father devised those requirements for your return to the States, you know. We were worried about you.''

Graham spoke up. ''You're worried no longer,'' he observed.

Three faces turned toward him. With evident surprise, Asa Bennett shook his head. ''No. Seeing you two together tonight has laid the last of my fears to rest. I believe you truly love each other, and—''

''Papa, really!'' Julia seemed mortified to be discussing such a private subject. She wrung her hands beside him. ''Can we at least shut the door before disclosing such delicate matters? Please?''

''No need!'' the elder Bennett blustered. Looking proud as the self-satisfied papa he was, he fixed them both with a meaningful look as he straightened.

''The whole town will know soon enough, anyway. I've decided to grant my approval of your engagement, Julia,'' Asa told them. ''And if you're to make that interview at *Beadle's* in time, you'll have to be married in a matter of days.''

It was ending, Graham realized. Now that Asa Bennett had granted his approval of his daughter's marriage, his time together with Julia would end.

He'd barely had time to absorb the dismal news before Asa delivered the final blow.

''Three days,'' he said, nodding happily at Julia. ''You'll be married in three days' time, to be precise. I've already spoken with the minister, tonight, and made arrangements for this Saturday.''

Of a habit, Graham reached for Julia's hand. She stood rigid beside him, her fingers cold, and he couldn't help but wonder if she was thinking the same thing he was:

'Twas much, much too soon.

Chapter Seventeen

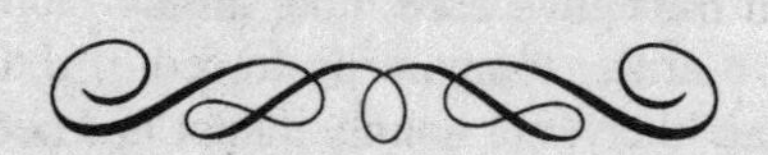

The following evening, Julia sat at the small writing desk in her chamber, pen in hand. Clad only in her nightdress, with her hair rolled in rags and a beautifying concoction spread over her face, she imagined she was a sight, indeed. But she'd been too busy with other activities today to see to this one, very necessary, letter. And no matter how late it was, writing it was a task she couldn't delay. Her longed-for position at *Beadle's* periodical depended upon it.

She still couldn't quite believe her opportunity had arrived. With her papa's approval of her sham engagement, the road to her dreams had opened. She would have the independent career and the secure, safely anonymous life in the city that she'd hoped for, away from everyone in Avalanche who had ever ridiculed her or turned her away. It was everything she'd worked for, and Julia knew she should have been elated.

Strangely enough, she was not.

But why? Everything was proceeding as she'd hoped. All Papa had demanded was that she find a husband before returning East, and now—or at least, as of the

Saturday afternoon two days' hence—Julia would have that husband.

However briefly.

Thinking of Graham, she sighed. When Asa Bennett had announced his approval, with Aunt Geneva beaming beside him, Julia's "fiancé" hadn't said a word. Instead, he'd merely clasped her hand in his and stoically stared straight ahead. Like a man facing a firing squad...or a drifter temporarily forced to settle in.

More than likely, her bounty hunter had been steeling himself for the ordeal ahead, Julia decided as she surveyed the crinkled wads of paper at her feet. Doubtless, Graham had been summoning up the necessary courage to bind himself, however momentarily, to one woman. One place. One future.

One pretended—but equally confining—commitment.

Well, it wouldn't be easy for her, either, Julia reminded herself defiantly. She'd never deceived her papa before. Breaking the news of her annulment to him—once she'd reached New York—would be one of the most difficult tasks she'd ever faced. Papa would be disappointed, especially having thought her so happy with Graham. Aunt Geneva would be, too.

But Julia had already vowed to go forward. The best she could do when the time came would be to devise an excuse for her marriage ending that would not lay the blame at Mr. Corley's door, and leave it at that.

Miserably, Julia kicked at a tossed-away early-draft letter with the toe of her slipper. She watched it skitter across the hardwood floor and come to rest at the edge of the loomed rug. If only she could cast aside her doubts as easily!

The trouble was, she'd begun to let her emotions rule

her, rather than common sense. During her time with the bounty hunter, Julia had found herself swamped more and more with unfamiliar feelings...unnavigable and dizzying feelings. Nothing in her logical life, orderly 'till now, had prepared her for such a thing. It was no wonder, Julia decided, that she was having trouble! She merely needed to return to reason, and let her usual practicality come to her aid.

To that end, Julia dipped the pen nib into her pot of ink and then in the wavering light from the nearby oil lamp, she considered what she'd written so far.

Dear Mr. Chamberlain,

I have most fortuitous news! As I'd so avidly hoped, I have at long last secured the means to return to the States, and in particular, to New York City. As you mentioned when we last corresponded, I am indeed interested in the etiquette columnist's position at Beadle's, which you so generously informed me of. If the following date and time would be convenient for you, it is my hope that I might meet with you on—

Squinting, Julia paused. She tapped the un-nibbed end of the pen against her lips, deliberating. "Meet with you on—"

She wrote a date one week hence. That would allow her time to be married, secure the funds her father had promised to release from her trust upon her marriage, and travel by train to the East. If she allowed no wedding trip with Graham...

With a frown, she scratched out the date. Wrote in a new one, a week later.

Regarding it, a small smile came to her lips. Surely

she could afford a few days' time to spend with her new "husband." Nothing demanded she end her sham marriage quite so precipitously, did it?

Julia's gaze fell on the stack of correspondence arranged neatly at the edge of her writing desk, and the feminine handwriting on the topmost envelope. It was the latest letter from Lucinda Druiry, boasting of her plans to secure the etiquette columnist position for herself. Groaning in remembrance, Julia struck out the new date and rewrote the earlier appointment time.

She examined her letter to the editor of *Beadle's*. Filled with strike-outs, corrections and tearlike blots of ink, it was, quite possibly, the sorriest rendition she had devised so far.

"Oh, this is no use!" Julia wailed, snatching up the letter and crumpling it. She tossed it over her shoulder to join the others. "What is the *matter* with me?"

As though her looking glass might tell the tale, she glared into it. Her beautifying-concoction-smeared face gazed back at her from beneath her frightful, rag-rollered hair. Outlined by the white horseradish-and-sour-milk potion that Aunt Geneva swore would make her complexion its palest and most beautiful, her eyes looked red-rimmed and confused. This, for an impending bride?

All at once, Julia wanted nothing more than to put her head in her hands and have a good cry.

Except she couldn't. There was still too much to be done. Once she'd finished with her letter, she would have to examine her dress for needed mendings, plan a menu for her wedding luncheon, see to packing her satchels for her return East...oh, it was all too much! Overwhelmed, Julia looked from her writing paper and pen to her wedding dress—formerly her mother's, in a beautiful shade of blue—to Lucinda's letter and her waiting opened satchels. And all she saw, in her mind's eye, was Graham. Resolute. Helpful. *Wonderful.*

She couldn't let him do it. She couldn't let him sacrifice the drifter's life he loved, for her. Not for so much as a day, and certainly not for any longer than he had already.

Suddenly decisive, Julia cast aside her pen, and hurried to the basin to wash her face. There was no sense fighting it. It seemed she'd have to let her wayward emotions rule her a little while longer...just long enough to call on Graham, and release him from their bargain.

Standing to the side of Bea Harrington's boardinghouse a half hour later, Julia nibbled nervously at her lower lip. She scooped up another pebble from the cold ground and bounced it in her closed gloved fist, preparing to toss it in the path six others had taken before it.

Against the bounty hunter's window.

The night breeze ruffled the skirts of her brown day dress. On the street some twenty yards distant, the occasional wagon or rider passed by, and piano music tinkled from Cole Morgan's Last Chance saloon. If anyone saw her here, they would surely think she was daft for standing at the building-side and throwing rocks. But the alternative—alerting Mrs. Harrington that Julia had come to call on her "fiancé" at the unspeakable hour of nine-thirty—was unthinkable.

"Please," she whispered as she pulled back her hand. "Be there!"

She threw. The pebble, like five of the six before it, pinged from the siding a good foot from the window, and fell harmlessly to the ground. Graham would have needed hearing like her family's old bulldog to have detected it.

"Arrgh!" Julia stomped her foot and scuffled sideways, looking for another rock to toss. Dust kicked up around her ankles, and her determined, muttered grumblings echoed from the buildings on either side of her.

"This will do the trick," she said a few minutes later. She hefted a six-inch rock, solid enough to fill her whole palm. "Let's see you ignore *this!*"

Suddenly, a hand clamped over hers. Julia tilted backward, maneuvered by the force of someone standing behind her. She spun, and found herself confronting a tall, dark figure in a black hat and duster coat.

"Mr. Corley! You scared me near to death! You're supposed to be inside." She nodded toward the darkened window, and frowned. "What are you doing here?"

He regarded the rock in their joined hands, and shook his head. "Stopping you from committing a terrible breach of etiquette, looks like. Or from spending the night in the town lockup, for destroying Bea Harrington's windows." He grinned. "What were you trying to do, brain me with this boulder? There are easier ways to get a man's attention than with mayhem like this, darlin'."

The endearment, his first for her, wafted through her mind like a feather on a breeze. Julia clutched it close, and vowed to remember it. Given what she'd come here to do, that last bit of affection held extra sweetness.

She dropped her rock, and brushed the dirt from her palms.

"I've come to—to tell you something," Julia said. She couldn't resist taking his arm, savoring the soon-to-be-faraway solidity of the bounty hunter's muscles beneath her fingers. "Something important. Is there a private place we can talk?"

He frowned. "Are you all right? If anyone's teased you over our wedding the way you feared they'd ridicule your papa's new hairstyle, I'll—"

"Oh, no! It's not that." Sweet heaven...he thought someone would find their wedding ridiculous? That was what she got, Julia supposed, for finagling a fiancé for the "oddity of Avalanche." Doubtless Graham had become the subject of a few jests himself, for becoming entangled with her. Still, the supposition hurt. "It's about you."

"Me?"

"Yes, and I...oh, I can't discuss this here. Someone might overhear, and then—"

"Shhh. 'Tis all right." As though sensing her turmoil, Graham pressed a kiss to her lips, then murmured reassuringly. "We'll go to my boardinghouse room. No one will bother us there."

He began to walk, bringing her along at his side. By rote, Julia came...then panicked.

"What if someone sees me entering your room? My father—my reputation—my books! I'll be ruined." At the boardwalk, Julia dug in her heels. "Perhaps we should retire to the municipal park, and find a bench to—"

"To freeze together on? You're already shivering. My room will be fine." Graham put his arm around her to warm her, and started walking anew. "I'll not let any harm come to you because of it."

"But that's why I'm here," Julia said, seizing upon the opening his words offered. "To make sure no harm comes to *you!*"

His expression was filled with disbelief. "You want to protect *me?* From what...a rogue soup-slurper at our wedding reception Saturday? A terrible shortage of neckties?" Graham laughed. "Julia, I've lived more than thirty years, most of it on my own. I need no protection."

Despite his jokes, Julia felt too beset to laugh. Assuredly, to look at him Mr. Corley did seem invulnerable. Big, strong, sure of himself. But behind his eyes lurked a sadness only she could help ease, and his broad shoulders and wide chest only hid his gentle heart. They could not prevent it from breaking, while he left behind the freedom he needed.

She had to go forward. To let him go. However much it hurt.

"I *do* need to protect you. I need to protect you," she insisted seriously, "from *me.*"

His sidelong glance examined her. Slowly, his grin faded. "We'll go to my room," Graham said, "and have this solved, once and for all."

'Twas bridal jitters, Graham figured, watching Julia pace up and down the narrow T-shaped strip of boardinghouse floor between his bed, the bureau and the window. It had to be ordinary wedding-day fears that had brought her to him now, especially at such an unfashionable hour. But why? Did Julia wish to hurry up their sham wedding?

Or call it off, altogether?

Against all reason, Graham found himself hoping she wanted him sooner, rather than never. 'Twas probably for the best that their brief marriage would be a false one, though. He knew nothing of settling down, of making a wife happy.

After so many years, it seemed likely to him that he simply did not possess whatever it took to be a staying kind of man—however much he found himself wanting to be, lately. The woman before him deserved better. Much better.

Near the window, Julia whirled. "Where were you tonight?" she asked suddenly.

"Working at the library," Graham said. He rested his forearms on his thighs, uncaring of his mud-splattered pants, and looked up at her. "And then riding. My poor horse has gone soft and unhappy, left in the stables day after day."

She gave a distressed sound, as though his answer pained her. He didn't understand it. 'Twas true he probably looked disheveled, exactly like a man who'd ridden hard though a Territorial spring night and back again. But surely his windblown hair, dusty boots and pants, and partly unbuttoned shirt weren't so offensive as that. Were they?

Julia drew in a deep breath. "He wants to be free," she said softly.

Graham frowned. "My horse? He's been stabled before. He'll survive."

At that, she looked on the verge of tears! Confused, Graham stood, intending to go to her. When he moved, though, Julia did, too—all the way to the window. She stood there with her back to him, and he didn't know how to respond. Acting on the notion he'd had before, he went to the basin and poured in some water for washing.

"It's a difficult thing, that I have to say to you," he heard Julia explain as he ran the wet soapy cloth over his face and neck. Her voice continued, haltingly, as Graham lathered his hands and forearms. "I know this is a poor time, so if—if you're busy with something else, I could try to—''

''No.'' He splashed fresh water on his face to rinse, and straightened. ''I'm busy with nothing but this. Go on.''

Blinking, he groped for a towel, and began scrubbing himself dry. There. Maybe now she wouldn't be so all-fired offended by the—

Soft hands covered his, grasping the towel. Lace from a drooping sleeve tickled his damp neck.

—sight of a man as nature had made him.

''Here, let me help you,'' Julia said, suddenly there. Ducking her head, she took the towel from his hands and began blotting the water that had wet the ends of his hair.

Dumbfounded, Graham let her. With gentle motions, she captured the moisture from his hair, a drip from his jaw. She began working downward, toward the opened neck of his shirt, intent on tending to the bare skin his washing had revealed.

''I'm so sorry,'' she said as she worked. ''I never meant for things to happen this way. And now you—you—''

Her voice choked on the words. He could see nothing but the crown of her head, and so could not gauge what had caused this new upset. He was most definitely dried by now, but Julia went on patting him with the towel, nonetheless.

''I'm fine,'' Graham assured her, at a loss for what else to do.

''No, you're sad!'' she cried. ''Like your horse.''

''Like my what?''

''Oh, mostly you hide it,'' Julia said, waving her arm. The towel flung to and fro with her efforts, nearly taking some of his evening's whiskers with it. He ducked to avoid it. "With jests and surprises and good humor. But I can see it in your eyes, an underlying sorrow. And it...oh, Graham. I'm *so* sorry for it."

She quit waving the towel, and wrung it despondently in her hands instead. She raised her gaze from it, and looked to him for a reply.

Whatever sadness you see is because I'm soon to lose you, Graham thought. But he could not say as much, and burden her with that. Especially along with whatever misery had brought her here tonight, to strangle the life from his poor towel.

And so he only moved nearer, and said instead: "There's nothing for you to be sorry for. My life is my own. I hold no one else responsible for the parts of it."

Julia sighed. "I might have known you would say that. Your chivalry may have been buried, but it is deep."

"What?" he asked, teasingly horrified. "'Tis not fair to mock your knight in shining armor. Especially when he's about to make an honest woman of you, two days hence."

She sniffled, and tried to smile. Tears threatened, though, he could tell. Alarmed by the notion, Graham took the towel from her hands and flung it beside the pitcher and basin. Then he led Julia to his bedside and urged her onto the coverlet.

"Here, sit down. Whatever you have to say, it cannot be so bad as all that."

"It is." She nodded vehemently, and accepted the handkerchief he salvaged from his discarded duster coat pocket. "It *is* so bad as all that, and I find myself horribly unwilling to come out with it. I'm sorry."

He'd never seen her like this. Scratching his head,

Graham searched his memory for a similar experience. He couldn't find one. He had never stayed with a woman long enough to encounter so many moods as Julia confronted him with.

"No more apologies," he demanded.

"I'll—I'll try."

"Good." That was progress. Encouraged, Graham straightened, and tried a new tactic. "Tell me what's wrong."

"I can't! I should leave. I shouldn't have come here to begin with. Your boardinghouse room, of all places! My goodness, I—"

Still chattering, Julia bolted for the door in a flurry of skirts. Graham beat her there, more befuddled than ever, and slapped his hand over the knob.

"Tell me what's wrong," he repeated, more sternly.

"I...oh, I suppose I must. It would be cowardly not to. And you deserve better than that."

With visible reluctance, she returned to the bed and settled in. She lay aside her handkerchief and reticule and smoothed her skirts. When Julia pulled off her gloves and set them aside as well, he knew he was in trouble. Serious trouble.

"I'd better sit down, too," he said, and did. The mattress dipped between them, then righted again.

She spared him a curious glance. Breathing deeply, she seemed to gather her courage.

"I'll tell you. But before I do..." Julia paused, blinking at him through hopeful blue eyes. "Please, may I kiss you one more time?"

She bit her lip. It seemed as though she believed he might not want to kiss her again, once she'd delivered her news. To Graham's mind, there couldn't have been a dafter notion.

"Yes," he said simply, for there wasn't a time when he did not want her. With him. Beside him. Even—for a man could dream—beneath him, as he loved her.

"You might think of this as a goodbye kiss," she murmured. Nearer now, she slipped her hand to his jaw to hold him steady, and dropped her gaze to his lips. "A goodbye to remember, I hope."

"But I'm not leaving until—mmmmm."

The rest of his words dissolved on the moan wrung from him when her mouth met his. Tenderly, slowly, Julia brushed her lips against his own, 'til Graham was nearly mad with wanting her. Then she touched her tongue to the seam of his lips and, delicately, swept inside.

Heat rushed through him with the force of the Territorial sun he'd ridden beneath to come here. Groaning with it, Graham brought his hands to her face and cradled her closer, losing himself in the wonder that was joining with Julia. Her confusing words, her inexplicable apologies, her bewildering troubles…all vanished beneath the sensations rioting through him.

The wanting he'd felt for weeks culminated in this moment, this kiss. 'Twas more than likely true that a drifter like him could not be a good husband to her, Graham knew. Not even for so short a time together as they would share. But he could give her this, a little pleasure to remember him by. And so he kissed Julia back with all the fervency his heart demanded, and then kissed her once more for good measure.

His blood pounded through him. His mind cleared of all but the sweetness of her lips on his, her hands against his skin, her body so near and so soft. Groaning, he surrendered to everything Julia seemed so willing to give, and did it gladly.

She splayed her hands against his chest, her fingers flexing against his shirt. Angling her head, Julia whispered something about, "Just one *more* last kiss," and then brought her mouth to his again. They rocked together, Graham thinking only too late to brace his feet against the floorboards lest they lose balance.

With a little moan, Julia deepened their kiss. The force of it sent them both tumbling backward, onto the bed. The pale coverlet billowed around them, then settled. Graham stiffened, expecting at any moment that Julia would rear up, alarmed to find herself—most improperly—sprawled atop her pretend fiancé.

To his amazement, she did not. Instead, her breath panted past his ear as she broadened her explorations to his neck and began kissing there. 'Twas as though some fever had taken hold of her, and only loving him could be the cure of it.

Grinning, Graham accepted his good fortune.

For all of five seconds.

And then his conscience asserted itself, and demanded that he take action. With an inner grumble, he captured Julia's head in his hands—noticing as he did that her hair had already tumbled into dark waves around her shoulders, lending her the look of a wild, innocent temptress. Gently he angled her face until their gazes met.

"Julia, I can't stand much more of this."

She blew a hank of hair from her eyes, and looked concerned. "You don't like it? I'm so very—"

Graham covered her mouth with his fingertips to forestall the apology that was surely on its way. "I love it." She frowned doubtfully, and he spoke again. "*Love it.* But if this goes much further, I won't want to stop. And you know what that means."

She did. He saw the knowledge in her eyes. And the curiosity, the heated interest, that followed. Damnation, but Julia's openness would be his undoing.

"You want an annulment, after our sham wedding," Graham went on, ignoring the way the truth pricked him. "So you'll be able to go to New York as a free woman. If we continue, tonight, that won't be possible."

Grudgingly, Julia rolled onto her back. She stared at the ceiling for a long, thoughtful moment, watching the shadows cast by the low lamplight. And then she smiled, with an impishness he never would have credited her with.

"Only if we...er, *continue* after we're married," she pointed out. "Then such...activities...would be grounds to deny an annulment. But now, well, we're free."

Graham boggled. Was she saying what he thought she was saying? His body leapt with eagerness at the very notion—even as his mind warned that hers was a dangerous idea, indeed.

'Tis merely your birthday wish, come true, the loudest part of him argued. *You wished for Julia. And now, here she is.*

A man couldn't argue with that, Graham decided.

But to be sure... "So now," he said, "you want—"

"A wedding night," Julia announced. She looked pleased with her startling idea. Pleased, intrigued and eager to discover where it would lead her. She sat up on the bed. "Please, Graham. Tonight, while we still have the chance...please, love me."

Chapter Eighteen

Levering upward beside Julia, her bounty hunter hesitated but a moment. Cradling her face in his broad hands, he tilted her head upward so their gazes met. His was intent. Serious. And oh, so very heated it made her skin fairly tingle with warmth.

"Are you certain?" he asked.

Her future hung on her answer, Julia knew. Ahead stretched days without Graham, lonesome days during which she'd have nothing but remembrances for company and missed chances for regrets. Here, *now,* she had the man she loved...close and caring and tempting as the devil with his roguish ways and slow hands.

It was hardly a choice at all. She'd choose the devil, and have as a consequence a night to remember for always.

This was not what she'd come here to do. She'd come, Julia recalled, to release Graham from their bargain. To set him free, to the drifter's life he loved. But faced with the overwhelming longing she'd been fighting for weeks, and with the means to satisfy it thoroughly within reach...Julia found she did not have the strength to turn Graham away. Not now.

Later, she promised herself. *After I've given him something of myself to take away with him.* And so she mustered a smile from the hidden part of her that loved him, and nodded her head.

"I'm certain," Julia said.

He remained still, searching her face. "This goes beyond our bargain," Graham said, lowering his hands. "We did not promise—"

"I'm certain," she repeated. With trembling fingers, she reached for the bodice of her dress, and unfastened the first button. The second. "Please, love me. Everything else can wait."

At least until after this...my goodbye.

His gaze followed the course of her fingers, his attention captured by their movement and by—Julia hoped—the glimpses of her body she revealed. She undid the third button. The next. And as she went, her trembling ceased, and her surety grew.

Making love with Graham was right, regardless of what propriety said. He held a piece of her heart already. It could not be wrong to give him more.

"Julia." He released a pent-up breath, his face harsh with the effort of restraint, and looked away from her gaping dress. "I cannot promise to stay. Understand that."

"Be with me *now,*" she murmured, catching hold of his hand.

Feeling its work-roughened strength beneath her fingertips, Julia gently tugged him closer. She brought his hand to her bosom and slipped it inside her dress. The thin fabric of her chemise was all that separated his warm palm from her skin, and her heart thudded with the thrill of his intimate touch. Still holding his hand beneath hers, Julia settled him firmly atop her breast, and bravely gazed upward.

"Please," she said. "Tomorrow will care for itself."

He groaned, making the slightest upward movement with his hand, as though savoring the feel of her in his palm. His expression was one of intent wonder. It eased her to see it. If he found her pleasing, if he...*no.* Graham had stayed with her all these weeks already because he saw something in her that others did not. She would not spoil the magic of this moment with wonderings about his thoughts.

Graham raised an eyebrow, and his familiar grin was back. "You do nothing halfway," he avowed. "'Tis a quality in you I admire. Especially now."

Julia smiled, too, and felt her worries melt still further. If he could jest with her, then Graham had accepted her wish to be with him. From here, there would be no turning back.

"I've never had trouble knowing what I want," Julia agreed teasingly. "It's the getting of it that's been a problem."

"'Twill be no problem tonight," he assured her. "I have all that you want, and more. 'Tis yours."

And with that, he set out to make it so. He kissed her again, and a million times more, now holding her close, now nuzzling her neck, now nudging aside her hair to cup her breasts. He stroked her slowly, without restraint. Before long, Julia lay beside him on the softness of the coverlet, writhing with the wondrous feelings he aroused in her. She ached to have still more of her dress unbuttoned. But when she reached upward with her hands to accomplish the task, Graham stopped her.

"Let me," he murmured, raising her hands to kiss

them. His mouth trailed from her wrist to her forearm, raising goose bumps in his wake. He brought her arms to the mattress and settled them there, then rolled upward beside her and regarded her tenderly.

"I have dreamed of you so many times," Graham said, his voice husky. "At first, I didn't know it was you. Only that I wanted this closeness, this union. Now that I've found you, Julia...ahhh, but this is sweeter than any dream."

He tended to her buttons, slipping them deftly from their places. All the while, he murmured wonderful things, things Julia ached to believe, and vowed to hold close to her heart. That he found her beautiful. That he loved the feel of her, the scent of her, the way she smiled. His tender words slipped 'round her, cradling her in a warmth that had only partly to do with his hands on her body and his breath against her skin. It was the nearest thing to true love that Julia knew she'd ever find, and knowing she would have to set it free only made it twice as poignant.

"I love...this," she whispered back, stopped in the last moment by the knowledge that declaring herself to Graham would only be a burden to him in the end. "I wish we could be together forever."

He missed her meaning, and nipped her collarbone playfully. "If I'm as successful as I hope, 'twill *feel* like forever."

Julia cradled his head against her, burrowing her fingers in the thick softness of his hair. All at once, she was glad he hadn't cut short those long dark strands. Their rugged wildness was utterly Graham, as beyond boundaries as the man himself. He needed taming by no one. Least of all her.

Moments later, he'd proved it anew. She lay clad in

her underclothes alone, her dress and corset cast aside to the bureau top and her shoes and stockings fallen to the floor. As though Graham had known the sudden shyness she would feel, he'd left the last, thin barrier of her chemise between them. Smoothing its delicate fabric with her hands, Julia tried to quiet her thundering heart, and turned toward him again.

"I find this most unfair," she said to shield her nervousness. "Here I am, nearly bared to you. And there you are—" she plucked at his shirt with a saucy gesture "—all covered from me."

Graham raised an eyebrow. "'Tis easily remedied."

Before Julia could so much as draw another breath, his shirt sailed through the air and landed on the bureau to join her things. They flopped together amiably, she saw, her feminine lace flung across his masculine collar and sleeves as though they were meant to be together.

She smiled at the notion, and turned to him. Her lighthearted musings instantly fled, chased by the wondrous sight of Graham, naked from the waist up.

"Oh, my!" Tentatively, she reached toward him. "Would you mind very much if I...touched you?"

"I'd mind only if you did not."

Reassuringly, Graham clasped her hand and tugged it to the center of his chest, in heartwarming imitation of her earlier request. Biting her lip, Julia spread her fingers over him.

His muscles, solid and hot, flexed beneath her touch. His crisp hair tickled her sensitive fingertips, and led her still lower, to his lean abdomen. Spreading her hand wide, she explored the whole length and breadth of his torso, from the hollow at his belly where his trousers stretched from hipbone to hipbone, to the warm curve of his collarbone and the unyielding firmness of his shoulders and arms.

"You're so warm. So strong. So different from me." Julia pressed a kiss to his chest and gazed up at him from her position stretched beside him on the bed. She teased a whorl of hair with her fingertip. "I can hardly wait," she said boldly, her shyness gone, "to see the rest of you."

Graham groaned and hauled her atop him. His kiss was thorough and deep, making her toes curl and her fingers clench on his upper arms. She was moaning when he'd finished...and still he wasn't done.

"You'll be the death of me," he said, his deep voice making his chest rumble pleasurably against her bosom. "With your lusty talk and that look in your eyes. Who knew you held such passion inside you?"

You did, Julia thought instantly. *On the day we met.*

But she only fluttered her eyelashes, and continued her explorations from her new position, half-sprawled atop him. From here, she could enjoy the rubbing of their legs, the solid press of his thighs...the unmistakable *rigidity* of him, threatening to utterly destroy the fit of his trousers. With the proof of Graham's desire so obviously at hand, Julia had expected to feel hesitant. Even fearful. But because this was the man she loved, and because tonight was the only one they would ever have together, she felt neither of those things.

She felt only love. And an eagerness to share it.

"I am passionate for many things," she told him, raising her foot to drag it seductively along his trouser-covered calf. She pressed against him, proving her claim. "It's only uncertainty that's made me hide it behind rules and proprieties. Until now."

"I'm glad you've come out. The brazen Miss Julia."

"The scoundrel, Mr. Corley."

"The beloved lady," Graham said, "of my heart."

Beneath his renewed smile and stroking hands, she stilled. *Beloved* whirled through her head, as intoxicating as the flicker of his tongue against her skin. Dared she believe it?

It didn't matter if she did, Julia told herself firmly. They were here, together, now. That was all that mattered. And so she lost herself in their lovemaking, and swore to remember it always.

"I hope this position suits," Graham said to Julia, long moments after she'd first suggested this night together. With a trembling hand he cast aside the last of her underclothes, removed during a lengthy exploration of her curves and secrets, and forced himself to breathe deeply. To continue moving slowly. Even if it killed him.

And it might.

"This position?" she asked.

Her voice sounded demure, despite its husky edge—and despite her bawdy position, naked and captured between his spread thighs. Thoroughly enjoying the glorious sight of her, Graham eased back on his heels so his straddled position would be comfortable for Julia, and nodded.

"Yes," he said, lowering his hands to his trouser-covered hips. He wanted his damned constricting clothes gone…but that would have to wait. He smiled so she'd know he was teasing her. Again. "You know I'm concerned with the condition of your knees."

"My knees?"

Her smile was innocently seductive. *Too* innocently seductive. She twirled a lock of loose dark hair around her finger, and looked up at him. More than likely, she was unaware of the way her bare breasts bounced enticingly toward him…but Graham wasn't. And he couldn't wait to show her how much he appreciated it.

"Your knees," he confirmed. Slowly, he trailed his hands from her hips to her breasts, and cupped her. Her nipples tightened beneath his thumbs, exciting him still further. With difficulty, he went on talking. "Do your knees feel wobbly, as they did when we kissed in the past?"

Julia considered it, mischievously narrowing her eyes. "I'm not sure."

"Hmmm. Let's see if I can help you make up your mind."

Graham lowered his head, and kissed her. He scooted backward and kissed her neck, then the top of her breast. Moaning, he drew her taut nipple into his mouth, and savored the wonderful feel of it against his tongue. Her breathing quickened as he went on loving her, and many moments ticked past before Graham could summon the will to stop for another question.

"How about now?" he asked, not raising his head as he pressed more kisses to the valley between her breasts, and moved to lavish equal attention on her other side. "Wobbly yet?"

Her answer was a strangled sigh.

"I'd better continue," Graham murmured. "Just to make sure."

Julia grasped his head and held him to her as he loved her. Again and again he stroked her, kissed her, licked her. She tasted good, like a sweet he'd been denied too long, and for the first time in his drifter's life, Graham could not get enough of a woman. *This woman.*

"Now?" he asked, somehow finding the strength to raise his eyebrow in question.

"Yes, yes!" she cried, finally surrendering their erotic game. She hauled him upward for a kiss. "Very, *very* wobbly! It's fortunate my knees aren't required to hold me now—" Julia paused, breathlessly clutching him against her "—for they'd surely fail in the task."

They shared a smile, one more tender and less teasing. Graham slid his hands to her hips and cradled her against him, kneading his fingers against her rounded derrière.

"Then it's a good thing I'm here to hold you," he said. "I'll never let you go."

Her eyes darkened, nearly black in the flickering lamplight. For an instant, Julia looked troubled…but then she wriggled beneath him, and gave him another impish look. Graham decided he must have imagined that moment's unease.

"Tonight I'll hold *you* just as tightly," she murmured, and followed the words with a tantalizing movement of her hand. "So long as you'll let me."

Her fingers caressed him through the rough canvas of his trousers. Graham jerked in surprise, then covered her mouth with his.

"Yes," he groaned when their kiss was through. "Anything. Everything. All that I have is yours."

"Thank you," she said primly, and began unbuttoning his trousers.

Graham held his breath in anticipation.

Several long minutes later, Julia was still at it. Head bowed, she wrestled with the fastenings. A muttered "blast it!" slipped from her lips, making him smile.

"This won't work!" She raised her hands as though

surrendering to the buttons' steadfast barrier. "You're simply too big for your britches."

Graham's grin widened. "Music to any man's ears."

"I didn't mean—" Her cheeks flushed. "Oh, never mind! I'll simply find another way to solve this problem."

She sat up, beautiful and bare, a determined jut to her chin. With a predatory air, Julia examined the contents of his boardinghouse room. Her gaze lit upon the bureau, where a pair of scissors lay half-buried amongst the writing supplies beside their clothes.

"Aha!"

"Oh, *no.*" Graham grabbed her just as she lurched upward from the mattress, setting the bed quivering. He tugged her backward, and rolled them both until she lay beneath him again. "I prefer my pants—and the rest of me—intact."

"But I want—"

"No."

"The problem is—"

He kissed away her next words, along with the rebuttal he didn't doubt would follow. "There's no problem." With eager fingers, Graham worked at his buttons and then proved the fact to her. "Believe me."

He guided her hand inside the gap he'd made. Closing his eyes, Graham let his head tip backward as Julia's palm covered him. Only the barrier of his thin drawers remained between them, and her touch was indescribably wonderful.

"Oh!" she whispered.

He looked to see her gaze, wide and curious, fly from his groin to his face, and then back again.

"Does this hurt?" she asked. "You're so...hard. That *can't* be correct."

Decisively, Julia began to withdraw her hand. Desperately, Graham stopped her. "'Tis correct," he groaned. "So very, very correct. Please, *don't stop.*"

She bit her lip, and studied him.

"'Tis the only way I can love you," he went on. "Truly."

Surely she didn't require an explanation of what was to come. And, soon enough, Graham realized she did not. It was not the mechanics of their joining that confounded her…it was his pants.

"You can't be comfortable," she insisted. "Your trousers must be disturbing your circulation. But that's easily remedied."

The last thing he wanted was a conversation. Or a return to her scissors-hunting. Especially now. But obligingly, Graham asked—or more truly, rasped:

"How?"

"You must be naked, as well," Julia announced. "Like me."

A man couldn't argue with that.

"You're the expert," he said on a grin.

He helped her with his clothes, untying the drawstring on his drawers as she stood and dragged his trousers over his hips and down his legs. They landed with a rustle on the floor, then were followed by the smaller bundle of his underclothes.

"You know what this means, of course," Graham told Julia as she returned to the bed.

"No. What?"

She kissed his chest and moved her way up to his mouth. Graham rolled her over. They shared a long, soulful kiss before speaking again.

"It means I'll have to begin anew. If you have the

strength to stand without wobbly knees then I've not done my job properly yet.''

In the moments that followed, he did. He held her close, and gave to her everything he could. Driven by the need to make Julia happy, to make her remember this night, Graham loved her with his eyes, his hands, his mouth. He caressed her until she was breathless again...and she caressed him, in her turn.

They were well-suited, he discovered, both passionate and uninhibited—remarkably uninhibited, in Julia's case. If he'd expected his etiquette instructress to remain prim and proper beneath the bedclothes, he'd been mistaken. It seemed that once Julia had decided their early ''wedding night'' was to go forward, she'd cast away her reservations, as well.

She was with him fully. Wholeheartedly. Giving, taking, and whispering of her feelings for him. She undulated beneath him, clutching at him for support. She quivered at his touch, and moaned her need for him. Now, in this, Graham was the tutor, and Julia, the student. But she was more...so much more, to him.

She was his love. He knew it, as he touched her. As he kissed her, and felt her turn hotter beneath him. As he looked at her, and saw his caring reflected in her eyes.

''You're beautiful,'' he whispered, cradling her cheek in his hand. ''So beautiful. It hurts to look at you, and to know—''

To know I'm about to lose you. Before he could say the words, Julia's lips pressed against his. 'Twas almost, Graham thought crazily, as though she yearned to keep the truth unsaid.

A small, stifled cry shuddered through her. With an

abrupt movement, he ended their kiss, and swiftly studied her face.

"Julia? What's wrong?"

She turned her head against the pillow. Closed her eyes. And then rapidly swept her fingertips over her lashes, as though dashing away tears. When she gazed up at him again, though, Graham could detect no sign of weeping. Only longing.

'Twas a feeling he shared. More deeply than he'd known.

"Just love me," she begged in a thickened voice. "Make me yours. Please, don't stop now."

He hesitated, fiercely aroused and acutely wary. Something, some inner sense warned him that something here was amiss. But however much he tried, Graham could not detect what it was. And so he cast aside his doubts, and concentrated on the moment instead.

Julia deserved only the best from him. And he was determined to give it. When she'd gone, at least she would have that much to remember him by...and he would share those memories, as well.

"If you're not sure—" he began.

"I am."

The upward tilt of her hips assured him of it, lured him with the slick heat of her most intimate, most womanly places sliding against him. Graham gritted his teeth, and resisted the need to join with her. Never mind that Julia, in her eagerness, tempted him with the seductiveness of a seasoned lover. 'Twas her first time, he knew. He would need to be gentle.

To begin, he covered her body with kisses, whispering all the while of the loving things he had planned for them. Julia squirmed and blushed beneath his frank words. Then she moaned and panted beneath their matching, sensual, actions. By the time he slipped his hands lower for a final time, and stroked her even more intimately, Julia was clutching fistfuls of bedding. She twisted the sheets in her hands and cried out to him, her voice husky with desire.

Graham answered her cry with a slowing of his pace, the better to savor her pleasure. He touched her with a kind of reverence, drinking in every sigh, every arch of her back, every flutter of her lashes as Julia closed her eyes with the feelings his movements inspired. Carefully, gently, he caressed her…and when at last Julia ceased quaking and stiffened in his arms to find her release, he felt her rapture as if it were his own. 'Twas as though their two hearts beat together, and would not function one without the other.

She sagged beneath him with a little sigh, her skin warm and faintly damp. Her arms came 'round to hold him close, a gesture Graham loved. The pulse in her temple thrummed against his cheek; the feminine allure of other, more private places snugged up against his shaft. Breathless with wanting her, Graham nonetheless took a minute to nudge her chin upward with his fingertips.

Her eyes opened. Vast and blue and filled with affection, they held a trust Graham devoutly hoped he could prove worthy of.

"Don't fall asleep just yet, darlin'," he told her. "There's more to come."

"More?"

He nodded. Settling himself firmly between her welcoming thighs, he braced himself on his knees and spread hands. Graham waited for her assent.

"Will it make me feel wobblier?" Julia asked. A

small smile crept onto her face. "Because I feel very, *very* wobbly right now, and I'm not sure—"

"Oh, yes," he promised. "It will."

"Oh, my!"

"I don't want to hurt you, Julia," he felt compelled to warn, knowing of her innocence. "But—"

"I understand."

She raised her hand to cradle his jaw, and swept her thumb tenderly over his cheek. 'Twas like a benediction, and Graham lowered his head to kiss her palm.

"Sometimes," Julia continued, "even good things hurt. I know that. Don't worry about me, Graham. I—I want you. Tonight. Now. No matter what else happens."

A shadow passed over her face, then vanished beneath a loving look. No doubt 'twas a trick of the light, like the others he had seen this night. Putting aside his thoughts of it, Graham held Julia closely and kissed her.

"I will never forget you," he vowed.

"Nor I, you."

Her words stayed with him, driving him onward as Graham carefully prepared her for him and then, finally, entered her. He stopped partway, breathing hard, and simply…*felt* her. 'Twas amazing, and agonizing, and as Graham slipped past her maiden's resistance and entered Julia fully, he was overwhelmed with emotion.

His body demanded release. His heart longed for union. And all sides of him were satisfied when Julia pulled him closer still, and whispered for him to love her. Graham did, long and well, his gaze remaining upon her face as he thrust and withdrew, and drove them both toward an ecstatic finish. Even as he felt his body clench and shudder, Graham kept his gaze upon her, and prayed that Julia would understand what was in his heart and mind.

I love you, he told her silently, with every increasing heartbeat. *I will love you always.*

Release burst upon him, and Julia cried out, too. At last, Graham allowed himself to lower his head to the warm curve of her neck, luxuriating in the closeness they shared. 'Twas unlike anything he'd ever known, and more than that by far, he realized.

'Twas very much…like coming home.

Chapter Nineteen

Long past midnight, Julia carefully and silently dressed. By the light of the waning moon, she gathered writing supplies from Graham's boardinghouse room bureau and sat on the floor near the window with them, determined to tell Graham in writing what she had been unable to say aloud.

You're free. Our bargain is done. Leave me when you wish.

She looked up from the paper, her fingers cold on the pen. Wistfully, Julia gazed through the shadows toward her bounty hunter's sleeping form. The hours they'd just shared had been wondrous, unforgettable...and all the more perilous for it. Being loved by Graham, and loving him in return, had only made her feelings for him stronger. She didn't know how she would find the strength to let him go.

Yet she had to. It would cost her the future she'd hoped for. It would probably make her twice the laughingstock in town, once word got 'round that bookish Miss Bennett had hired herself a fiancé—and then had proved unable to keep him. And it would undoubtedly disappoint her papa and Aunt Geneva, who would be forced to hold their heads high in spite of it all.

But despite everything, Julia loved Graham too much to be the cause of his unhappiness. Not so long as she could cure it. It came down to that, no matter what else. And so she dipped her pen all over again, and bowed her head to do the deed.

Graham murmured in his sleep and turned. The bedclothes rustled, reminding her of all the shameless pleasures they'd shared. Julia held her breath, waiting, half praying, for his drowsy invitation to rejoin him in their bed.

It never came. Instead, Graham's breathing lengthened and deepened, and Julia dared to continue writing. When she'd finished, she raised herself on shaking limbs and held her note to the moonlight to read it.

She frowned, feeling heartsick. This was cowardly of her, she knew. But Julia feared that, faced with Graham in the morning, she would be unable to release him from their bargain. Again. This had to be the best way.

Imagining Graham's certain relief when he opened her missive gave Julia the courage to fold and deliver it. He would be glad to be free, she reminded herself. Happy to have no obligations, no roles to play, no lies to tell.

No fiancée to court, and pretend to love.

Drawing in a deep breath, Julia stood beside the bed. Graham sprawled in a square of moonlight, his hair dark against the pillow, one arm outflung as though he dreamed he cradled her against him still. Even in repose his features were strong and blatantly masculine, softened only a little by sleep. She yearned to touch him, to press a kiss to his brow or hug him close, one last time.

She couldn't risk it. Instead, Julia carefully placed her note on the empty pillow she'd left, and stepped back. Tears blurred her vision and clogged her throat. Fighting against them, she indulged in the only solace she dared.

"I love you," she whispered.

And then she left, too blinded by tears to look back.

Graham awakened to the sound of wagons rumbling past his boardinghouse window, and a feeling of unease. Still stretched out in bed, he felt his muscles tighten instinctively with readiness. Stealthily, he snaked a hand beneath his pillow, and located the handle of the knife he kept there. He wished his Colt was within reach, too. This wary feeling had saved his life more than once in his bounty hunter's days, warning him of an ambush before it could strike. He would not ignore it now.

He waited, slowly taking in his surroundings without moving. The bedclothes were warm and twisted 'round his legs, the room bright with the rising sun. Its brilliance washed over his closed eyelids. The scents of coffee and sizzling sausage wafted beneath his door, and probably permeated the whole boardinghouse. Muffled thumps and indistinct voices could be heard downstairs, in Bea Harrington's kitchen. Everything seemed as it should be.

Then why this feeling of unease?

Julia, he thought suddenly, and remembrance of the night they'd shared came rushing back to him. 'Twas Julia's presence that made this morning feel different, and not a nearby danger at all. Going limp with relief, Graham withdrew his fist from the handle of the knife. Now that he thought of it, Julia's fresh orange scent still lingered amidst the sheets surrounding him, although her weight was so scarce compared to his that it obviously barely registered in his mind.

Smiling, he contemplated how best to awaken her. With a kiss? A gentle stroking, moving from her knees upward, 'till she quivered again, and cried out in his arms? A husky "good morning," with a wink to promise more? 'Twas more than possible that Julia, more wanton than he'd known, would want to kiss *him* awake herself, after all.

Truly, he was a lucky man, Graham decided. He'd found a woman to love, to laugh with, to confide in. He'd confessed his dreams of a lending library to her, and she'd safeguarded them—then helped make them real. He'd revealed his orphan's past, and she'd wanted him all the same. For Julia's sake, Graham had dared to risk the dangers of life in a settled town, choked with families and convention and a lamentable lack of desperadoes to be tracked...and he'd survived. Not only that, he'd actually enjoyed it, if the truth were told.

Yes, Julia was the answer to a question he hadn't even known how to pose. And for that she deserved a knees-upward awakening that was slow, seductive and thoroughly heartfelt.

His mind made up, Graham smiled still wider. He could get used to this sort of awakening, he decided as he rolled over to begin. He could grow to love this life, he thought further as he shifted the rumpled bedclothes aside to reveal Julia.

An empty indentation in the mattress met his gaze.

Confused, Graham wrinkled his brow and swiftly examined the room. 'Twas vacant, save the furnishings and the clothes he'd tossed away so eagerly last night. *His clothes,* only. With a growing sense of foreboding, he lay his palm in the indentation beside him. He spread his fingers, and touched the place where Julia had last lay. His grin faded. His gaze lifted to the pillow where he'd last seen her smile.

And that was when Graham discovered the note.

Julia reached the church at the edge of town, and sat on the steps with a bone-deep weariness. After leaving Mr. Corley's boardinghouse room, she'd gone home to get some rest, but sleep had eluded her. Restless and sad, she'd eventually arisen, washed, and dressed, and had set out on foot to try to sort through her tangled feelings.

Now, with thousands of steps behind her, Julia was no closer to the peace she'd hoped for than when she'd first set foot onto Main Street before sunrise. Wearily, she propped her elbows on her upraised knees and rested her chin on her palms. Just beyond her resting place, business owners opened their shops and farmers' wagons trundled slowly past. Birds twittered with a cheeriness Julia thought she'd never feel again.

What was Graham doing now? she wondered. With every horse and rider that passed, her heartbeat quickened as she imagined it was him. Surely now that he was free, he would waste no time in leaving Avalanche behind. But despite her expectations, none of the men who rode by raised their hats to reveal her bounty hunter's rugged face, charming smile and warm dark eyes.

"Miss Julia, is that you?" asked a small voice nearby. "Are you lost?"

She looked to the side to find Libbie O'Halloran standing close by, her ginger-colored hair twirled up in braids. In her hands, she held a length of what looked like clothesline, attached at one end to...Herbert?

The bantam rooster bobbed his head, his red comb flopping. Beside him a similarly leashed hen pecked at the ground near Libbie's feet.

Are you lost?

Yes, Julia wanted to cry. *Lost, and lonesome. I just never knew how very alone I could be, until now.*

"Yes, Libbie, it's me. And no, I'm not lost." For the girl's sake, Julia tried out a wan smile. "Good morning. Taking Herbert and his friend for a walk, are you?"

"That's Matilda, his ladylove. They don't like to be separated."

"I see." Libbie's serious tone warned her not to make fun, and Julia did not. "Well, even chickens can fall in love, I suppose. Are they both yours?"

"No. Only Herbert." Fondly, Libbie picked him up and cradled him in her arms. The rooster calmed at her touch, and miraculously submitted to the treatment. "Matilda belongs to one of my friends. We discovered they're fond of each other, and so she lets me walk them together sometimes."

"Naturally," Julia said, as though taking two chickens for a walk were the most ordinary occurrence in the world. "It's kind of you to accompany them."

Libbie shrugged. "Everyone needs a helping hand, sometimes. Even a lady like you. Why, Patrick told me that if he hadn't—"

She broke off, a guilty flush pinkening her cheeks. Rapidly, Libbie sat Herbert down beside Matilda and gathered the clothesline slack in her girlish fist.

"Hadn't what, Libbie?"

"I shouldn't say. He prob'ly meant it to be a secret."

Julia studied the girl. Then she patted the church step beside her spread skirts. "If it's about me, you should probably tell me."

''Well...Patrick says he's the one who brung you and the bounty hunter together. He says if he hadn't done all that spying for you—''

This time, it was Julia's turn to have pink cheeks.

''—Mr. Corley woulda left town right quick, afore you could catch him.''

''He's right, Libbie.''

''What?'' The girl's mouth was an O of surprise.

''And further—'' She might as well just come out with it, Julia decided. The whole town would know soon enough, anyway. ''It turns out Mr. Corley *will* be leaving town, after all.''

''But what about your wedding tomorrow? My ma hemmed me a dress to wear, and everything!''

''I'm sorry,'' Julia said, and meant it. *Oh, how she meant it.* ''As it happens, Mr. Corley is a special kind of man. A drifting kind of man, who likes to be free. That's why he—''

''He likes to be with you,'' Libbie disagreed stubbornly. She shook her head, her pigtails flying over her skinny shoulders. ''Just like Herbert likes to be with Matilda. I know it!''

''I wish that were true.'' With a sigh, Julia gazed out over the still-busier street that ran into the distance before them. ''I *truly* wish that were true. But I'm afraid Herbert and Matilda have something...extraordinary together. Real love doesn't happen easily, or every day.''

For a moment, Libbie looked thoughtfully at her. Then she settled her small hand atop Julia's, and squeezed.

''It will be all right,'' the girl said solemnly. ''I never want to admit when I'm lost, either.''

Lost. Libbie's repetition of her earlier notion caught

Julia off-guard. Before she could correct the child's mistake, though, Libbie went on talking:

"All you have to do is stay right where you are," she said, nodding for emphasis as she dispensed her advice. "If you go wandering around, nobody can find you. That's what my ma always says. But if you stay put, somebody you love will track you down. And everything will be okay."

How I wish it could be, Julia thought. But she only hugged Libbie close in reply, and whispered her thanks.

"Do you want me to send somebody for you?" Libbie asked. When Julia shook her head, the girl's brow wrinkled. "Patrick could prob'ly find Mr. Corley for you again. 'Specially if you have more of those chromo cards he likes collectin'."

"No, Libbie. Thank you, though. You go on and finish your walk," Julia said. She took her arm from the girl's shoulders, and gave her an encouraging nudge. "I'll be fine. Maybe I'll just stay here, like you said."

"You ought to."

Clucking to her chickens, Libbie waved and walked away. Julia watched until she'd rounded the corner out of sight. Then she rose.

She couldn't stay here. If she knew what was good for her, Julia would stay lost, at least for today...at least until Graham was gone for certain.

Graham's eyes burned as he finished dressing and pulled on his hat. 'Twas like a handful of grit had been tossed in his face, and his eyes were protesting mightily. Doing his best to ignore the feeling, he buckled on his gun belt and strode across the room to collect his saddlebags.

His gaze fell on the scrap of paper lying on the empty

bed. Julia's damned note. Swearing, Graham deliberately looked away and moved past it.

His heart twisted, though. His fingers moved clumsily on the cracked leather of his riding gear. His throat clogged, feeling tight. With a frown, he hefted his things, putting more muscle into the work than was needed.

Obviously, he'd spent too much time in this town. He'd gone soft, Graham figured. Dangerously and unfamiliarly so. The best remedy to that was striking the trail, and soon. After all...he had nothing to remain in Avalanche for.

Not now.

He slung everything onto his shoulder and headed for the door. Partway there, a scraping sound caught his attention. His saddlebags had dragged across his bed, sending the cursed note wafting into the air like a particularly unwelcome goodbye salute.

Graham snatched it back. He scowled, tempted to crush the thing in his fist and hurl it away. On the verge of doing so, something inside him made him unfold it again. Like a drunk staring into the bottle of Old Orchard that would be his undoing, Graham read Julia's note again.

Dear Mr. Corley, she'd written. He grimaced all over again at her high-handed formality. Leave it to the etiquette instructress to pretend they hadn't moaned in each other's arms all last night.

> I'm sorry to deliver this news in such a cowardly and ignoble fashion. This may be the most difficult letter I have ever written, and although that is no excuse for what I have done, please know I deeply regret ever hurting you.

Graham tightened his fingers on the letter. It shook, subtly, as he continued reading.

> I never meant you any harm. It wasn't until I knew you that I understood the magnitude of my mistake.

Here the letters grew blurry, as though she'd somehow smudged the ink. Given that she must have written her note in semidarkness while he slept unaware nearby, it was no wonder it was less than pristine. Graham scanned a few lines that wobbled in his vision, then came to the most damning part of all:

> In the end, it comes down to this. Knowing you as I do now, I cannot bring myself to marry you. Not even for so brief a time as we had planned in our bargain. I'm sorry.

His eyes burned more fiercely, as though the grit had been tossed yet again. Graham looked away, blinking. Why the hell had he wanted to learn to read such things, anyway? If this was his reward, he regretted the whole damned notion. Perversely, and because he couldn't help it, he looked again, to the end of the note Julia had written:

> I release you from our bargain. You are free.

He crushed the paper, obliterating Julia's flowing signature—and the words, *With deepest admiration and fondness,* penned directly above it. Graham felt his mouth lift in a cynical curve, and cared not a bit. If he was to strike the trail as he'd planned, he'd need whatever toughness he could muster. He grasped it with both hands, needing that mean edge to his soul.

'Twas preferable, he thought roughly, to the hurt that had pierced him before it.

Adjusting the burden he shouldered, Graham headed again toward the door. At the last moment, he stuffed Julia's note into his duster coat pocket, then squared his jaw and stepped into the hallway. Before leaving Avalanche, he had things to do. Calls to pay.

And a message of his own to deliver…to the woman who'd left like a thief in the night, carrying his heart along with her.

Chapter Twenty

Afternoon shadows were lengthening over the dusty streets of Avalanche by the time Julia finally gave in to the inevitable. No matter how much she walked, she couldn't escape the truth, and she couldn't avoid explaining that truth to her papa any longer, either. Tomorrow was supposed to be her wedding day. As the father of the bride, Asa Bennett would need an explanation for why the wedding he'd agreed to would not take place.

With a heavy heart, she trod down Fir Tree Lane toward home. A fair number of people passed by her as they paid calls and ran errands. For them, it was a sunny spring day, with clear skies overhead and a soft southern breeze. For Julia, it was the first day of her new future, tied to a town where she wasn't really wanted, and compelled to devise something new to fill her days. Given that reality, the weather mattered little to her.

Nearly home, she turned up the brick walk to the front door. As she did so, a distant movement captured her attention. Holding her breath, Julia turned. Several houses away, a tall, hat-wearing figure strode down the street in the opposite direction, his battered duster coat streaming behind him with his rapid movement.

Graham?

Automatically, Julia started to follow. She squinted. Could it really be him? Hesitantly, she grasped the gatepost.

"Julia? Is that you?"

She started at the sound of Geneva's voice. Looking over her shoulder, Julia spotted her aunt standing in the opened doorway, a concerned expression on her face.

Reluctantly, Julia returned to the walkway, squaring her shoulders as she did. It was time to have done with this, once and for all.

"Yes, Aunt Geneva. It's me." She traversed the steps and hugged her aunt's purple-begowned figure, gratefully inhaling the familiar scent of roses that clung to her. "There's something I must tell you, and Papa, too. Is he nearby?"

At the livery stable, Graham finished saddling his horse and checked his supplies one last time. He'd already settled his boardinghouse bill with Bea Harrington, paid a few calls, and visited the express office, where he'd sent wires to both Frankie and his bank in Baltimore. Now, with most everything that needed doing accomplished, Graham faced the assembled men surrounding him.

The stable owner, Tom, cleared his throat. "Sorry to see you go, Corley."

Graham clapped a hand atop his shoulder. "I know better. You'll be sorry only to see my stabling fees vanish."

The surrounding men laughed. One of them, a nearby farmer, stepped forward.

"We'll be sure and take care of the lending library, like you asked us," he said. "If we take it in shifts, the way you planned, it should work out right fine. And Richards here won't have a stranglehold on our books anymore, neither."

Laughter and jests filled the room. At their center, Wilson Richards angled his head, good-naturedly accepting those quips which came his way. Although Graham's lending library had deprived the man of his monopoly on *The Adventures of Tom Sawyer* and other reading supplies for the men in town, Richards had recovered well. In the end, he'd even donated a dictionary and several books on Arizona Territory law to the collection.

"Best of luck to you, Corley," he said now.

They shook hands, and parted on good terms.

Avalanche's sheriff stepped forward next, flanked by Mayor Westley. He inclined his head toward Graham, and gave him a no-nonsense look.

"You reconsider that deputy offer, you hear?" he commanded. "I could use a man like you, 'specially for posses and such. We might not get whole passels of desperadoes riding through Avalanche on a regular basis, but we do take care of our own."

"I appreciate the offer," Graham told him, putting forward his hand. The sheriff took it in his crushing grasp, and they shook. "All the same, I've stayed here too long."

The gathered men shuffled their feet and nodded. A few muttered agreement. None of their eyes met his, though, and Graham knew why.

He hadn't explained about Julia.

They were understandably curious, but he hadn't been able to bring himself to speak of her. What could he say? That Julia had decided he wasn't good enough to wed her, even temporarily? That she'd released him with a letter before she embarrassed herself with a drifting man who had no notion of family, and wasn't likely to get one?

Hell, no. With confessions like that, a man didn't need a rogue bullet to lay him down. He took care of the shooting himself.

"Ride safe," Jonas Farmer said from his place beside the unlighted potbellied stove. He raised his callused hand. "We'll welcome you, if you come back."

Graham nodded, keeping his expression stern. With luck, no one would detect the dull ache that had dogged him since entering the livery stable this morning, to find word of his leaving had already spread through town, and every man he knew had stopped work to gather there for a goodbye. 'Twas uncommonly good of these men, men he had known but a month and would likely never see again. He would miss them, too.

"I'll not be coming back," Graham said gruffly. He dragged on his hat and, followed in twos and threes by the men of Avalanche, led his horse into the livery stable yard. "A bounty hunter can't afford to return to the same town twice."

They all nodded, making Graham feel twice as low-down for the falsehood he'd just delivered. It wasn't bad enough that he'd deceived everyone here with his courtship of Julia Bennett. Now he had to leave this place on a lie, as well.

With a disgusted frown, Graham swung into his saddle.

Amidst the well-wishes surrounding him, he gazed into the distance. Despite his sorriest hopes, no yellow-clad woman with a bonnet big enough to topple her over hurried down Main Street. No feminine voice called for him to stay, in the same husky tones he remembered from last night.

'Twas true then.

He was free.

He should have been glad, Graham told himself as his horse shifted beneath him, impatient to be gone. He should have been relieved, not to be expected to deliver on a staying kind of promise, even for so short a time. If he'd been right about himself all along, he wouldn't have been capable of settling down with Julia even for a day, anyway.

For the last time, Graham pushed back the niggling curiosity that had plagued him…could he have done it? Could he, a foundling child and lifelong wanderer, have found the strength inside himself to commit to a whole new life?

Well, now he would never know. Savagely, Graham turned his mind to other things, and made himself stop looking for Julia. He'd lost her. For all he knew, he'd never had her to begin with. Not truly.

He raised his hand in a solemn salute to the men who'd befriended him. He took one final look around the only town where he'd ever felt the beginnings of peace. And then, with a muttered curse and a mighty scowl, Graham Corley rode away from Avalanche and toward a future he didn't really want.

His last thought, as he struck the winding trail leading outside of town, was a self-mocking one: As he'd blown out his first-ever birthday candles, Graham had wished for Julia, he recalled. Now, he knew better.

He'd wished for Julia, and had gotten her—for one long, magical night. He should have wished, Graham realized now…for Julia to want him, in return.

* * *

Julia had scarcely finished explaining the whole awful truth of her misbegotten plan to wed Mr. Corley, annul her marriage to the bounty hunter, and then travel to New York alone, before her papa interrupted her.

"And you thought this scheme of yours was a sound one?" With obvious astonishment, Asa Bennett lowered his cigar and gaped at Julia over its smoldering tip. "Whatever possessed you, child?"

"I—I wanted to please you," Julia said. "You wanted me to be happy. You wanted me to have a husband, and I...well, I'm afraid none of the men in town would oblige me. I...asked."

There. The embarrassing, awful truth was said. None of the men in Avalanche had been willing to take oddball Julia Bennett to their hearts. Not even for money. And now, the two people whom Julia most wanted to think well of her knew it. Papa and Aunt Geneva knew exactly how undesirable she was to everyone in town.

No doubt they soundly pitied her.

Or would, once they recovered from their anger.

Her voice barely echoed from the papered parlor walls, so low and miserable was it. She cast her papa a pleading look, twisting her hands on the handkerchief she'd pulled from her reticule. It was one of Mr. Corley's, tucked there after he'd comforted her last night. She felt like never letting it go.

"And I wanted to be away from here," Julia continued, still hoping to make her family understand. "Far away. I'm happiest in the East, Papa. Where no one knows me."

Where no one dislikes me for being a person I cannot help being.

"Being unknown is preferable to being with your

family?'' Aunt Geneva asked. Her wounded look cut deeply. ''We knew you would be stimulated by attending Vassar, and a higher education was what your mother wanted for you, too. But *this*...I never expected you to turn away from us completely.''

''It's not that!'' Julia cried. ''Please, you must understand. I would have missed you both. Terribly. And of course I'd have come back for visits. But you and Papa...you have your own lives, Aunt Geneva. You cannot be responsible for mine.''

Aunt Geneva twisted her lips, seeming to begrudgingly accept the truth of that. They talked further, at length, about Julia's plans, her thwarted desires to be accepted in Avalanche, her finding Mr. Corley in the municipal park, and striking her bargain with him. By the time Alice had brought them all tea and sandwiches, and every crumb had been consumed, Julia and her family had reached a tentative accord.

''I have to confess,'' Aunt Geneva said finally, brushing a sprinkle of sugar from her skirts, ''that Mr. Corley did not seem to be fulfilling a bargain when he was with you. He seemed to be falling in love with you.''

And you, with him, her expression added.

Julia's heart softened. She wanted to weep with despair.

''Of course it seemed that way to you, Aunt Geneva,'' she said quietly. ''We were still amidst our bargain then. Graham—Mr. Corley—can be profoundly persuasive, when he wishes to be.''

My, could he be persuasive!

''Nevertheless, I have my doubts.'' Aunt Geneva gave a resigned shrug, and sipped her tea. ''I may be a spinster, but I've known a love affair, or two, in my time.''

Beside her on the parlor love seat, Asa Bennett didn't raise so much as an eyebrow at his sister-in-law's blithe admission. In fact, he seemed utterly unsurprised by it. As Julia watched, her papa lit another cigar. He tipped the ashes into the nearby dish, and regarded Julia thoughtfully.

''Judging by what you've told me,'' he said slowly, ''your scheme with the bounty hunter ended this morning.''

Julia nodded, fighting the heated blush that rose to her cheeks. She'd mentioned only to her papa and Aunt Geneva that she'd gone walking for most of the day to think things through, and that she'd left a goodbye note for Graham early this morning, breaking their engagement. The circumstances preceding that, she'd chosen to omit. She wasn't ready to share the private hours she'd spent with Graham...and even if she had been, Julia would have thought it unwise to confide such intimacies as that.

Her father cleared his throat, ending her musings.

''Then Mr. Corley was *not* fulfilling his end of your bargain,'' Asa Bennett continued, ''when he came here to speak with me an hour ago. Nor when he left this, for you.''

Her papa withdrew a roughly folded envelope from his suit coat pocket. He tapped it thoughtfully against his palm for a moment, then slid it across the parlor table toward Julia.

She stared at it, mesmerized by the sight of the familiar, masculine scrawl that labeled it with her name.

Graham, here? But why?

''Mr. Corley was here? Only an hour ago?''

Asa nodded.

Then it *had* been him she'd seen walking away! A

new regret seized her. She could have followed him, could have made certain for herself that he was all right...no, Julia told herself. Doubtless Graham was fine without her. Happier, perhaps.

With trembling fingers she picked up the envelope. Curiously reluctant to open it, she turned it over in her hands as her papa and Aunt Geneva watched.

"Did he say what this is?" she asked.

Her papa blew out a stream of richly scented cigar smoke, and shook his head. "Only that he wanted you to have it. I thought it was merely a bridegroom's note...although it's a bit bulky for that."

Julia rubbed her thumb over the envelope. It *was* bulky, as though filled with something more than a single sheet of paper. It would serve her right if it was a happy note, requiring reams of paper to describe Graham's relief accurately. But there was something about the sharp slash of her name as he'd written it on the front...something decidedly *un*happy.

Decisively, Julia slit the seal with her fingertip and opened it. Drawing in a deep breath, she reached inside and withdrew the contents.

A pile of bank notes filled her hand.

She stared at them in confusion. "Money?"

Aunt Geneva leaned forward to retrieve a piece of currency that had fallen to the rug. She returned it to Julia. "Several *inches* of money," she clarified with a bemused expression. "More than I've seen in quite a while."

"More than used to be contained in your trust, I'll wager," Asa commented.

"Used to be contained?" Julia snapped her head up, her gaze swerving from the befuddling pile of money

to her father. "What do you mean, *used to be contained?*"

Her papa and Aunt Geneva shared a fretful look. He breathed deeply, then stared at the glowing tip of his cigar for a long moment.

"I'm sorry to have to tell you this, Julia," he said. "But your trust money is gone—"

"Gone?"

"—spent to finance your education in the East." His shoulders sagged a bit as he squinted at her through a tendril of smoke. "It simply didn't extend as far as your mother had hoped, and there was only so much I could contribute. My pharmacy is doing well. Especially with the new soda fountain. But not that well."

"What?" Utterly at a loss, Julia gawped at him. "But—but you were planning to release the rest of the money to me when I married. You said you—"

He waved a hand. "I'd hoped you would forget about that. And I wish I could have. Why do you think I insisted on your finding yourself a good husband?"

"It was because we were worried about you, that's true," Aunt Geneva said. "But also because your trust money had already been spent. We needed to make sure you would be taken care of."

Taken care of. That's what Julia had intended to do for herself, with her plan to return East and secure a position at *Beadle's Magazine*. Now, suddenly, she saw things in an entirely new light.

"I hope you can forgive me," Asa continued, gazing at her fondly. "For misleading you this way. I didn't want you to worry, and that's why I—"

"Oh, Papa! Of *course* I forgive you!" Still clutching the thick wad of money, Julia leapt from her chair and went to her father. She lowered herself beside the love seat and hugged him close, savoring the security of his familiar embrace. "How could I not?"

"Perhaps because I'm an impossible, meddling schemer who thinks he knows what's right for everyone around him?"

She laughed, as did Aunt Geneva. Smiling, Julia leaned away and regarded her papa affectionately. "At least now I know *I* come by such traits naturally," she teased.

Aunt Geneva laughed louder.

"Except in my case," Julia added, "I also always think I'm right about things, too."

"Doesn't everyone?" Geneva asked, raising a brow.

"Guilty," Asa said, grinning. "Except I *am* right."

A loving feeling filled the room, turning the parlor cozy and welcoming where it had at first been dark and stifling. With a great sense of relief, Julia returned to her chair to ponder Mr. Corley's unexpected offering.

She ran her thumb over the edge of the currency stack, watching as the high-denomination bills fluttered past. Truly, this was a great deal of money. More than she'd ever seen, all in one place. But why?

As she examined it, a scrap of folded paper fell out. Frowning, Julia bent to retrieve it.

"A note?" Aunt Geneva asked.

"I think so." Julia unfolded it, her heart pounding. "We'd been practicing handwriting so that Mr. Corley could correspond with his friend Frankie, and…"

Her voice faded as she glimpsed the brief message.

"What does it say?" her papa asked.

"Asa, really!" Geneva scolded. "I'm sure it's private."

"It's…" Julia gazed at it, then ran her fingertips tenderly over the harshly angled writing. Already she missed Graham, and he'd scarcely left. "He means for me to have this money," she said slowly. "To head East as I'd planned. He wants...he wants me to be happy."

Geneva sighed. Her papa grunted and smoked his cigar. Julia closed her eyes, the note's message already a part of her memory forever.

Follow your dream. I believe in you.

Graham had left her this money as proof of that belief, knowing that once she'd ended their engagement, her trust funds would not be released to her. He'd met her sacrifice with one of his own. The realization of it humbled Julia...and made her understand something more, as well.

Her dream was not going away, or leaving Avalanche. It was not living in New York, or writing an etiquette column for *Beadle's Magazine*—her books kept her quite happily occupied, now that Julia considered it, and she didn't really require anything more. Her dream was being accepted, being *loved.* And she'd already found that.

Found it, and set it free.

"I think I've made a terrible mistake," Julia said suddenly, rising from her chair. Currency floated to the floor at her movement, but she paid it no mind. "A terrible, terrible mistake."

Aunt Geneva raised an eyebrow. "Exactly what did you do to earn those greenbacks, child?"

"Oh, Aunt Geneva! It's nothing like *that.*" Stifling a chuckle at her aunt's ribald-sounding suggestion, Julia began stuffing the money back into the envelope. "But I was wrong, all the same. I can see it so clearly now."

You can't admit you're wrong, she remembered Graham telling her. *So long as you close your eyes to it, it will continue to be true.*

He'd been right, Julia saw now. But today, her eyes had been opened. She would not go back and repeat her mistakes of the past. Because of her time with Graham, she'd learned a great deal about herself…and she'd grown, too. Grown into a woman who gave love, accepted love—and understood when drastic action was called for.

''What are you going to do?'' her papa asked.

Geneva leaned forward. ''Yes, what?''

''I'm going to follow my dream,'' Julia announced. ''My *true* dream. And I'm going to need some help to do it.''

Chapter Twenty-one

Nestled into the side of a mountain range as it was, Landslide, Arizona Territory was not quite as picturesque as its neighboring town of Avalanche. Where Avalanche was pine-and-oak-studded and almost entirely painted, Landslide's ramshackle buildings were dug halfway into the steep rock face or perched partway on stilt supports. And instead of farmers and merchants, its streets and houses were filled with miners who worked Matt Chance's famously productive copper mine, along with a few renegade souls who'd chosen to mine alone.

Its saloons and gambling houses sported a far greater number of miscreants and desperadoes, though. And its freight wagons were dogged by a much larger contingent of thieves, all hoping to secure a piece of the Chance family wealth for themselves. Those were the things that had drawn Graham Corley to town, and they were the things, he pondered now, that just might convince him to stay.

He'd have near-steady work, he told himself as he strode away from the bank where he'd just collected his latest fugitive capture reward. None other than Matt Chance himself had offered Graham a position protecting payroll shipments and safeguarding the transportation of mining officials to and from town. And chances of running short of female company were slim, thanks to the four brothels doing brisk business here.

Whiskey, women and work. Yep, in a town like Landslide a rough-and-tumble drifting man like himself could have everything he wanted, Graham figured. He pocketed his money and continued onward, pulling his hat down to avoid being drawn into unwelcome conversation. *Everything except what he truly needed.*

Julia.

He'd thought of her often, over campfires during too many lonely nights, and in the empty spaces between one town and the next. She was never far from his thoughts…nor were the things she'd taught him. Not reading, or writing, important as those skills were. But other things. Things about himself.

He *could* settle down, Graham knew now. Not in spite of his past, but maybe because of it. His wandering days had fulfilled something he'd needed, and in the end they'd shown him something more. They'd taken him to Avalanche, where he'd dared to stand still for the space of many days' worth of riding. He'd survived it. He'd thrived on it. And Graham had changed beneath its influence.

He'd become a man who understood his own capacity for commitment.

Too bad he'd hidden his newfound talents so damned well, Graham thought as he continued down Landslide's hilly, twisted Main Street. He'd covered them so thoroughly that Julia had never found them. She'd believed he wanted freedom more than he wanted her.

I release you from our bargain. You are free.

Damnable, unwanted freedom.

Scowling, Graham surveyed the town surrounding him, noting the new house construction to his right and the Little Lola's tall timber headframes at the copper mine in the distance. This was as good a place as any to make his future, he decided. No matter what revelations he'd had, Graham Corley was not a man who crawled back to a woman and asked for second chances.

Julia had let him go. She hadn't wanted him enough to confront him, face-to-face, and figure out where they stood. Given that, he had no reason not to stay where he was.

Besides, 'twas still possible he'd misread her motives. 'Twas beyond likely that Graham had wished for another excuse for her letter ending their engagement, aside from not wanting him, and so had concocted this namby-pamby reasoning—about her misunderstanding his hidden, newfound abilities to stay put—in order to save face.

In order to save his soul.

No. Until he heard Julia Bennett tell him she wanted him, from beneath one of her outrageous hats and preferably in front of dozens of witnesses, he would stay away, Graham vowed. There was nothing more a reasoning man could do.

With that decided, Graham switched directions and fixed his gaze on the towering spire of the Little Lola mine. He headed for Matt Chance's office, his future decided. Like it or not, he'd already become a staying kind of man. If he couldn't have Julia, then he'd stay wherever he was, and make the most of it.

On a bluff far outside Avalanche, Julia reined in her horse and gazed into the distance. Somewhere out there, Graham waited for her. Or *didn't* wait for her, if she'd damaged their love beyond repair. Either way, she had to keep looking until she found him.

She tightened her grasp on the reigns and straightened her spine determinedly. No matter what it took, she would correct the mistake she'd made. Julia had sworn it. Her vow was as good as the four-inch pile of money still secured in her saddlebags, awaiting return to its rightful owner.

The sound of approaching hoofbeats snagged her attention. Looking behind her, Julia spied Isabel, Abbie Farmer, Aunt Geneva, Katie O'Halloran and a half-dozen other women from town, all riding toward her. In their wake rode another half-dozen men, husbands and fathers who'd accompanied their group.

Dust rose, glittering in the strong territorial sunlight, as everyone reined to a stop. Chattering voices surrounded Julia.

"Has there been any word?" Julia asked, loudly, to be heard above the din. Everyone quieted, including those who had recently rendezvoused after fanning out to search for word of the bounty hunter. "Any sign of Mr. Corley?"

Several people looked at each other, then away. The horses shifted restlessly.

Julia took their silence to mean that no one had information about Graham's whereabouts. Again. She lowered her head, feeling despair rise within her. When she'd first struck upon this plan, she'd been encouraged. She'd hoped everything would soon be settled, given the circumstances.

Given the fact that Julia had been able to raise a full-up posse, to help her trail her love.

Considering it now, it seemed no less unreal today than it had five days ago. She'd left her papa's house on a wave of decision, determined to somehow locate Graham and confess her love for him.

First, she'd been compelled to call on everyone invited to the wedding, and inform them, quickly, that it had been delayed. Foolishly, Julia hadn't been able to bring herself to say the words, "the wedding is cancelled." Instead, she'd optimistically substituted the hopeful phrase, "the wedding is temporarily postponed," and had left it at that. She hoped, at this moment, that she wouldn't be forced to recall her own buoyant prediction.

To her amazement, everyone she'd visited on that day had come to her aid. It seemed that, while making certain Graham was welcomed in Avalanche, she'd made herself welcome, as well! One by one, friends and neighbors had stepped forward to help Julia find her runaway groom, and further—they'd voluntarily formed a posse to accomplish it. That posse milled around her now, apparently unwilling to deliver whatever news they'd discovered.

"No word, then?" she asked.

Everyone looked toward Isabel. As Julia's closest friend, she was likeliest to be chosen to deliver the bad news. With a sigh, she nudged her mount forward. She stopped beside Julia, and looked down as she patted the black gelding's neck.

"Yes, there's word," Isabel said quietly.

"All this searching wouldn't have been necessary," interrupted Katie O'Halloran before Julia could speak, "if the men had only informed us the bounty hunter was leaving town! We could have stopped him afore he did. But *no.* They had to keep it a secret, at that livery stable of theirs, and—"

"Hush, Katie!" her husband said in his thick brogue. "That's all been settled."

To judge by the renewed chattering of the women—and the grumblings of the men—it hadn't. The ladies of Avalanche remained convinced all of this could have been settled much more quickly, had the menfolk confided in them. At the moment, they were angling for a Spring ball to take their minds from the issue, but the men hadn't quite agreed. Yet.

Amid the swirl of conversation, Isabel looked at Julia. "We've had word that Mr. Corley has taken a freight wagon robber to Landslide, some five miles distant from this spot. Two days ago, he—"

"Five miles from here? What are we waiting for?" Julia interrupted. "Let's go!" Encouraged, she lifted the reins to set her horse in motion toward Landslide.

Isabel stopped her with a hand on her arm.

"Have you considered…well, that he may not want to see you?" she asked reluctantly. "After all, you *did* refuse to marry him, Julia. Are you sure about this?"

That explained her posse's initial reluctance to disclose their findings, Julia realized. They'd all been trying to protect her—the former misfit of Avalanche—from disappointment.

"I've never been more sure of anything in my life," Julia said. And then she spurred her horse and headed down the bluff.

Settling down in one place was pure hell, Graham decided on the sixth day of his newfound commitment to staying in Landslide. No matter that the town held the same things of any other—people, buildings, businesses and houses. It lacked one crucial element. *Julia.*

And Graham was having a devil of a time doing without her.

Frowning, he lowered his hat and took a seat on a boulder that jutted to the side of the Landslide mercantile. He set the bottle of whiskey he'd been carrying at the boulder's base, making a face at it as he did. Drinking at his nightly poker games had seemed a good solution to his constant ache for Julia, but so far his attempts had gained him nothing more than fuzzy mornings and a series of headaches. 'Twas past time to put the bottle aside.

Scrubbing his hands over his face, Graham contemplated his next move. He could wire Baltimore for the cash to buy some property outside Landslide, get started on a house, begin the work he and Matt Chance had discussed. He could take advantage of his unwanted freedom and visit the brothel, the dance hall, or the saloon. He could…he could swear he'd just glimpsed a flurry of yellow, off to the right behind the millinery.

Julia, he thought instantly. *She's come.*

But that was daft. Landslide was a good thirty miles from Avalanche, a long ride even without the mountainous trails. There was no reason a'tall why a fancy lady like Julia would be…exiting the millinery shop even now, and striding toward him?

He straightened with a jolt. Truly, his eyes were playing him a fool. But sure as he sat there, that was his Julia coming toward him, her ruffled yellow dress swishing in the breeze. She even had on one of her gigantic, flower-bedecked hats. And she was smiling, too. Julia looked, Graham saw, exactly as he'd wished she would, when she came to tell him she wanted him.

Ahhh, but this could not be! Scowling, Graham snatched up the bottle of Old Orchard, and poured the whole thing into the dusty ground. The sour scent of the whiskey rose around him, but even that couldn't mask...the scent of oranges?

A shadow fell over him as he stared, dumbfounded, at the bottle he held. Heart pounding, Graham looked up.

''Hello,'' Julia said, almost shyly.

It seemed his vision could speak. Deciding to play along, Graham thrust the bottle back into its place on the ground, and cleared his cottony throat. ''Hello.''

Hesitantly, she touched a hand to her hat, steadying it as she pushed something through the ribbons and fabric flowers at its crown. A glimmer of gold sparked from between her fingers, and Graham recognized the thing she held.

'Twas the hatpin he'd given her.

His pulse thrummed anew. A new, entirely lunkheaded hope rose within him. Could it be that he hadn't imagined her at all?

Graham stood.

They gazed at each other for the space of several breaths, both with—he was sure—identically disbelieving expressions on their faces. He yearned to touch the tendrils of silky dark hair framing Julia's face, to catch hold of her hand and tug her closer for a kiss. But that would dissolve the illusion, Graham figured. And so he did not.

Lord, but it was good to see her.

A flurry of movement behind Julia caught his attention. A woman ran from the millinery shop, a paper fluttering in her hand. Breathlessly, she came to a stop just beside them, and tapped Julia on the shoulder.

''You forgot your receipt for your new hat, miss,''

the woman said, holding out the scrap of paper. "I thought you might want to have it."

Julia murmured her thanks. As the woman returned to the shop, she tucked the receipt into her reticule and then regarded Graham calmly again.

He let his gaze rise to her head, where the decorations on her wide-brimmed hat fluttered in the breeze. "You bought a new hat, just now, for this meeting?" Graham asked.

"Of course," she said with a smile, as though doing such things were as natural as breathing. "Just because I've only now ridden into town doesn't mean I can't look my best for you."

He gawped.

"'Tis becoming," he managed to say.

And then he knew. 'Twas her. Truly. He couldn't possibly have conjured up something so feminine-frilly, so touching and so thoroughly Julia, all on his own.

Joy filled him. Julia had come for him, Graham realized. She'd followed him, and now—now he did *not* intend to let her get away again. She could write a dozen letters, launch a thousand pretend-engagement schemes, wear any kind of outlandish hat she wished. Nothing would change his mind. Not even...bringing along an audience to their reunion?

Momentarily puzzled, Graham glanced over her shoulder at the group milling there. And then he recognized them—at least a dozen Avalanche residents. Familiar men and women all, they stood whispering and smiling and trying *not* to seem as though they were watching Graham and Julia's encounter with avid interest.

"Aren't you wondering why I'm here?" she asked.

Graham's attention swerved back to her. The joy in his heart multiplied, bringing a wide smile to his face.

"No," he said. "I know why you're here."

"You—you do?"

Although Julia had seemed relieved to see his smile, now she looked visibly discomfited. There was no cause for that, Graham knew, although he understood it and wanted to reassure her. Gently, he captured her gloved hand in his, and stroked his thumb over her palm.

"I do." He allowed his smile to broaden, even as he felt her quiver beneath his touch. There would be more of that quivering later, Graham vowed. Also more moaning, more stroking, more pleasure. For both of them. But first… "You've come to finagle yourself a bridegroom."

She looked shocked, and tried to withdraw her hand. "I have *not* come to *finagle* anything!" She fussed with her reticule, trying to open it one-handed, and finally gave up in frustration. "I've come, first of all," Julia told him firmly, "to return your money. I can't accept it. It's in my reticule, every last bit, but I—"

"You've come to finagle yourself a bridegroom," Graham repeated. He lowered his voice, and raised his eyebrows meaningfully. "Namely, me."

"Graham! Listen to me. My days of scheming for what I want are over with. I've learned so much, and now I know—"

"I don't want the money," he said, to make her stop fidgeting during this important moment. "No, thank you."

"Well, I can't accept it. And furthermore—" She blew out a gusty breath and tried again to withdraw her hand so she could get into her reticule to retrieve his bank notes. Julia only succeeded in bringing them closer together, so their clothes whispered and their bodies nearly touched.

She glanced up at him, startled. "Furthermore, I have to insist, again, that I'm not trying to finagle you into anything! I don't know where you got such a notion, but I assure you—"

Graham shook his head. "You are. 'Tis obvious to me that any woman who would be willing to gather a posse—" he nodded toward their spectators "—and track down her chosen man would also be capable of finagling him into marriage."

She opened her mouth, looking bowled over. "Graham! Honestly, I...well...*well.* We should deal with the matter of your money first."

He ignored her natterings about the money. 'Twould belong to them both to share soon enough, anyway.

"'Tis also obvious," Graham went on, "that any woman who could turn a rootless drifter into a settling-down kind of man deserves to be listened to. So I'm ready to hear your proposal."

"You—you—my *proposal?*"

"Of marriage," Graham clarified helpfully. She really was *too* easy to tease, this woman he loved. He'd have to rein that in eventually...maybe after their second or third child had arrived. He released her and removed his hat to achieve the proper air of solemnity. "Go ahead."

"I...I..."

"I can see you're a little tongue-tied. 'Tis surprising, in a woman who knows her mind well enough to tell a man she wants him, in broad daylight, before a dozen witnesses."

"Seventeen!" Aunt Geneva piped up, moving

slightly forward in anticipation. "There are seventeen of us!"

"Thank you," Graham called. He winked to their audience, then turned to Julia again. "Fear not," he said. "I only left Avalanche, and you, because I believed you wanted me to. 'Tis obvious now, though, that you want me with you."

"I want you with me?"

He shook his head, grinning again. He tossed his hat onto the boulder behind him. "'Tis not a question, darlin'."

"I want you with me." Julia tested the words, and apparently found them to her liking. She clutched his shoulders and rose a little on tiptoes. "I *do* want you with me!" she cried more loudly. "That's why I'm here! I missed you so much."

"See? I knew it," Graham said. Damnation, but he loved this woman. "And...?"

"And?" Julia wrinkled her brows.

"You may continue finagling me," he offered.

A blush rose to her cheeks. Truly, she looked even prettier than he remembered.

"Ummm."

"Tongue-tied again?" Graham asked. "Then I will have to help you."

He grasped her hand, and lowered to one knee in the dust. The seventeen from Avalanche gave a gigantic "awwww" sound, and went on watching.

"Graham! What are you doing?" Julia asked.

"I'm *staying,*" he said. "With you."

"But—" A sudden indecision flashed across her face. "But you said you're not a staying kind of man."

"Not true." He shook his head. "I simply hadn't found...anyplace that felt like home yet."

''Oh, Graham...''

''With you, I have.''

''Oh!'' Julia squeezed his hand, and a sheen of tears brightened her eyes. ''Do you really mean it? When I wrote you that note, I didn't understand. I didn't mean to—''

'''Tis behind us,'' Graham told her. ''It's all right now.''

She sniffed. ''Then you forgive me?''

''Forgive you?'' From his position on bended knee, Graham gave her a renewed, undoubtedly spoony grin. ''Of course I forgive you. *I love you.*''

A little cry escaped her. Bending slightly, Julia pressed a kiss to his mouth. Her cheeks were damp with tears now, and her lips trembled faintly against his. But Graham welcomed her, all the same, and held her close for a long moment. Then, he urged her to straighten.

''I love you, too,'' she whispered as she did, clasping his hand in both of hers and cradling it against her. ''With all my heart. Forever and ever, and ever.''

'Twas not quite fair for a man to feel so much happiness as he did right now, Graham thought. But so long as he did...all he wanted was to share it with Julia.

''Then I surrender,'' he said. ''You have finagled me.''

Her answering smile was part loving recognition of his teasing, part loving chastisement. She rolled her eyes at his antics. ''I did *not* come here to finagle you. But so long as I have...''

''So long as you have, you may as well agree with me,'' Graham said. He cast her a tender smile, and took his time to savor her nearness. ''And so long as you have already shown me more happiness than I have ever known, and so long as you have already made me feel the luckiest man in all the territory, so long as you have done all that...you may as well consider this, too.''

''Consider what?''

''That I love you, and I will love you until my dying day. That nothing I do will ever feel complete unless you are by my side. That I need you with me always.'' Graham cleared a suspicious hoarseness from his voice and went on. ''That you are my heart and soul, and I will not so much as let you leave my sight again until you answer this one question.''

''Question?'' Julia asked.

Because she was crying, the word sounded garbled. But Graham knew what it was. His heart had wished for this moment too many times not to recognize it, when it came.

''Yes, question. Are you ready?''

Julia sniffled, and nodded. The crowd behind them pressed nearer. Even the sounds of the bustling town surrounding them seemed to grow quieter.

'''Tis this,'' Graham said, wrapping his fingers around hers more firmly. ''Will you be mine, Miss Bennett, and make this day complete? Will you marry me, and make me an honest man?''

''Oh, *yes,*'' she breathed. ''Yes, I will!''

She lurched forward, cradling his face between her hands and pressing small, fervent kisses to his lips, his cheek, his whiskery jaw—anyplace she could reach.

''Yes, yes, yes!'' Julia cried, and she gave a little jig. ''Nothing could make me happier.''

Their first celebration couldn't wait. Graham rose to his feet, and hauled Julia into his arms for a proper kiss. As the groom-hunting posse from Avalanche roared their approval, he held close the woman he loved, and did all he could to show her how happy she'd made him.

When their kiss ended, they turned to face the group. As they did, a renewed cheer rose to the skies—sunny skies, the first he'd truly shared with Julia. From here on, Graham vowed, the sun would shine on all their days.

He scooped up his hat and dragged it on his head, then held his hand out for Julia to take. "Our lonesome days are over," he said. "From here, 'tis nothing but shared happy days and shared loving nights. Agreed?"

"Agreed." Gleefully, Julia seized his hand.

And with their fingers clasped, they swung their arms and strode toward their friends and family, walking together...together into a loving future.

Outrageous hats, bristly jaws, etiquette rules, gun belts, and all.

* * * * *

LISA PLUMLEY

When she found herself living in modern-day Arizona Territory, Lisa Plumley decided to take advantage of it—by immersing herself in the state's fascinating history, visiting ghost towns and historical sites, and finding inspiration in the desert and mountains surrounding her. It didn't take long before she got busy creating lighthearted romances like this one, featuring strong-willed women, ruggedly intelligent men and the unexpected situations that bring them together.

When she's not writing, Lisa loves to spend time with her husband and two children, traveling, hiking, watching classic movies, reading and defending her trivia-game championship. She enjoys hearing from readers, and invites you to contact her via her Web site at www.lisaplumley.com.

HHIBC605